RADIOHEAD
plus Special Guests

THE FORUM
Friday 24th March 19
Doors Time: 7.00 p.m.
Ticket Price: £8.50 (Advance
£9.50 (Door)
STANDING DOWNSTAIRS

1059

WEDNESDAY 1st SEPTEMBER 1993
ADMISSION £5.00 ADVANCE

N5 1RD

20

(HIGHBURY + ISLINGTON TUBE)

001

NRISE PRESENTS

DIOHEAD

special guests
AY 12th MAY 1993
£6.50
ACADEMY
OF L
LET S

SJM CONCERTS in association with
present
radiohead
Plus Special Guests
Saturday 4th November 1995
£9.00 Advance/£10.00 on Door
Doors 7.00p.m. – 11.00p.m.

STALLS
STANDING

00747

adione

plus
The Julie Dolphin
RTSMOUTH PYRAMIDS
ESDAY 4th OCTOBER 199
Doors 7.30pm
TICKETS £7.00 Advance

PRESENT
TIM'S BIG THREE-O
IRTHDAY PARTY
FEATURING:
D. Js – LUVERLY LIGH
– CHEAP BAR 'TIL 1
IAL LIVE GUESTS:
ESS

DER
TICKET 2 50

SJH CONCERTS PRESENTS
** RADIOHEAD **
AT
THE ASTORIA
157 CHARING CROSS RD

TICKE
2 50

faithless
? the
Wonde Boys

WEDNESD
jericho 21XMSTMF
tavern £6.00 9

radiohead
standing on the edge

alex ogg

B🌱XTREE

First published 2000 by Boxtree
an imprint of Macmillan Publishers Ltd
25 Eccleston Place London SW1W 9NF
Basingstoke and Oxford

www.macmillan.co.uk

Associated companies throughout the world

ISBN 0 7522 1843 3

9 8 7 6 5 4 3 2 1

A CIP catalogue record for this book
is available from the British Library.

Typeset by Blackjacks
Printed by Mackays of Chatham PLC, Kent

Plate section picture credits (left to right, top to bottom):
Dean Ryan; Dean Ryan; Dean Ryan; Andy Willsher/S.I.N.;
Michel Linssen/Redferns; Paul Bergen/Redferns;
Ebet Roberts/Redferns; Simon Ritter/Redferns; Ebet Roberts/
Redferns; Ebet Roberts/Redferns; Jon Super/Redferns;
Roy Tee/S.I.N.; Erik Pendzich/REX; Brad Miller/Retna;
Roy Tee/S.I.N.; Youri Lenquette/Retna.

contents

preface

'You have to feel sympathy for anyone who attempts to make gripping reading from the Radiohead story,' noted Alexis Petridis in a review of the last shelf-filler to emerge on the subject. The point is taken, and I hope that such generosity of spirit and sympathy extend to *Q*'s reviews page when its journalists are confronted by the next tome cartwheeling down the production line.

Writing a biography about a rock band as literate as Radiohead is asking for trouble. Their drummer is a trained copy editor, for heaven's sake. Yet Radiohead are important enough to merit serious critical appraisal and that's what's been attempted here. The band themselves were approached about contributing but declined. It's not hard to understand why. I only hope they're not offended in any way by the resulting volume. Not because I'm a lily-livered excuse for a rock biographer, but because they're essentially decent people trying to retain their integrity in a cut-throat business. What they've achieved is a triumph for the good guys, and I wouldn't want to tread on that in any way. For part of the story I'm as dependent on third-hand testimony as previous biographers. Articles by John Harris, Jim Irvin, Steve Malins, Paul Lester, Jon Wiederhorn, Simon Williams, Andrew Mueller, Ronan Munro, Dave DiMartino and sundry other journalists were filleted for useful extracts. Similarly, books by Jonathan Hale, Steve Malins and Nick Johnstone. However, an attempt was made to balance this with the testimony of those who have known or worked with the band. One thing characterized most of the two dozen or so interviews I conducted while researching this book: the subjects were initially suspicious of my motives, and then universally keen to convince me of what honourable, decent human beings Radiohead are. Nobody had any axe to grind. I genuinely hope any relationship they have with the band hasn't been compromised in any way by their contribution.

This book is dedicated to Hugh or Ellie,
whoever decides to put in an appearance first.

acknowledgements

Salutations first and last and always, and again, to Dawn Wrench.

Many people were helpful above and beyond the call of duty in the preparation of this volume. Firstly, thanks to Chris 'Muffin' Taylor and Andy Smith, without whom I'd never have found several of the people listed below. I hope your faith in me wasn't misplaced. I'm enormously indebted to both of you.

Thanks to all at ITFC, especially renaissance man Martin Keady, who helped greatly with the early chapters of the book. My gratitude to everyone at Oxford Music Centre, especially Mac, Ronan Munro and Dave Newton, who all found time in busy schedules to talk. Apologies to all three, and to the cleaners at the Euro Bar in Oxford especially, for disgracing myself after being plied with huge quantities of cheap whisky. Meeting people who are still involved in this game because they love music is as humbling as it is unusual. Richard Cotton put me in touch with Nobby of the Candyskins, who graciously delayed his Christmas shopping to contribute. Amelia Fletcher, elder stateswoman of the Oxford music scene, was also kind enough to agree to talk with me.

Lunatic Calm's sHack not only provided a key contribution, despite his busy schedule, he even typed it all up for me. Many thanks. Those members of Abingdon School I corresponded with, even though some decided not to contribute to a book written without the band's express consent, deserve acknowledgement for their time. Take a bow, Richard Bakesef, Graham Scott and Andrew Tracey. Also, I must mention my e-mail collaborators: Christy the K-ROQ fan, Mr Scott at Stagecoach, James Sleigh (and Sarah, natch), the Rev. Tyler

Jacobson, Dai Griffiths, Andy Bell, Al Spicer, Paul Cobley, Helen Gould and Pauline Eyre, the representatives of Murray Gold, and the best friend a boy could have, Sue Pipe.

Several journalists who have covered the band were kind enough to submit to personal interrogation. Jack Rabid, proprietor of the finest music magazine on the planet, answered questions, as did John Mulvey at *NME*. Both Jim Irvin at *Mojo* and John Harris at *Select* were enormously helpful, and this book would be much poorer without their informed comments. Raise your glasses also to John Robb and Pat Gilbert, and to Bill and Marion Ogg for that matter.

Dean Ryan and Mark Sargeant were tremendously helpful in the later stages of the book, and special thanks to Peter Cole for obliging me in all manner of respects. Among other things, he provided invaluable contact addresses for superfan Barbara Violani and Lee Potton, who helped look over the manuscript. Kathryn O'Neill put me in touch with Jamie Drummond, whose input was greatly valued (more importantly, so is his work with Jubilee 2000). Stuart Osborne was always on hand to answer queries, even if few of them concerned the subject at hand. Phil and Mel (Leytonstone mafia) put me in touch with Fiona Conway, to whom thanks also. To all those Radiohead Web sites whose archives and opinions I have spent many pleasant hours filleting, my gratitude. Finally, my gratitude to editors Jenny Olivier, whose idea this whole project was, and Guillaume Mutsaars, who saw it through to completion, as well as copy editor Richard Dawes.

Writer Alex Ogg lives in Leytonstone, London, with his partner Dawn. His previous books include *The Hip Hop Years*.

introduction

'People sometimes say we take things too seriously, but it's the only way you'll get anywhere. We're not going to sit around and wait and just be happy if something turns up. We are ambitious. You have to be.'
Thom Yorke's closing remarks in Radiohead's (then On A Friday) first interview with Curfew fanzine in November 1991.

'His only real problem was that he couldn't see that there was enough interesting material or that anyone would be interested enough to read it.'
A friend relates Colin Greenwood's response to being approached about contributing to this book.

The above quotes tell us something of the nature of Radiohead – a band at once driven by ambition and at odds with the humanity-sapping compromises that accompany mainstream success. Throughout their career they have downplayed audience and media deification while openly recoiling at the codes of behaviour and excess expected, even demanded, of a major rock band. Yet while they take every opportunity to underscore their normality and domesticity, their songs dissect the minutiae of everyday neuroses with surgical precision. As a result they've struck a chord with a global audience that ranges from convicted murderers to thousands of Internet-loony acolytes. More importantly, they've produced a body of work that distils the essence of the nineties – delineating the alienation, fear and longing of the pre-millennial decade while managing to celebrate our fascination and detached amusement with a world spinning beyond our control.

They are polite, well-behaved English middle-class boys, learned and self-disciplined, yet their records see them constantly teeter on the edge of nervous breakdowns and anxiety attacks. Once jokingly self-diagnosed as 'neurotics anonymous', they played urbane Englishmen on tour, before tiring of constant allusions to their college-educated, bridge-playing past. Jokes about testosterone-free tea-drinkers who read the *Independent* on the tour bus rather than play video shoot-'em-ups wore thin when they were swallowed as wholesale truths in a thousand promotional interviews. Yet there is some substance in these stories, in so much as Radiohead remain ill at ease with the prescribed hedonism of the rock 'n' roll lifestyle.

What has made Radiohead the greatest band of their generation? They possess an innate musical adventurism that has helped shift British rock from its consumptive reliance on the past. While early in their career their influences were worn on their sleeves, their appetite for invention and restless creativity has produced successively more ambitious, panoramic records. Thom Yorke's lyrics depict protagonists overcome by feelings of worthlessness, hypochondria, insecurity and indecision – a wellspring of despair and anxiety that is occasionally the source of exquisite gallows humour. His empathy with the characters that populate his songs, not least himself, is so richly felt (rather than merely observed) that the emotional resonance is unparalleled in contemporary rock. Early in their career, lead guitarist Jonny Greenwood abused his guitar in a manner which, famously, left his knuckles bleeding. Their best work eschews sentiment in favour of a heartfelt emotional dialogue that's as raw-nerved as Jonny's fingers. While they avoid the trappings of the overwrought rock band, for the few hours they appear on stage, Radiohead deliver performances of genuine intensity and drama. In an era when British music was awash in irony, archness and complacency, we needed a rock band who meant it.

Radiohead's records – spanning apologetic despair and vertigo-inducing mood shifts – offer an emotional elevator that plunges from dizzying heights to terrifying depths within seconds. In short, it's the sound of the last great guitar band of the century. To belatedly answer Colin's question, the group – proudly nondescript, uniformly unpretentious, undemonstrative and attention-shy – have produced some of the most remarkable, even unimaginable, rock music of the past decade. And that's why people are interested.

-one-

meeting in the aisle

Thom Yorke
The newborn chick

Radiohead singer Thom Yorke's childhood adventures have been well documented, often much to his disdain. After far too much prurient intrusion, his early years are now a closed subject, though the basic facts have been established. His left eye was paralysed at birth, the eyelid left completely shut. It was initially considered a permanent affliction, until a specialist suggested grafting a muscle into the socket to effectively give Thom a bionic eye. By the time he was six he'd endured five major operations. He was forced to wear an eyepatch, about which he was remorselessly taunted – especially when he was moved to a new school. 'I ended up half-blind and had to wear a bandage over my left eye which had become lazy from the extensive surgery. The doctors messed up. I had to walk round looking like a pirate for over a year. I was laughed at in school. And as if this wasn't enough, we moved house twice that year, which meant that I had to change schools twice as well.' Later he discovered that New York songwriter and poet Patti Smith, with whom he formed a mutual appreciation society, endured a childhood similarly blighted by childhood illness and stigmatizing eyepatches.

Thom's problems are almost certainly caused by one of two conditions – congenital muscular fibrosis, which prevents eye muscles from functioning properly, or weakened muscle connections resulting in the eye being held in one position. Optical practitioners have subsequently judged that, for all the minimal benefits in aiding the recovery of 'lazy eye' syndrome (which is actually a misdiagnosis of Thom's condition), patches can cause such irreparable social damage that they have largely been abandoned. Although he is not totally blind in his left eye, it is of use only in preventing Thom 'walking into something'. Aside from the physical disfigurement, the sequence of operations ensured he also had to spend protracted periods in hospital. 'Hospitals are fucking horrifying places. We were next to the geriatric ward as well, so we used to get these senile old men coming in, walking into things and throwing up. There was no television, no phones, just the radio.'

Thom Yorke was born on 7 October 1968 in Wellingborough, Northamptonshire. However, his early years were spent in Scotland, where his father sold chemical-engineering equipment. His enduring memory of this period is of the time he spent on a nearby beach, where he stumbled upon the half-buried artefacts of Second World War coastal defences. He was instructed in boxing by his father, who had been a university champion, to little effect. Every time his father landed a blow, his fragile son would simply fall over. More profitably, Yorke Senior bought Thom his first steel-stringed guitar when the boy was four. Frustrated by his inability to comprehend it, and with his fingers bleeding from his efforts to master the instrument, Thom threw it against a wall and destroyed it. He contented himself with building Lego models instead, exhibiting an early spatial awareness that must have better pleased his father than his pugilistic efforts. Aside from his time in hospital, he claims his mother always remembered him as a happy child, forever immersed in drawing and construction, and rarely bored.

His parents brought Thom and his younger brother Andy to Oxford when he was eight. At roughly the same time, he was given a Spanish guitar to play. Finding this less injurious to his fingers, he decided he was destined to become the new Brian May after a friend purchased Queen's *Greatest Hits*. After enduring an early diet of Scottish dance tunes, the sophistication and complexity of 'Bohemian Rhapsody' entranced him. This discovery helped relieve the pain of being the new boy with the eyepatch at Standlake Church of England School, near Oxford. Thom formed his first band at age ten in 1978, before moving on to Abingdon School, also in Oxfordshire, in 1980. Inevitably, he was given the nickname Salamander because of his bad eye. 'I got into a fight with the guy who originated the name but that didn't stop it. It was a very malicious school and everyone had very malicious nicknames, so Salamander was par for the course.' This was the first of a number of fights he became embroiled in. Unsurprisingly, given his unimposing frame, he lost them all. That, in a nutshell, is the impotently combative Thom Yorke's schooldays.

Thom is the unlikely lead singer of an unlikely rock band. At five feet five inches tall, he finds that the adjective 'diminutive' (or more cruelly, 'gnomic') accompanies almost all profiles. In fact, an MTV book recently pithily noted that Radiohead as an entity 'are shorter and less attractive than most musicians'. Others have detected something John Lydon-esque about Yorke when he works up to a good stare, or picture him with the aspect of 'a newborn chick'. More recently, when he neglects to shave, he resembles a shrivelled-up Boris Becker. Yet there is something endearingly unkempt and unready about his appearance, like a stray dog in need of a loving home and more considered grooming. We've seen the blond mane, the hair extensions, and more recently the care-in-the-community skinhead look. 'There is irony, there's implied irony and there was my hair,' he admits. 'My image changes were a result of a low boredom threshold and a lack of confidence in what I look like.' His fretfulness is reflected in his poor posture and seeming discomfort at inhabiting his own skin. Less well documented than his defective eye is an ear problem. There is a history of deafness in his family, and he also suffers from fluid in the ears, which makes air travel uncomfortable.

It's an easy cliché to describe such a complex artist as a man of contradictions, but some fully realized personality conflicts are clear. He admits to restlessness with the humdrum normality of modern existence yet grasps at the fabric of the everyday for emotional renewal and subject matter. He despises the inhumanity of Western capitalism but has to square that with enjoying extreme wealth and loving to shop. He craved attention as a young man but is now revolted at its relentless invasive stare. He's worried much of the time, not least about wasting his life worrying, yet despairs of accusations that he's a whining, spoilt rock star. He promotes similar schisms in onlookers. To some he is the key author of the culture of complaint; to others one of the last sane voices in the wilderness. As Pat Blashill once wrote for *Spin* magazine, 'Thom Yorke is one paranoid android: freaked out by cars, haunted by houses, suspicious of everyone. You couldn't ask for a better rock star.'

Thom is often viewed as an English Michael Stipe, a major rock star with an agenda rooted in maintaining his own dignity and perspective. The comparison extends beyond a propensity to play fast and loose with hairstyles to a shared personal and musical register. As well as R.E.M. being a defining influence on the sound of Radiohead, Stipe's ability to maintain his balance within a fanatically followed rock band has provided Thom with an instructive role model. It has allowed Radiohead to emulate R.E.M.'s example as radio-friendly unit-shifters 'who give a shit'. Like Stipe, Thom's relationship with fame is best described as ambivalent. 'I still get days when I want to clock in all my billions of utterly useless executive air miles and fuck off for ever to a shack in Kare Kare in New Zealand with its alien plant life. But then what?' What indeed.

For his sins, Thom gets saddled with more preposterous theorizing and intrusive analysis of his character than any of his bandmates, and presumptions are readily made about him that are either flippant or simply ill conceived. But sometimes he has encouraged that line of questioning. He once confessed in an interview that he has always felt distance between himself and the group dynamic. 'There's a pervading sense of loneliness I've had since the day I was born. Maybe a lot of other people feel the same way, but I'm not about to run up and down the street asking everybody if they're as lonely as I am. I'd probably get locked up.' Many have postulated that the early chasm between him and his schoolmates caused by his eye problems is what makes him such a lightning rod for 'outsider' narratives.

His manager, Chris Hufford, believes Thom's personality is easily divisible from his public persona and has been widely misconstrued. 'Thom cannot stand going through the motions, and when he catches himself doing it he gets furious with himself. Thom is a highly strung, emotional person. He's also incredibly shy, and he can go off on one when he feels something's been put the wrong way, so people immediately say he's a manic depressive. That's understandable because they only see him in his public role when he's highly stressed, but he's not like that at all.' Thom himself admits to being tetchy, unpredictable and bad-tempered in the wrong circumstances. 'I'm always losing my temper and it's very rarely justified. I always feel myself doing it but I can't stop it. Everyone else knows too and no one comes near me. My friends now have the ability to carry on a normal conversation while I blow my top. I should go into therapy, shouldn't I?' He admits that, unlike the rest of Radiohead, he wasn't brought up to be polite under duress.

Music has always been Thom's prime motivating force. Though horrified at some of the charlatans that populate his artistic spectrum, and aware of the pitfalls of taking it all too seriously, he is at heart a fan and advocate of pop music. Beyond the purchase of those first two guitars, his parents never encouraged him to pursue music. In fact, he would regularly pretend to be staying at a friend's house whenever On A Friday (the band who became Radiohead) staged gigs. He loves recording studios, and has claimed he'd be happy to spend months on end in them if it limited the long grind of the promotional tour. He defends music as the most vital and important art form of the century, a far more immediate and embracing currency than any comparable means of expression. More rarely acknowledged than his singing – he possesses the most emotionally resonant voice in contemporary rock music – are his abilities as a guitarist. As bandmate Ed points out, 'He's a really great guitarist. He plays terrific rhythm, but he doesn't like to talk about it because he thinks he sounds like Brian May.'

Thom's other interests in his adolescence included cars. Before he developed a disabling phobia about the twentieth century's most dangerous and avaricious form of transport, he was the scarcely proud owner of a beat-up Morris Minor with a door that wouldn't close. A car crash later provided much of the lyrical scope for songs expressing bewilderment at our reliance on automobiles and naked fear at the vulnerability of passengers. Unarguably the most excitable member of a particularly stoical group, he is readily engaged by new concepts and ideas, and regularly extols the virtues of whatever books he's immersed in – like Sogyal Rinpoche's *Tibetan Book of Living and Dying*, texts by and about the Situationists, and Lester Bangs's *Psychotic Reactions and Carburettor Dung*. Many of his lyrics are triggered by such books.

For musical role models look to R.E.M., Elvis Costello and Tom Waits. All these citations reflect the kind of impeccable taste that makes you suspicious about his relationship with the grinding mediocrity of British cultural life in the late twentieth century. 'I am proud of my pretensions,' he freely admits. All are consumed in the obsessive manner of the hard-bitten fan, which he stubbornly remains. He once claimed that, aged sixteen, he left *Raindogs* by Tom Waits on repeat on his Walkman before going to sleep. But then he also has the tiniest propensity for exaggeration, once enthusing that he didn't sleep for six months after meeting Elvis Costello.

Thom is the member of Radiohead who has endured the most press censure for his attitudes and behaviour. Some journalists have mistaken boredom for irritability, while many others have, more self-revealingly, adopted the line that he really has nothing to complain about and should 'go away and count his millions'. But there have also been self-acknowledged temper tantrums, fits of pique, capricious exhibitionism and the like. Some writers have detected a surly attitude to interviews, and Thom has, at various points, gone on record to say he hates photographers. 'Thom couldn't give me ten minutes for a quick interview and wasn't exactly the most pleasant person I've ever met. I think all this success in America has gone to his head,' is one typical comment from the pages of *Submerge* fanzine. One can only wonder whether he was antagonized by the original approach of the journalist, but the impression remains that Thom finds the whole process of explaining himself tedious and unproductive.

His resentment at the intrusion reached a zenith halfway through promoting *OK Computer*, when he pulled out of interview engagements completely. The justification is easy to understand – receiving the most attention of all the band members, he is the one who suffers fools least gladly. 'I get people coming up on the streets in Oxford saying, "Can I have your autograph?" Sometimes I'll say yes and sometimes I'll be really, really rude because they'll catch me when I'm not being Thom Yorke from Radiohead, like in a restaurant or something and it'll be, "No, piss off." But then to have people come back and say, "We heard you're a bit difficult, a bit weird, you're not very easy to talk to." It's the circumstance that people are talking to you in, when people come up and they want a little bit of you, their two cents' worth.' At the moment everyone, your author regretfully included, wants their two cents' worth of Thom Yorke.

Ed O'Brien
The healthy-looking one

Tall and physically imposing, unflinchingly polite and diplomatic, Edward John O'Brien was born on 15 April 1968 in Oxford, the son of an affluent medical family. He is thoroughly at ease with his comfortable background, unapologetically acknowledging the 'inherently middle-class' nature of Radiohead. His father is an osteopath, which may or may not be the reason Ed has the best posture in this band of gym-dodging Quasimodos.

His love of music began in 1977. While older boys were riding the first wave of punk, Ed was lapping up Elvis movies screened on British TV following 'the King's' death. Elvis on repeat was enough to convince Ed that music would be his salvation. His parents split up when he was ten, and though the family nucleus splintered he remained close to his father throughout, while lodging with mater. His parents actively encouraged their son's involvement in music, which makes him unique within the band. In fact, his father's enthusiasm has become legendary. There are amusing tales of O'Brien Senior being desperate to discuss the new Primal Scream album or debate whether Throwing Muses or Kristin Hersh solo is the superior article the moment his son walks in after completing a tour.

After his parents enrolled him at Abingdon School, Ed excelled at drama, notably in school productions such as *Julius Caesar*, where he managed a towering portrayal of Brutus (at least inasmuch as he was taller than anyone else in the show). He is the only member of Radiohead to possess anything approaching sporting mettle, and was a mainstay of the cricket team throughout his scholastic career. As a supporter of the forces of darkness, Manchester United, he remains the most vocal football fan in the group. He also gives the impression of being the one least discomforted by his time at Abingdon School.

Aside from sport and academic pursuits, he developed a fixation with Morrissey and the Smiths. It was the latter's Johnny Marr who inspired him to take up the guitar, in which he is self-taught. '[Marr] was an amazing, brilliant rhythm player, rarely played solos, so full of sounds. Even something as obvious as the intro to "How Soon Is Now?" – that brilliant tremolo [especially notable on the John Peel session version]. Of course, I'm nowhere near as technical, but I'm also into sounds, pedals, rhythmic textures, and arpeggio stuff.' The first guitar Ed ever bought was a Rickenbacker, 'because Marr, Weller and Peter Buck all played them. And they were great rhythm guitarists. I always associated leads with cock rock. The only lead guitarist I like is Jonny Greenwood. He doesn't have that cock-rock stance.' Being a rhythm guitarist in a band of three guitarists, of which one is a widely acknowledged musical polymath, Ed finds his contribution is often overlooked. But arguably the best guitar line in Radiohead's entire catalogue, the arpeggio that underpins 'Street Spirit (Fade Out)', belongs to him. So too the treacly power chords in 'Planet Telex'.

After Abingdon, Ed worked in a pizza parlour, and on one occasion served Stephen Hawking. He was subsequently a waiter at Brown's restaurant in Woodstock Road, Oxford. It's been said he was the only member of Radiohead sufficiently handsome to get a job there. Thereafter he read economics at Manchester University. His interest in finances and the machinations of the music world (he has read Fredric Danne's exposé of the industry, *The Hitmen*) saw him conclude that the way to really get on was to become a lawyer. But rather than take a conversion course, he spent a year after college travelling around America on a Greyhound bus, Jack Kerouac style. It is still his favourite country.

Like the rest of the band, despite his more four-square image and physical presence, he forswears any indulgence in rock 'n' roll hedonism, as he explained while touring America. 'This absolutely beautiful girl comes up and says, "My parents are away, do you want to come back with me and do loads of coke?" I didn't have a girlfriend at the time and we had a day off the next day, but I was just flabbergasted. I was very polite, but I thought of us as a very moral band and I said no, because I wasn't sure what the others would think of me.' It's indicative of the tough moral base of the band, but also typical of a group of young men who grew up in an all-male environment. As Ed has noted elsewhere, 'We're not into bonding. We're friends and everything, but because of maybe our upbringing or the school that we went to, we don't tell each other our problems. We deal with them ourselves. It's the only way you can deal with them.'

On stage Ed is the most effusive member of Radiohead, and his bandmates still tease him about one gig in North Carolina where he disappeared completely over the lip of the stage, falling into the orchestra pit before spending an age trying to clamber back to his rightful position. Other peculiarities about Ed O'Brien include his sleeping habits. Not only does he talk, he apparently shouts in his sleep. However, the consolation is that, according to Colin, 'He can do wicked Sean Connery and Darth Vader impressions first thing in the morning.' He is also considered, alongside Phil, the go-to guy on band matters fiscal.

After Colin, Ed O'Brien is Radiohead's most garrulous and forthcoming conversationalist. When Thom and Jonny were promoting *The Bends* with a free gig at London's Eve Club in 1995, long-term fan Peter Cole found himself chatting with Ed behind the mixing desk. 'He never shuts up! He can put nervous fans very much at ease. All the times I have spoken to him, he's always asking, "Enjoy the gig?" "What do you suggest we release as the next single?" "What do you think of the new songs?", etc. He never stops. Meanwhile, I'd missed half of Thom and Jonny's set.'

Despite appearing to all and sundry as the most healthy member of the band, Ed is arguably the one who smokes most heavily, and is rarely pictured without a tab in his hand. He's also, legendarily, 'the cocktail king' – responsible for performing wonderful feats with cranberry juice. In the early days of the band, Ed was the *de facto* manager, impressing many with his calm, polite approach, and lack of discernible ego. Caitlin Moran's description of him as 'very much like Fraser, the moral mountie from BBC's *Due South*' is probably as accurate as any.

Colin Greenwood
He went to Cambridge, y'know!

Born on 26 June 1969 in Oxford, Colin Greenwood is famously considered to be 'frighteningly intelligent' by the rest of his band-mates. Studying came to him like a natural second language throughout school. He holds a degree in English from Peterhouse, Cambridge's oldest and smallest college, famed for its successes in science and humanities and the establishment of choice for that great oxymoron – the Tory intelligentsia. His thesis was on the work of Raymond Carver, the American poet and short-story writer – one of dozens of authors he's acknowledged in print. Yet, for all that, he's never shown any desire to contribute lyrics to Radiohead.

Colin is a cornucopia of trivia on the band, able to spout Israeli chart positions at the drop of a hat. And he likes to talk. It would not be too unkind to suggest he can 'go on a bit'. For this reason he's become Radiohead's director of communications. Thom: 'Colin's great at talking to people when no one else will. He's our secret weapon. We wheel him out and he just doesn't shut up for half an hour. I can't even smile when all I want to do is punch someone in the face. Colin could smile while sticking a knife in your stomach. That's a huge compliment, by the way.'

A record nut of the same fervency as Thom, Colin grew up with a penchant for post-punk bands like Magazine, XTC and Wire, as well as Joy Division/New Order. This was largely thanks to a big sister with taste; his big brother preferred Iron Maiden and the new wave of british heavy metal. 'I guess some of us were into the pre-adolescent stuff, like Japan and Rush, but not for me. My first bands were New Order and Joy Division and the Fall, 'cos I had an older sister who wouldn't let me listen to anything that was heavy metal.' As he grew older he'd put on make-up and sneak off to see the Fall and Alien Sex Fiend. The Greenwoods' father died when Colin was seven, so perhaps that accounts for the degree of parental laxity.

Before the band went professional, Colin worked at Oxford's Our Price record store in an attempt to 'broaden his musical knowledge'. He was to be frustrated, however, by his manager's fondness for playing a steady diet of soft metal on the shop stereo. His sister would have been horrified.

Colin got his first guitar at the age of thirteen, purchasing it with his own money. However, he's the least 'muso' musician of the band. He once confessed to spending most of his private time studying English literature and history, and 'occasionally' playing the bass. Despite this, he elected to take music lessons between *The Bends* and *OK Computer* in order to improve his technique, given the complexity of new material they were writing. On stage, being quite the least demonstrative member of the band, Colin tends to hide somewhere near the drum kit.

However, he's the most gregarious member of the Radiohead entourage, claiming he doesn't like to be alone much and suffers from insomnia caused by an overactive mind. He's also mused about the possibility of returning to academia when the ephemeral world of pop music is done with. He once joked that he intended to set up a rock 'n' roll fellowship at Peterhouse. The entrance exam would include sections on joint-rolling and how to deal with groupies. Some American journalists assumed he was being serious. Despite his social largesse, alongside Thom, Colin is the one most capable of hitting dark moods, which caused them to clash on several occasions, until both learned to be 'careful' around each other. On tour he tends to room with Ed, because 'we're both smokers and we both have a soft spot for country soul music.' He also prefers to travel with the road crew.

'His posture is as dismal as Joey Ramone's; at times he folds his arms behind his head and slumps so furiously that he seems to be sinking into the crevice between the couch's cushions,' noted Sandy Masuo in *Request* magazine. Colin shares with his comrades a lack of visible clothes sense, though he did purchase a Paul Smith designer suit when Radiohead were allocated a stylist by their record company, which he singularly failed to carry off.

Phil Selway
The sensiblest of the sensible
Phil was born on 23 May 1964, in Hemingford Grey, Cambridgeshire. Amiable, soft-spoken and courteous as he is, it is

entirely possible that his nickname of Mad Dog is ironic. That doesn't stop band members from teasing prospective studio staff with tales of his Incredible Hulk-esque transformation from mild-mannered charmer to avenging hellhound should he miss his morning cuppa. His steadfastness can be demonstrated by the fact that, before the group's momentous appearance at Glastonbury in 1997, he was the only one who didn't display any nerves. In a rare concession to esotericism, he once claimed he owned a parrot, called Bert, who could recite *Pablo Honey* in its entirety. He fits the Radiohead thematic of poor health in a half-hearted fashion – though he often goes for five-mile runs, he has 'dodgy knees'.

Phil first got his hands on a toy drum kit at the age of three. He learned percussion at school (though he was only formally trained in the tuba), enjoyed it, and decided that would be the course his life would ideally take, influenced by drummers such as Stewart Copeland of the Police and the Jam's Rick Buckler. However, he was not so confident that he neglected his academic studies.

Phil is recalled generally as 'agreeable' or 'quiet' during his college years (Liverpool Polytechnic, now Liverpool John Moores University), where he drummed in productions by C. F. Mott's drama department of *Return to the Forbidden Planet* and *Blood Brothers.* A video exists of the former – and it is, indeed, an ugly spectacle. The *Forbidden Planet* 'band' also included one Jon Fiber – later a member of Liverpool underachievers the Vernons (one LP on Probe Records). Phil subsequently completed a postgraduate diploma in publishing at Oxford Brookes University, before working as a desk editor for a medical publisher in Oxford. The fact that he had a proper career in publishing while all his bandmates were in dead-end-waiting-for-Radiohead-to-happen jobs is indicative of his grounded nature – even though he, like all the rest of the band aside from Ed, actively defied his parents' wishes by going into music. He obviously benefited from his time in publishing, however. When he is cajoled to appear on Radiohead's bulletin board, he's more than likely to tsk tsk over grammar and respond, 'Spell-check, SPELL-CHECK!'

Naturally enough, given his equitable nature, he now serves as band social worker. Indeed, while at college he gave some of his time to the Nightline phone service for distressed students in Liverpool. One of the referral agencies used by Nightline was the Samaritans, of whom Phil remains a committed advocate.

Within Radiohead there is great competition for the status of least rock 'n' roll personality. Thom has the odd tantrum. Ed rocks out on stage. Jonny's looks are too sculpted. Phil pips Colin on the basis of quoting fewer books. Asked about his contribution to Radiohead, he plays a stoically straight bat. 'My approach is to try to do what's right for the song musically, rather than just stamp my ego all over it.' Which is just as well, as the man demonstrably has no ego. I asked fellow drummer and journalist Jack Rabid about what Phil Selway brings to Radiohead's table. 'He brings extreme creativity in the parts he selects – for example, he often bypasses the expected four-four beats and parts – and when he starts slamming, he slots in perfectly with Colin's big hammer sound. The perfect drummer for a band looking to stretch rock a bit, without destroying it.'

You get the feeling Phil enjoys the anonymity of being the band's 'clock on, clock off' drummer. He was once stopped by a fan outside a gig on Radiohead's first stint in America and asked if he was a roadie, or just a hanger-on. 'Oh, and can you get me Thom's auto-graph?' However, that seemed to all be behind him after a semi-official 'Phil Is Great Fan Club' was formed by employees of Epic Records in Osaka, Japan. It published newsletters and badges, and made him his favourite meal of steak and potatoes. In just two years the membership shot up from twelve to fifteen. It's since disappeared, though.

Jonny Greenwood
It's hard work being a musical prodigy

Colin's younger brother was born Jonathan Greenwood on 5 November 1971 in Oxford. Some two and a half years Colin's junior, he is the colour-blind son of a tone-deaf mother. Quite what part this played in his musical development is a moot point. As they grew up together, Colin would tease his sibling by switching coloured crayons while he was drawing, which resulted in 'disturbing pictures'. And that's about as fierce as the sibling rivalry ever got.

Jonny adapted to music from an early age, his grandfather teaching him banjo from the age of three. The Greenwood homestead rejoiced to the sounds of popular musicals and the classics. A year after his father died, Jonny bought his first single – Squeeze's 'Cool For Cats'. He committed it to memory and recited the verses to any family member willing to listen. The first instrument he took to was the recorder, before he graduated to viola and piano. After appearing in a succession of school and county orchestras, and joining big brother's rock band, he taught himself to play the guitar. Although he inherited some of Colin's interest in the post-punk generation, he has the broadest listening tastes of anyone in the band, enjoying everything from jazz and funk to classical music. He's a particularly big fan of the Blue Note jazz archive. As Colin admits, 'He's always lived in his own musical little world.'

For most critics, it is Jonny's expanded musical vision that has stretched the range of Radiohead beyond common-or-garden angst rockers on the indie/alternative treadmill. Yet he rarely gets the credit for being the lateral thinker he is. For example, while all his bandmates were aware of the ignominy associated with pre-punk rock, he took time out to investigate all the unfashionable bands – especially Pink Floyd. And while he freely admits that most progressive rock deserved all the bad press it got, he was able to find something in them of value. His self-confessed low boredom threshold (he's said to be the band's most restless, impatient member) is the principal reason why Radiohead have been able to push the envelope in terms of their sonic structure. His influence on *OK Computer* is particularly significant.

Those in the know credit Jonny with being the most original guitarist of his generation, but that kind of acclaim sees him run for the shelter of Radiohead's group dynamic. 'I don't think you could even ask me to quit Radiohead and play guitar for another band. I don't think I could do it. It would probably reveal me to be the bluffer that I believe I am. That's how it feels. I wouldn't have the confidence to do anything but this.' Yet Jonny's repulsed by the idea of being a guitar hero. It's no exaggeration to say that the most accomplished, imaginative guitarist we have is positively embarrassed at his profession. 'If I tried to do a Bernard Butler, I'd drown. If I tried to write and sing... We're holding each other up. There are no budding solo artists in this band. Noel [Gallagher], bless him, is going up and down the blues scales, and technically I'm not doing anything faster or more impressive than that, really.' Butler himself has professed to being a fan of Jonny's playing. 'He's a god. He's great. He's *the* modern guitar player, his playing seems to come from nowhere.'

It's not the only compliment Jonny's playing has attracted, yet he remains demure in the face of the garlands. In an interview with, of all publications, *Guitar Magazine*, he once claimed, 'There's just revulsion sometimes about being around people who love guitars so much. I find many of them love their guitars but they don't like music. That's really weird... Our guitars are more clitoris substitutes than phallus ones. We stroke them in a nicer, gentler way.' That may be true, but as journalist John Robb notes, 'Even if you're not a fan of the band, it's always worth buying the new Radiohead record, if only to find out what Jonny's doing on it.'

A non-drinker ('because I don't like drunk people, and I like to feel nervous on stage'), Jonny's the only member of Radiohead without a degree, managing just a couple of months at Oxford Poly (now Oxford Brookes University), studying psychology and music, before the others kidnapped him. His mother, naturally, was concerned. According to his brother, 'She got a bit better when she saw us on *Top Of The Pops*. Mind you, she thinks everyone on that programme's a drug-taking lunatic. Actually, she's not happy unless she's worrying. Very Radiohead, that.'

Rolling Stone once described Jonny's features as 'an extreme exaggeration of Aerosmith guitarist Joe Perry's already caricatured good looks', which was presumably intended as a compliment. Others mutter about the stark contours of his cheekbones. That much-over-used adjective 'androgynous' has also crept in from time to time. In terms of wardrobe, he's immersed himself in the chic Japanese labels Milkboy and Mighty Atom. And girly blouses used to be a big thing, too. Indeed, the brothers are said to be so in touch with their feminine side, they're sometimes nicknamed the Greenwood sisters.

Jonny's mild-mannered off-stage personality is in sharp relief to his wholehearted commitment on it. On a given night he may be found using his head for leverage while he bends the neck of his guitar to achieve the correct degree of distortion. It is a technique which demonstrates scant concern for his physical well-being. So much so that these days he wears a wrist brace. 'It's conceited to deny there's any affectation,' he told *Q,* 'but having said that, I enjoy putting the arm brace on before I play. It's like taping up your fingers before a boxing match. It's a ritual.' On stage, Jonny's hair drapes over his guitar, physical being and instrument forming a single visual entity. It's from this fused silhouette and hunched, contorted frame that much of the constant experimentation and reinvention of the band's catalogue on stage emanates, which is a big part of the reason why Radiohead are such a unique live band.

Hobbies? Jonny likes to fly kites and on tour has crosswords faxed to him. 'It's mental masturbation, I suppose. I'm not proud of liking them. I found a book full of half-finished crosswords when I was sixteen. My father died when I was five or six, and it was half filled out by him, so I used that as the basis for understanding how to do them. I've still got it somewhere. It's massively anal – it's kind of doubly satisfying, filling out a grid, and solving these massively witty clues.'

In a group of highly articulate young men, when Jonny deigns to speak, he's also the group's rapier wit, especially in the company of his brother. His one-liners have seen off many an inquisitive journalist. As Phil recalls, 'He's excellent entertainment value. He usually costs less than a video. The only problem is you can't take him back to the shop when you're sick of him.' Sadly, many of the comments attributed to Jonny in interviews are unreliable, owing to his habit of inviting family friends, relations, journalists and passers-by to conduct telephone interviews in his stead. Next to Thom, he has the least interest of any member of the band in indulging in interview psychoanalysis. He's also, arguably, the most resolute in his thinking. When asked what Radiohead is all about, he is to the point, economical, but terse: 'You aim to have high-quality standards for yourself, and you strive to make music of importance.' That's his job. Talking to journalists, he judges, is not.

-two-

please sir, can i have some more fx pedals?

'The search for excellence, if thoughtlessly pursued, can bring undue pressure to bear on some individuals, and it is important, therefore, that pastoral care should be seen as an essential and central part of our arrangements at Abingdon. We see each boy as an individual, and we try to teach each individual to see himself as a valued member of the community, with a share in its responsibilities and opportunities. A friendly, direct and positive attitude, free from pretensions but reasonably aware of the social arts and graces, characterizes Abingdon boys and makes the school a happy, as well as a purposeful place.'

Michael St John Parker, Headmaster, in his introduction to Abingdon School's prospectus.

The embryonic Radiohead, as the world now knows, first assembled at a public school in Abingdon, Oxfordshire. In the process a bond was created which saw the members travel together through adolescence into adulthood. Colin has spoken several times about the group's transition 'from short trousers to long trousers'. 'I think the way we got together is unusual,' he admits. 'When we started, we were fifteen years old in a boys' school that wasn't that much fun. So we tried to use music as a way to find our own space away from it and kept doing it all the way through college.'

Abingdon School, which dates from at least the thirteenth century, is an independent school of approximately 750 boys, aged eleven to eighteen. There are places for day, weekly and full-board pupils; the members of Radiohead were day-boarders. The prospectus provides colourful pictures of the site's well-kept buildings and thirty-seven-acre greenfield setting. The fees for Abingdon, from September 1999, are £2,223 per term for day students and £4,098 for boarders. This is considered modest by English public-school standards. The current chairman of governors is the Conservative shadow chancellor, Francis Maude.

The headmaster is a man recalled by Thom as 'a power-crazed lunatic who banned music and walked around in robes impersonating a bishop'. Michael St John Parker was offered a chance to defend himself in this book but declined, saying, 'I don't think that I can offer anything that would be of very much value to you.' Thom, in particular, developed a hatred for the old-fashioned patriarch. Speaking to former pupils, you get the impression that the scholastic sensitivities were of the 'Oh, and Jenkins, your mother died' hue. Thom later wrote a song about his nemesis entitled 'Bishop's Robes'. As well as decrying the 'bastard headmaster' and insisting he was 'not going back', it included references to children tearing themselves apart on school playing fields. The lines about children being groomed as killers may have something to do with the public-school tradition of training children for the armed forces via the Army Cadets, a body which remains active in the school to this day.

Thom Yorke was never military material. Instead, he found his salvation in the school's well-equipped music rooms. By the time he reached Abingdon, he was already a veteran of one musical group – aged ten, he'd wired up a home-made electric guitar while his friend made noises dismantling old TV sets, which would often give him mild electric shocks. The spectacle occasionally attracted an audience of wholly bemused friends and onlookers. A year later he'd written his first song, 'Mushroom Cloud'. Rather than being the anti-nuke diatribe its title suggests, it concerns the perplexing beauty of the cloud formations following a nuclear strike. By the age of twelve and with a few good kickings from his peers under his belt, Thom had joined Abingdon's school punk band, TNT. He took over as singer 'because nobody else had the bottle' to do it. 'I started singing into this little stereo mic tied to the end of a broomstick handle. Everyone just started falling about laughing, and that was that. That was my introduction to singing.'

Thom later revealed that, as a reluctant academic, music gave him a chance to shine, and to be the centre of attention. 'We just started making tapes when we were younger. First me on my own, and then me and Jonny, and then with the others. And we'd play them to people, and they'd really like them and they'd take them home and they'd actually play them at home and I was really into this. Or I'd be at a party or something and someone would give me a guitar and I'd play a song. I mean this is all when we were sort of fifteen, sixteen, and it was the first time that I found something that I really loved and I suppose that I just loved the attention, so I wanted to be famous, I wanted the attention. What's wrong with that? But there is also something really seriously fucking unhealthy about it.'

The experiment with TNT proved abortive. In truth, Thom was the member least impressed by the punk phenomenon. 'Punk rock was important to the other members of the band. I kinda missed it the first time round. Maybe it was good for a month, then all the crap came out, like any movement, really.' It left him to devote his energies, temporarily, to school productions and the drama department. He didn't act, preferring to provide musical accompaniment to plays such as *A Midsummer Night's Dream*. He was still looking for people in the school with whom he could form a more satisfying band, if not bond. Ed O'Brien ('I thought he was cool and looked like Morrissey') was his first recruit, after Thom saw him crossing the playground carrying a guitar case.

Ed first encountered Thom when he overheard him playing improvised jazz guitar with a friend. Ed: 'There was this tense dress rehearsal, and Thom and this other fella were jamming freeform cod jazz throughout it. The director stopped the play and shouted up to this scaffold tower thing they were playing on, trying to find out what the hell was going on. Thom started shouting down, "I don't know what the fuck we're supposed to be playing." And this was to a teacher.'

Thom recruited Colin Greenwood 'because he was in my year and we always ended up at the same parties'. Colin and Ed met independently during another school production, this time Gilbert and Sullivan's *Trial by Jury*. While Ed was relatively at ease with the school's ethos, both Colin and Thom were noted around the establishment for their ambivalent regard for school uniform and authority. Both were committed Joy Division fans, though they were too young to attend the band's gig at the Apollo in Oxford, supporting the Buzzcocks. Colin also played bass in TNT for a short time. He was offered his spot in Thom's band on the condition he learned to play low-slung bass like Peter Hook.

Colin: '[Abingdon] had a great music school where we would all run and hide away from the tedious conformity of timetables and uniforms. There, we jammed endlessly around Joy Division and New Order covers.' Thom wrote angular lyrics to accompany his embryonic songs and melodies. With Thom, Ed and Colin each playing a guitar, the trio performed their first set at a friend's birthday party – accompanied by a drum machine and muted applause. From there the group added drummer Phil Selway, the elder statesman of the band, who was in his final year when he joined. He was considered a better bet than the group's ailing drum machine. Phil: 'It was one of those Dr Rhythm things which always stalls after around ten bars. Of course, you get a drummer and he stalls after eleven bars.' Phil was currently playing with Abingdon school band Jungle Telegraph, as well as other Oxford-based groups.

The night after the three-handed birthday party debacle, Ed took Phil for a quiet drink and asked him if he'd be interested in switching allegiance. He agreed to attend a practice session. At this audition, the first thing Thom said to him was: 'Can't you play any fucking faster?' Phil remembers the incident well, and recalls that he did, indeed, upgrade his tempo. 'First impressions are so important, and such was my initial greeting, as drummer, from the band. Despite having been at the same school for years, we'd had no contact until the exchange of ideas at my first rehearsal at the music school. We had been in different years, and most certainly weren't a gang ... aside from Thom's hair, little has changed. We still argue about tempo and, finally, are in a gang of our own – thankfully without any bizarre initiation rites.'

The quartet began to rehearse together on the last day of each week at the nearby Clifton Hampden Village Hall. This weekly sched-ule saw them christened On A Friday, for want of a better name. They were forced to borrow a key from an old lady who lived round the corner for each of these practices, having first convinced the local vicar they were an aspiring jazz combo. That could hardly have been further from the truth. Colin: 'Thom wrote some great songs, and the few gigs we played involved us all wearing black and playing very loud. Some things never change.' One of their first gigs was as part of a twenty-four-hour school marathon. The largely improvised performance included the Beatles' 'Dear Prudence', fashioned after Siouxsie and the Banshees' recent cover (a version that would later inform Radiohead's 'My Iron Lung').

At this early stage, influences included the Smiths, New Order, the Cocteau Twins and the Waterboys. The appeal of being in a band was obvious. Phil: 'When you're at school you get into a band and you get to be kind of a cool person in your year...' This was self-evidently important to Thom, who even went through a New Romantic stage, complete with 'honey hair and lipstick'. Colin, however, denies that he was ever a full-blown Goth. The core members were often augmented by other musicians. Among those who occasionally joined these sessions was Colin's younger brother, Jonny, presently a member of the Thames Valley Orchestra. Bored with merely watching, he was soon itching to assume full member status. He subsequently claimed that he could see the value of Thom's songs in the school's music room even then.

Thom was writing prolifically now, often taking his guitar to parties to entertain his peers. However, his songs did not receive immediate recognition. 'When I was much younger, I did this four-track demo, and this girl, a really close friend of mine, listened to it and said, "Your lyrics are crap, they're too honest, too direct and too personal, and there's nothing left to the listener's imagination" and I've had that somewhere in the back of my head ever since.' Later Thom elaborated on this oft-quoted observation to *Q*: 'She was right. When I first started I wasn't really interested in writing lyrics. Which is strange in a way because if I didn't like the words on a record, if it wasn't saying anything, I would never bother with it again. But at 16 your own songs are half-formed and you don't really expect anyone to hear them, so you don't care what the words are. A big step for me was starting to work with Jonny and the others. And that would be a month after my friend said what she said.'

Thom's readily acknowledged discomfort with women was a by-product of his years in a single-sex school. In fact, his initial observations of the opposite sex were that they were 'so wonderful I was scared to death of them'. That impasse was hardly bridged by the school's intolerance of social encounters. 'Me and my friends invited these girls round. We were in the bogs, smoking, drinking and generally having a good time – when this right cunt of a teacher caught us. He made us phone our parents and say exactly what we'd done, and said we were going to be expelled. It wasn't a big deal but it completely destroyed my parents. They thought I was going to be a drug-taking lunatic from hell.'

Thom's confusion over women continued after school. He has commented several times that beautiful women scare him, and that he is disgusted at the reactions they provoke in others. Later he clarified his position. 'It's not just beautiful women. I totally fear all women. Ever since I've been at school, I would go for five months without talking to a girl my own age. I don't think it's misogyny. It's the total opposite. It's blatant fear.'

After a year of rehearsals, Jonny had pestered his sibling to within an inch of his sanity, and Colin finally relented, inviting Jonny along and telling him to bring his harmonica. Colin: 'It was a way of keeping an eye on him. He was only thirteen – it was a difficult age.' A week after On A Friday's first rehearsal as a quintet, they played their debut gig at Oxford's Jericho Tavern. Jonny sat by the side of the stage for most of the set until he got the nod from Thom. Thereafter Jonny purchased a keyboard, while the group considered adding further components to their sound. As a result they recruited, from the related Abingdon Girls' School, two sisters to play saxophone (they were sometimes joined by a third, male saxophonist). A keyboard player was tried out then jettisoned, his position taken by Jonny. Throughout 1986 Thom would go to Jonny's house to work together on original material. This was the basis of a songwriting partnership which only truly blossomed five years later.

At this stage, however, On A Friday were still very much a 'school band'. Jonny later admitted as much to *Q,* qualifying it by saying, 'We weren't the school band in the sense of playing to all our friends at parties. We wrote songs and played for five years but not really in public more than once a year really... It took five years to learn how to play, though. We were in the same room but we weren't necessarily playing together.'

In their final year together all the group except for Ed were subjected to parental pressure to concentrate on their studies. They obliged, Thom winning prizes in music and art despite the fact that he 'couldn't read music or paint'. Phil had already left, but Colin, Ed and Thom said goodbye to the school with appearances at the annual Symposium Revue, a final-year production in which leaving students traditionally baited teachers. Thom played a song, solo, on acoustic guitar. It's not hard to imagine the sentiments he wanted to express.

Eventually it was time for the senior members of the band to pursue their college courses, leaving Jonny behind to finish school. As well as completing his studies, he also wrote songs with Thom's younger brother, Andy, who was also enrolled at Abingdon. Together the two briefly forged another school band, the Illiterate Hands (which included Radiohead's lighting designer, Nigel Powell). More famously, in 1994 Andy Yorke and Nigel Powell founded the Unbelievable Truth, another group with an unwieldy moniker, this time taken from the Hal Hartley movie.

Thom meanwhile took a sabbatical year before going to university, starting a job at a clothes shop – Cult Clothing in Friar's Entry, Oxford – where his blond hair continually agitated his manager. 'I used to sell suits for him. This guy was the floor manager of our department, which was menswear. I couldn't afford any of the suits that I was meant to be selling, so I used to turn up in an Oxfam suit – which was quite smart – but I still had long blond hair and he took an instant dislike to me...' Thom left after being wrongfully accused of stealing a suit. 'I handed my notice in, which was quite a good moment, but I wish I'd told his boss to fuck off. He had this twisted little mouth and you could tell he was desperate to make everyone's life hell.' When asked about Thom's time with the company, manager Gary Kingston would say only: 'He was here for less than a year. He was very responsible, but totally into his music, to the exclusion of just about everything else. You could tell that. He actually brought in a few tapes to play us at various points. A nice, quiet lad, but it was obvious his interests lay elsewhere.'

Despite their impending college careers, and the distractions that would inevitably follow, the members of On A Friday agreed to keep the band together and to meet up regularly. While that pact alone is noteworthy, the fact that the members of the band kept to its letter and spirit is doubly impressive. The idea was to keep their parents happy by securing the degrees that had been earmarked for them, yet they always insisted that 'the band was the thing'. It's hard to imagine any other group who could have put their career on hold for three years, then reassembled with the ink on their degree certificates still drying, to pick up where they left off. The myth of rock 'n' roll, after all, is to defy parental wishes, rather than deftly outflank them. There is an echo of John Major about the Radiohead story. In this case it's not the circus boy who ran away to be an accountant, but the strong-willed youth of middle-class Oxford fulfilling their familial obligations before setting out to do what they always said they would. In this fashion, On A Friday continued to exist not just as an idea but as an entity during the years 1988 to 1991.

Colin had secured a place at Peterhouse College, one of the fusti-est of Cambridge University's hallowed halls. Peregrine Worsthorne was educated there, as was Tory right-winger Michael Portillo. As Peterhouse's Web site proudly proclaims: 'Recent graduates include the former Conservative minister Michael Portillo and the bass guitarist of the band Radiohead, Colin Greenwood. Moreover, while the college understandably emphasizes the highest academic standards, we have never taken a narrow view of personal attainment. After all, Peterhouse was the college of Sir Christopher Cockerell, who left with a third-class degree and yet went on to invent the hovercraft.' The Worsthorne–Portillo–Greenwood connection is interesting. When Portillo declared he had had homosexual affairs while at college before standing for the safe Tory seat of Kensington and Chelsea in 1999, a patronizing article by Worsthorne claimed that such relationships were natural for an undergraduate, and in fact, had his halls been populated by women, he may never have concentrated on his academic studies. Colin, too, admitted to 'dabbling' while at the college.

Despite the growth of further education, an Oxbridge degree still carries great kudos in large sections of British society, a fact Colin was well aware of. 'The thing about Cambridge is there's a lot of pressure on you to be known for something, whether it be journalism, theatre, music or academic studies. It requires a certain amount of confidence to deal with a place like that and if you haven't got it then it can be a bit nightmarish.'

As well as playing in college bands, Colin profitably secured the job of Peterhouse entertainments officer. In his final year he had the responsibility for booking bands for the Peterhouse Ball, opting for Humphrey Lyttelton and the James Taylor Quartet. His position also gave him the chance to book shows for On A Friday on the university campus, an opportunity for nepotism that he evidently abused at every opportunity.

Martin Keady was manager of King Of Thailand, one of several bands Colin played bass for during those college years. However, Keady never saw much in the way of potential in the group. 'They were not great. It's possibly not unkind to say there were Dire Straits elements in there. The band was originally called Junkyard Angels, after the Dylan song, and they formed to get gigs at college balls, and were very successful at that level.' Among the gigs that Colin secured for the band was an affluent party on a rooftop in Kensington – noted by all present as their 'Beatles at Apple Records' moment.

Keady remembers that, on at least one occasion, King Of Thailand, who also included a saxophone player, were joined by Jonny

Greenwood on violin. 'They played one gig in the bar at either Queen's or Emmanuel College in Cambridge in late 1989. Jonny was the best thing about them – despite being only seventeen, he was absolutely exceptional. You could tell he was an extremely gifted musician.' Colin, meanwhile, was noted around campus for 'looking the spitting image of actor Christopher Walken'.

The other group that Colin played in was Momma Hung Me In The Closet (But I'm Still Feelin' Funky), a covers band that ran concurrently with King Of Thailand and turned out to be a repository for the great and good. They too played the university events circuit, proffering blues and funk standards (at this stage Colin was said to be 'very influenced' by jazz and funk, as well as indie). The lead singer, Scott Handy, subsequently became an actor with the Cheek By Jowl theatre company. Murray Gold, who played keyboards with both King Of Thailand and Momma Hung Me In The Closet, is now an established TV composer, having worked on the BBC adaptation of *Vanity Fair* and the serial *Queer as Folk*. Another member of the band was Andy Collis – now better known as journalist Clark Collis – who was among Colin's closest friends at Peterhouse, where he was known as 'the ultimate beer-monster drummer'. He now writes for *Select* and *Mojo*, and has contributed several articles about Radiohead. Strangely, though it was not his college, a photo of Colin can be found in a colour montage in the current prospectus for Homerton College, Cambridge.

Thom started at Exeter University, studying English and art, in October 1988. He, too, joined a number of bands. The atmosphere at Exeter was both creative and pretentious, the college famed for being a bolt hole for upper-middle-class students who couldn't get into Oxbridge. Thom himself had been rejected by both Oxford and Cambridge, though his younger brother Andy (who studied Russian and spent a year in Moscow) and several of his friends went to Oxford. Exeter suited Thom well enough, though he had reservations about some of his fellow students. 'I was embarrassed to be a student because of what the little fuckers got up to. Walking down the street to be confronted by puke and shopping trolleys and police bollards. Fucking hell. I used to think, "No wonder they hate us." If I was

29

going to throw up, I did it in the privacy of my own room.' That didn't stop him from pulling the classic student party trick of nearly dying from alcohol poisoning on at least one occasion.

He was well aware of the town–gown divide from experiences in his home town. 'It was the same in Oxford, seeing these fuckers walking around in their ball gowns, throwing up on the streets, being obnoxious to the population. The little guys in the bowler hats will clear up their puke and make their beds for them every night. They don't know they're born and they're going to run the country. It's scary. Of all the towns in the country [Oxford is] one of the most obvious examples of a class divide.' He was to learn first hand how deep the enmity between locals and students could run. 'In my first year at college I went through this phase where I was into this grand-dad hat and coat I had. They were immaculate and I was into dress-ing like an old man. But I went out one night and there was these three blokes, townie guys, waiting to beat someone up, and they found me. They said something, I turned around, blew them a kiss and that was it: they beat the living shit out of me. One was kicking me, one had a stick and the other was smashing me in the face. That put me off fighting a bit.'

The inherent lack of discipline at the college, following the grind of Abingdon, ensured he would keep his academic studies at arm's length, at least for the first two years of his studies. One aspect of the course, however, did grab his attention. 'When I was at college the only artwork I ever really loved was something with this dodgy broad term of "Outsider Art", which was basically by completely untrained people who'd never been to art college or who were mentally unsta-ble.' The Outsider Art or Art Brut movement bred an awareness of forms of creative expression that exist outside accepted cultural norms. The movement began with research by psychiatrists in the early part of the century. *Raw Vision* magazine offers the following definition: 'The work of Dr Morganthaler documented his patient Adolf Wolfli, a genius who produced countless thousands of works from a small cell in his Swiss asylum. Dr Hans Prinzhorn collected thousands of works by psychiatric patients and his book *Bildernerei der Geisteskranken* (*Artistry of the Mentally Ill*), published in 1922, became an influential work amongst Surrealist and other artists of the time.' Surveying Wolfli's disturbing work, you can see where Thom and his friend and later collaborator Stanley Donwood draw much of their inspiration from for Radiohead's artwork – especially the blank, emotionless faces, combined with images from magazines and newspapers.

Thom: 'One of my favourite artists was this paedophiliac bloke [Wolfli – though there is some doubt as to whether he was convicted of any offences], and he did these scribbles which most people would say were like the doodles you do on the telephone. But there was something underneath it. There was something about the way he could pick up a pen and put it on a piece of paper, which sounds really wanky but I'd much rather study stuff like that than all the endless fucking Saatchi & Saatchi art... I'd much rather go off and explore stuff that didn't come out of that context at all, because that context is self-referential and boring. I think the same thing is true of the music industry at a lot of points.' The similarity doesn't end there. Much like rock music, the actual texts and canvases of Outsider Art were often overlooked by those more interested in its macabre, freak-show aspects.

Thom's art degree offered him a licence to indulge himself which he exploited with relish. 'Everything [I painted] was brown. So that kind of made me stop. All I did was paint Jesus all day for no good reason, and they weren't even good paintings. They were sort of yellow, murky brown, and quite miserable. That's why I ended up using computers, because then, technically, you can cheat. You've got more licence because no one else is doing it. In the final degree show there was a portfolio with all the final-year artists in it. And each one had "future plans", and I just put "pop star".'

His most visible activity came as a minor celebrity DJ at Exeter's student venue the Lemon Grove. Thom's DJing (at the Big Club night) was 'an excuse to spend loads of money on records, and be a cult figure or something. It was great for my ego... When I started the club we had 250 coming every week, and it was quite embarrass-ing. The first time I did it, I basically had twenty-odd albums of mine and a few odd singles, absolutely nothing. I kept having to play them. I went out the next week and borrowed £250 from the bank and bought all these records. About four months later we're getting 1,000-plus people a week.'

He was, as ever, honest about his pretensions in an interview with *The Big Takeover*. 'I think the main criterion of that was power. The power over the fact that you can play whatever the fuck you like, ball-dance or not. Yeah, I used to buy a lot of records, but I think when people ask you what your influences are, that's sort of a weird question as well, because obviously they change all the time, don't they?' Thom would often share a stage with Felix Bunton of Basement Jaxx. Bunton, who gravitated to the role of DJ after subsisting on tapes of the Police, Sister Sledge and a disco collection, recalls: 'After doing that they asked if I could do it again, so I thought I better get some records. That was when I was partnering with Thom Yorke – me playing dance music and him playing indie music.'

A fellow student, now known as sHack, who would later form the band Lunatic Calm, was working as a security guard at the same bar. 'I don't specifically remember a first encounter [with Thom], but Exeter was a fairly small, campus-based university and it was only a matter of time before you ran into like-minded people, and Thom was no exception. The Lemon Grove DJ spot on a Friday night was a much sought-after gig and the year-on-year line-up while we were there now reads like an alumni of Exeter's muso-talent – before Thom DJed there, Frank Tope (now deputy editor of *Muzik*) was the DJ. Then Thom found himself with the job for a year, followed by me, followed, I think, by Felix of Basement Jaxx. The DJ booth was a good meeting point for people to mull over the new tunes that were coming out at the time, and prior to getting that job, a lot of us worked the doors as security for the night, which was pretty low-impact work, save for when the Hell's Angels decided to pay us a visit now and again.'

Thom's sets included current indie faves as well as a smattering of dance records. He was particularly interested in Belgium's R&S label and hardcore pioneers the Ragga Twins and Shut Up & Dance. sHack: 'Thom did an excellent job as a DJ, transforming the Lemon Grove from a quiet night out for rare groove and Salsoul fanatics into a raging weekly sell-out for those with a passion for all things indie. It was around the Madchester time, when guitar music rediscovered "groove", and you could slip pretty effortlessly between the likes of the [Happy] Mondays and [Stone] Roses, through 808 State and A Guy Called Gerald, and into the proto-hardcore of Shut Up & Dance and [Joey] Beltram. Acid house was still enjoying its heyday, and although much of that would have been too minimal to work at these nights, I remember it being the sonic backdrop for a lot of parties and after-hours sessions.'

The two like-minded individuals quickly formed a band together, called the Headless Chickens. That was later abbreviated to Headless when sHack heard a New Zealand band with the same name in session on John Peel's BBC radio show. The line-up featured Thom on vocals and guitar, sHack on bass, vocals and keyboards, John Matthias on electric violin and viola (he would later contribute to *The Bends*, co-ordinating the string arrangements), plus a drummer who took the stage in a dress and motorcycle helmet. Howie, also later a part of Flicker Noise and Lunatic Calm, contributed guitar, while Laura Forest-Hay added backing vocals. Thom and sHack wrote the material between them. sHack: 'Playing music that had a contemporary dance angle to it was much more of a challenge than buying it and playing it to people, as the equipment was expensive and we, of course, had no money whatsoever for such luxuries. We did, however, have access to guitars, basses, a couple of keyboards and a couple of drummers. In the interests of creativity, we formed the Headless Chickens. I was also really into extreme hardcore at the time – the likes of Electro Hippies, Sore Throat, etc. – and that style figured in what a lot of bands were playing in the area, which is how we became involved in Hometown Atrocities. This was a loose affiliation of four or five people who lived in Exeter and who had an interest in bringing bands we liked into town, and at the same time helping our own bands do support slots for the likes of Snuff, Fugazi, Senseless Things, Cowboy Junkies, etc. After we'd done a few of these shows as the Headless Chickens, we occasionally supported bands passing through the Lemon Grove, and even did one or two of our own shows there.'

Hometown Atrocities, whose activities extended beyond music, was jointly founded by Thom and sHack, who recalls: 'Exeter was essentially a pretty Sloaney place, with lots of people winding up there as a second choice after failing to get in at Oxbridge. This gave rise to a substantial conservative – big and little 'C' – outlook, which of course galvanized anyone with opposing politics into action. It was also a time when student protest was as vigorous as it had been at any time since the sixties, on the back of eight or nine years of Thatcherite rule. Whilst bigger universities can be very divided on the left, Exeter saw a loose coalition of Socialist Workers, Marxists, eco-warriors and anarchists, all of whom knew each other, and all of whom were very willing to undertake direct action at the drop of a hat. We were involved in a number of covert night 'operations' that included occupations of the chancellor's office, of Barclays Bank, and the storming of the town hall. More often than not, Thom was a feature of these events. [As an art student] he would have been surrounded by more than his fair share of like-minded activists who'd bring a creative flair to their protests.' Thom's political commitment also took him to anti-fascist demonstrations outside Exeter City's tiny football ground, where the pasty-faced students were duly set upon by unimpressed skinheads.

The Headless Chickens' gigs included one set at the Lemon Grove around October 1989, where they shared a stage with a number of local acts. They played a set of thrashy originals, plus a thirty-second thrash-punk version of the Everly Brothers' 'Dream'. 'It just went: "Dream! Dream! Dream!" all the way through,' according to spectator Martin Keady. Thom had blond, spiky hair and played guitar and performed backing vocals. 'They were a very aggressive band, superb standard, way above college level. It was obvious they had potential,' recalls Keady. John Matthias's electric viola added a distinctive dissonance to the sound. 'It was just amazing, long instrumental jams with the viola and guitar feedback. I remember Thom Yorke riffing alongside the viola at deafening volume. You'd see so many ultimately indie eighties' bands around then. The Headless Chickens – they had this amazing energy about them, and the noise and sense of performance was a league away from student bands, especially at that time.' Although Thom wasn't the lead singer, 'he had a very compelling presence, even then', concludes Keady.

The Headless Chickens were featured on a 1989 'various artists' EP, 'Hometown Atrocities #1'. sHack: 'The EP was a four-tracker, featuring a track each from Exeter-based acts, most of whom were involved in Hometown Atrocities in some way. Our tune was called "I Don't Wanna Go To Woodstock" (although we'd change that to Glastonbury in the summer to get under the skin of the hippies that used to go) and it was basically a good-natured and completely point-less attack on long-haired loafers.' 'Woodstock' was taken from a suite of experimental songs written by sHack and Thom, credited as Tom (*sic*) Yorke on the EP's insert. There was also a projected single, 'Beautiful', which never saw release. sHack: 'There were a lot of tracks we co-wrote, and then a fair few that we brought individually to rehearsals, although the band was always seen as a sideline or a diver-sion to the many other things we were involved in. Writing with Thom was one of the most exciting prospects musically at that time – we'd hole up in my house, spark ideas off each other and have a couple of new tracks done in as many hours, and then take them to the band when we had the opportunity. In fact, around the time we split – with him going back to Oxford for On A Friday duty – we'd just spent a painful few days in a local studio trying to record this track "Beautiful", which was a cracker, but never came out quite right. Of the future Radiohead output, I remember "High & Dry" being around for a long time and I wouldn't be surprised if we played it as a band.'

The Headless Chickens/Headless lasted for some thirty gigs. Thom also played briefly in sHack's Flicker Noise, a group who evolved at the end of his time in Exeter and again featured later Radiohead collaborator John Matthias. sHack: 'Thom only did a couple of shows with us as Flicker Noise – we played a huge rave in Exeter's Great Hall which featured an opening track not too dissimi-lar to 808 State's mighty "Cubik", with Thom playing a ridiculous rock 'n' roll guitar solo over the top. He was really interested in the technology of making music without the need for a band and would come up to my loft flat on Queen Street where we'd attempt to piece together electronic tracks with little more than a four-track and a couple of very basic keyboards.' Afterwards Thom decided to honour his commitments to On A Friday. Flicker Noise subsequently recorded an acclaimed debut single, 'Information Is Power', while Lunatic Calm are still active, having just recorded their second album after extricating themselves from their original deal with Universal.

Thom's interest in academia had only returned in his second year, at which time he made use of Exeter University's newly installed Apple Macintosh computers, scanning images and completing simulated mosaics with them. 'The only good painting I did in the first year was this guy blowing his brains out. In the second year I got into taking sixteenth-century Italian paintings and ripping them off. I was really lazy and I didn't like getting all messed up, so when my college bought all these computers I was in heaven. I just stole images and fucked about with them, smudged them. I became this ideas person. For my degree show I scanned the whole of the Sistine Chapel into the hard disc, changed all the colours and called it my own. Gave it away as photocopies.'

In Liverpool, Phil largely shunned the college band circuit, which was populated by groups such as Charlie Don't Surf, The Men Who Couldn't Play, Wake Up Afrika and the Vernons. Ed, an hour away in Manchester, had also found a plum post as entertainments secretary at the Owens Park complex of student halls of residence just over a mile south of the city centre. Just like Colin in Cambridge, it meant he could arrange gigs for friends. Candyskins guitarist Nick 'Nobby' Burton remembers: 'He booked us two or three times, and he was very generous. He'd buy these enormous riders of beer from Sainsbury's and we'd all get shitfaced together – at the taxpayer's expense. Afterwards he'd take us round Manchester. I remember going round and looking at all the baggy trousers, which were very much the vogue at that time.'

Such distractions might have turned many an impressionable head, but Ed would only reiterate how important On A Friday remained to each far-flung member of the band. 'We were all at different universities around the country, and the commitment was pretty unbelievable in that we'd get back every three weekends. We'd all come back to Oxford, and Oxford's not – you know, I was in

Manchester and Manchester's such a great city. Why would you want to leave Manchester for weekends, when there's so much going on? The only reason was 'cos of the band.'

-three-

oxford and all that: the cowley road mafia

'The dreaming spires had never really been a rock 'n' roll town. But by the nineties there was a whole explosion of activity in the city. There are so many reasons why something finally went off here, it's hard to imagine why it had never happened before.'
John Robb, The Nineties: What the Fuck Was All That About?

Oxford's proximity to the capital lends it a major advantage over other regional bases – it's close enough for London-centric A&R staff to travel to. The university city has been a sustaining influence on Radiohead throughout their career, and has remained a fertile breeding ground for a succession of cutting-edge bands – Supergrass and James Lavelle, instigator of the Mo' Wax label, are among its other celebrated sons. In 1997 Oxford's influence and status were confirmed when it became Radio 1's 'Sound City'. For a town of just 120,000 people (80,000 when the students are away), the output is astonishing. It has been estimated that Oxford has more signed bands per head of population than any other town or city in Britain – even Tony Blair had a group when he was studying there. And though much of its citizenship is migratory owing to the high student population, a comparison with its old rival Cambridge (which has produced hardly one worthwhile band in twenty years) argues against a student bias. Indeed, few successful Oxford bands have any associations with the university at all.

Oxford's music mecca is sited squarely in the Cowley Road area to the south-east of the city – the 'Haight Ashbury' of the Thames Valley. As *Nightshift* magazine put it, Cowley Road is 'where it all happens, apparently. Unless you're a Uni student straight out of public school in which case it's where all the scary drug pushers, muggers and lefty bohemians hang out. A myth we're more than happy to perpetuate to keep bastards out. Also, anyone who uses the phrases "Cowley Village" or "Cowley Strip" had better watch their backs – pretentious hippy wankers.' The laddered streets spinning off to right and left house students, postgrads and young couples, while the central artery is lined with cafés and junk shops, and cheap restaurants with novel strategies about avoiding licensing laws. There is also an unusually high proportion of care-in-the-community cases wandering around, as documented in the Supergrass song 'Strange Ones', as well as one of the largest populations of homeless people outside London. More salubrious areas to the north of the city attract a wealthier clientele and the better-off student. *Select* editor John Harris attended the university and records the juxtaposition of two very different cultures. 'You've got Little Clarendon Street down to Jericho Street – it's very much wine bars, and it's where all the Sloaney people hang about. Ed was a waiter at Brown's, which was the epitome of that. And Thom never thought he fitted in there. "Prove Yourself" is all about that – "I can't afford to breathe in this town." All those lines, even up to "Subterranean Homesick Alien" – "I live in a town where you can't smell a thing/You watch your feet for cracks in the pavement" – a lot of that is about Oxford. I don't think you can understand Radiohead if you don't understand Oxford. Bizarrely, they've stayed there, so they can't hate it that much.'

Oxford was not always a haven for musical quality or risk-taking. During the punk and post-punk years it offered little of value. Indeed, up to the mid-eighties its most successful export was Mr Big, an AOR horror who placed 'Romeo' in the Top Ten in 1977. Nearby towns and villages offered greater rewards. Abingdon was the birthplace of the Inspiral Carpets' Tom Hingley (who met his future band members when Abingdon band Too Much Texas supported them at the Jericho Tavern), while nearby Banbury produced techno ace Richie Hawtin. Other famous sons of Oxfordshire include U2's Adam Clayton (born in Chinnor) and the Bonzo Dog Band's resident eccentric the late Viv Stanshall (Shillingford).

After a false start with early-eighties' Killing Joke impersonators Play Dead, the contemporary Oxford music scene began with Amelia Fletcher's Talulah Gosh, kingpins of the *NME*'s C86 movement, who later became Heavenly and eventually Marine Research. Talulah Gosh's early sets were shambolic efforts (hence the media term 'shambling bands') that were the product of enthusiasm and independence rather than serious musical content. And because of that, they were fun, even liberating.

According to Amelia Fletcher, there was little happening in Oxford before this. 'No, not really. There were loads and loads of bands, but no one ever dreamed of ... if you got to play London, that was a really big deal. At that point journalists didn't come to see bands here at all. Pete [Momtchiloff], our guitarist, had been in bands for years, always playing to the same people, the same venues.'

A whole fanzine culture erupted around bands like Talulah Gosh, the Shop Assistants, the BMX Bandits and the June Brides, all reared on old Buzzcocks singles and the DIY spirit of punk. Some of the music was fairly unappetizing, especially when it stopped being a cover for musical amateurism and instead cloaked a lack of ideas. Fletcher: 'When I listen back to some of the records, a lot of them are awful. Lots of them were rubbish.' Regrettable, too, was the coyness of some of the childlike sentiments expressed by the C86 bands. However, the movement offered a template for a self-supporting local band scene. Fletcher: 'I never lived through the punk thing or the New Romantic thing, but it was probably like that. But it did seem like there was a scene in every town.'

The difference with Oxford was that, unlike the vibrant indie culture extant in places like Leeds and Edinburgh, it was close to London. Fletcher: 'It does help. A lot of people will come to see gigs in Oxford. In a way, it's as easy as seeing a band in London because of the buses. It should be the other way round, there should be lots of people prepared to go to London, but it doesn't work like that.' The introduction of the London–Oxford Tube following deregulation in the 1985 Transport Act – a cheap bus system that runs practically round the clock between the two cities – made a huge difference. 'You could go to London to see a band and not worry about being left on a deserted Paddington platform at one a.m.'

Dave Newton, later manager of Ride and a key figure in Oxford's musical history, started a magazine entitled *Local Support* in July 1986. Newton: 'It ran from 1986 to 1989 and then evolved into *GIG*, which ran through to 1990. I've got the copy from January 1987, still, with the On A Friday demo review.' However, first impressions were not great. 'My memory of them at the time was that they were a school band. They had thirteen or fourteen tracks on the tape. I just remember they sounded like R.E.M. That's obviously what they were looking for. They just kept turning up at various gigs throughout the whole of 1987. We did one live review from the Old Fire Station, which is now a theatre and bar. I remember that because they had two or three girls playing saxophone. The support band that night [the Illiterate Hands] actually had Jonny in, before he was part of On A Friday, as well as Andy Yorke.' Local musician and promoter Mac was similarly unimpressed with On A Friday's output. 'They were much better when they came back. They were awful before university. I do remember thinking some of it was quite Orange Juicey, the Postcard-label type of stuff.'

Shortly thereafter Mac, then a member of the Clamheads, began to promote shows at the Jericho Tavern. This offered, for the first time, a legitimate outlet for aspiring local groups, as Amelia Fletcher recalls: 'About 1988 he started doing stuff. There were very few indie bands about, no one wanted to promote them. If big bands came, they played at the Apollo or the university. There was no place for medium-sized bands at all before that.' Andy Smith, bass player with The Bigger The God, has fond memories of the venue. 'The Jericho Tavern was basically a pub, the upstairs room was the band's bit. You went round the back of the pub, into a dingy car park, with all your gear if you were in the band, carrying Marshall amps up rickety stairs.

The first time I went there it made a big impact. I'd only ever been to major gigs, I'd never seen such a low-key gig before. We went down there to check something out. I was standing at the bar and could almost touch the band. Great venue, good sound. Fantastic gigs.'

Mac recalls how the Jericho came about: 'I was in a band, we couldn't get gigs, so I started putting our own on. The Jericho thing arose purely because we went through this Cockney geezer called Bob Woods. He was sent in to sort the pub out. He loved music, and me and another guy, who was into perm rock, started promoting. And he said to that guy, "You're doing my music from now on." And I said, "Right, just do a straw poll in the pub, of those people who've come to the gigs we've already done, and ask them who they'd rather have do it." He did that, then the next day he walked in and said, "You're my new music manager!"' The venue quickly grew, as bands grasped the opportunity of playing a venue other than the soft-rock-orientated Dolly. Mac: 'The Jericho had been a quite hippyish venue, there was a club called the Mad Hatter that used to happen there. And there was the Club Avocado, which was all old men playing and shit. There was nowhere for young people. The Jericho started out, you could play two rehearsals and get a gig, you'd probably get £20 out of it. They realized the more of their mates turned up, the more they got. Which is the only way it can work out.'

The Jericho quickly became the focal point of the local music scene. Mac: 'Dave had set up *Local Support* and he promoted every Friday night. They had things like [New Zealand band] the Chills play, and they gave Carter [the Unstoppable Sex Machine] their first three or four gigs. Things like the Primevals and those sort of bands. It was that thing that if you put a Creation Records artist tag on top of the poster, fifteen more people would turn up for the gig. These days, you put it on and they'll run in the opposite direction if they've got any sense. They used to do that on Fridays, then I took it on and eventually we got it up to seven nights a week. Two or three bands a week, every night of the week, with increasingly bigger names. Then it got to be too much. We realized we could make more money doing three or four nights a week. We did the Blue Aeroplanes and Hoodoo Gurus and Primal Scream. Supergrass played as the Jennifers. There was also a really good thrash scene in Oxford then, bands like Madam Adam. There were always really good bands. As soon as the Jericho got up and running, the bands had to get better to get a gig. Before, you had to go and hire a hall and play social clubs.'

Another factor in the more receptive climate for young bands was a new generation of Oxford-based music journalists. Among those was John Harris. 'I was at Queen's College, which is on the high street. In 1989 and 1990 I was working for *Sounds*. That closed in Easter 1991. I started working for *Melody Maker* in 1992. It was somewhere between those times that Ed used to send me one or two letters. There's a load of pigeonholes in college; he'd come in himself and stick it in my pigeonhole. It never ever came through the post. I was kind of known, there was the Oxford scene then, it wasn't really big, but there was Mac from the Jericho. Dave Newton, who was Ride's manager, Ronan [Munro], who wrote *Curfew*. There was an indie shop, Manic Hedgehog. I was the resident writer. Nice thing to do when you're at college. Ed used to send me these A4 letters on On A Friday notepaper. Very nice. And never was anyone better suited to the quasi-managerial role than Ed. If he hadn't been a musician he could have been a career diplomat. He was just fantastic. He wrote me a letter asking me to see On A Friday, and because the name was terrible I must have thought: "No way – this is the essence of a local band."'

Surprisingly, the nerve centre of the emergent Oxford music scene was Our Price – the famously overpriced, understocked and snottily staffed high-street retail outlet. It is now the site of a Horne Brothers suit shop, but at the time it provided a lifeline for Oxford. Among the people who worked there before Colin Greenwood were Amelia Fletcher, Dave Newton, Ronan Munro (whose job Colin filled) and Steve Queralt of Ride. Amelia Fletcher: 'I would fill the shelves with indie releases, and that created a market for those sorts of records in the town. Previously there were only two market stalls and Manic Hedgehog, and when Our Price arrived in Oxford it was like magic for us. We'd stock it with the June Brides' singles, and we could sell them really easily.' Dave Newton: 'There were three Our Prices in town for a while – it was a major employer. We got moved around a bit. I worked there for eight months, then I got moved to another branch.' Although the identities of the perpetrators are best obscured, favoured scams involved falsifying the autographs of Goth super-groups in order to sell CDs to Mission fans, and mailing 'returns' straight to the sales staff's home addresses.

Talulah Gosh were undoubtedly the pre-eminent Oxford band of the mid-eighties, but the group who truly put Oxford on the map was Ride – a briefly fashionable and stylish rock group whose rise gave Creation Records a desperately needed pre-Oasis breakthrough. In fact, without Ride it is unlikely that Creation Records would have had any of the cultural impact it enjoyed. Fletcher remembers the day that Ride signed to Creation. 'I worked with Steve Queralt at Our Price. He wrote this resignation letter. He told me he'd done it, and I said he was insane. "No, I'm going to do music." I didn't believe him and I made him open up the letter and show me it.'

Fletcher acknowledges the great leap forward that Ride consti-tuted. 'There was a scene in Oxford, there was us, but we were John Peel rather than Radio 1. Creation had been going a while, but they hadn't taken off.' Newton: 'Looking back, it seems quite remarkable, but it didn't at the time – we were just doing what came naturally. It happened by accident. We did *Top Of The Pops* and everything, but it didn't feel odd at all. It felt real. We made it so quickly; if we'd done it more slowly we might have spent more time thinking about it. The first gig was January 1989, the first single was January 1990. That charted, then the next one charted. Those first two years were great fun. And then you play Europe. It seemed like it happened with a plan – what we're going to do in 1991 is work very hard on America – but it was actually, "If we want to do America, let's go." It was new ground for Creation, they hadn't had that kind of chart placing at all.'

Ride's breakthrough proved to the local music scene that it was possible to reach a national audience. Newton: 'I hope, looking back, that what happened was quite an inspiration. It must have been. Before then, the limit for any local band was headlining the Jericho Tavern. That was as big as you could get. On A Friday were a bit of an oddity, because even though they'd played quite extensively, it was only completely at cult level. But they were never more than a popular local band. But Ride – Andy was at art college, and he went to art college because he wanted to form a band; all his favourite bands had formed at art college. So he finished school and went to art college, and lo and behold it happened. It was almost a Channel 4 four-part drama of how a band forms – from their first practice to *Top Of The Pops*. The Ride story was just like that. I hope retrospectively that the band were thought to be leading the way. They had something too, the first two albums, this was not like any other band. And if you're not like any other band you always have a chance to make your mark on history. The catalogue still sells well now, I'm quite amazed by how it's held up.' Dave Newton's commitments with Ride meant he had little time left to devote to *Local Support*. Ronan: 'I was doing T-shirts and merchandise for Ride, but when I got back off tour, Dave was getting too busy to do the paper, so I set up *Curfew*.'

Local journalist Mark Sargeant recalls: 'You could see that there was a scene bubbling up at that time. Then, like now, really, the bands would be at each other's gigs checking each other out. It was pretty close-knit. If someone had a really good idea you could be sure that someone else would be using it pretty soon after!' Ride's impact was immediate. For a while in the late eighties it seemed the whole world revolved around textured guitar bands, but as John Robb notes, this was a misrepresentation. 'Perhaps it is no surprise that Oxford was going to be shoe-gazing central. The dreaming spires were perhaps evocative of dreaming music. Mind you, the housing estates that surrounded the city, including the notorious riot-torn Blackbird Leys estate, were having no truck with all this town-centre action. They were into banging techno.'

Ride arrived in 1990 to the unfurling of a series of music paper front pages, hysterical expectations, triumphant gigs and a place in the 'grown-up' charts. Nobody, however, was paying much mind to On A Friday. Newton: 'There were a lot of local bands about, as there are now. I did a compilation of local bands on a label called Jericho Records [*The Jericho Collection*, released in 1988 and featuring the Anyways, Clamheads, Wild Poppies, Shake Appeal – whose members went on to form Swervedriver – among eleven local outfits] and they didn't feature on that. You'd have thought On A Friday would be on that. They weren't considered in that league, they were simply "that school band".'

Mac remembers his first meeting with Ed, the group's acting manager, at the Jericho. 'I was actually looking after the whole pub as relief for the manager. Ed came in one lunchtime and gave me a tape, said the usual kind of stuff. I said, "What do you do?" "I work at Brown's. I'm a waiter there." It's quite a popular, student-based restaurant in Oxford. They have the most incredible waitresses, blonde, long legs, short skirts. When he said he worked there, I thought: "Fuck me, I'll get this lot on. All the waitresses will turn up." They always drink like fish when they go out together as well. I listened to the tape, I thought that was great. "Stop Whispering" was the best track. I had another tape from them that sounded very Haircut 100. I had heard that one before, so I kind of knew about them anyway. They'd been around a bit then gone away. So the Brown's thing swung it.' As Dave Newton points out, bands with good connections at the local hospital who knew loads of nurses were also marginally more likely to get gigs.

Mac: 'Ed was a really nice guy as well. He was very polite. They were just getting such huge crowds. The first one, there were a few waitresses, but they only go and see their mate's band once, they don't become fans. They stood there dancing like the models in the Robert Palmer video, a whole front row of blondes. On A Friday put a lot into the gig, and they were just easy to work with as well. And they were local. All the sorts of things that would make you want them back. No hassle, and you end up with some money at the end of the day.'

Newton: 'After *Curfew* started, On A Friday became *the* established local band. They must have gone off to college and come back. They played in the holidays as well. I don't know what their perspective was on it, but from ours, they weren't one of *the* bands that things were expected of.' Ronan Munro, however, believes reports of On A Friday's shortcomings were exaggerated. 'I remember them as being very good. I remember thinking Thom's voice, in particular, was excellent.'

Shortly after Ride came Swervedriver, the next of a rash of Thames Valley bands to revel in My Bloody Valentine-style guitar washes, ostensibly generated by effects pedals. 5:30 also caused a few ripples in the British music press, though their *Quadrophenia* influences were a little premature with the Britpop scene still a few years away. Several other Thames Valley acts were signed in Ride's wake, including Slowdive, the Candyskins and the Mystics (whose Sam Williams later worked extensively with Supergrass). All released at least one good record, but most had their careers blighted by record company mismanagement or falling out of fashion with the music press at crucial points.

As well as playing together, the bands all socialized together too. Phil: 'It's pretty much the rule for everyone to know each other. Musically, it's very non-competitive, and if you do fall out with someone for those reasons, it's your social life gone immediately.' John Harris: 'There was one pub, the New Inn on Cowley Road, where they'd hang about. It was really a nice set-up because it had none of that bitchiness that you tend to get. Manchester, for instance, local band-wise, was very bitchy. I think that allowed Radiohead to come through with that degree of speed. They had places to play and people to write about them. *Curfew* put them on the cover. What you tended to find, Oxford bands, though no one had heard of them in London and they weren't signed, they'd pull crowds of 400 or 500, if not more. Most local bands have about twenty followers. By the time they come out of London, they're not used to playing big audiences. I think Radiohead were starting to know what that felt like because Oxford already had that vibrant scene.' Dave Newton and Ronan Munro were huge fans of the Shop Assistants. When they promoted a gig by spin-off group the Motorcycle Boy, they managed to whip up enough enthusiasm to pull a crowd of over 200. Everywhere else the group played, they were lucky to get audiences in double figures.

Oxford now has one of the most highly developed musical infrastructures of any city, ranging from venues like the Zodiac to events including the Truck Festival, Oxstock and the Punt – a movable feast held over one evening at seven venues. *Nightshift*, Ronan's follow-up venture to *Curfew*, documents local developments, its author still masking his identity behind a series of *Dr Who*-inspired pseudonyms such as Dale Kattack – Dalek Attack. Labels like the highly regarded and engagingly irreverent Shifty Disco (set up by Dave Newton, Ronan, Mac and former Candyskins manager Richard Cotton in 1997) are known on a national level. However, there was a danger in the mid-nineties that Oxford's musical growth might be compromised by the lack of a suitable local venue. A few metres along Cowley Road from the New Inn, the Zodiac is sited. Formerly the Co-op Hall and the Venue, the venture was financed with capital from Radiohead, and members of Supergrass and Ride, in the mid-nineties.

As the story goes, the groups liked the place so much, they bought it out. This allowed them to offer it to other aspiring local bands – a small investment back into the scene that made them and with which Radiohead still strongly identify, despite their global appeal. Compare and contrast with Oasis's 'Wanna borrow a tenner?' kiss-off to their former acquaintances.

The Jericho Tavern had been shut down after a multinational renamed it the Philanderer & Firkin and give it a million-pound refit. Radiohead, alongside Supergrass, Pulp, Ride and others, were involved in a failed campaign to save the venue, reasoning that they would have never got started without it. Mark Sargeant: 'They had a gig every night of the last week. It was a rearguard action, but after it closed and reopened, for years nobody would play there. They tried to get live music back there but the only things they did were blues and jazz bands. Nobody would touch it because of what happened.'

It was Dave Newton who brokered the deal to set up the Zodiac. 'Nick and Adrian, who used to promote at the Venue, owned the PA and leased it to the landlords. Basically, the place was falling apart, and it was all going to collapse. That was at the same time as the Jericho Tavern ended.' Newton recalls the anxiety of those days. 'There was a very big fear. Ronan stopped writing about the local music scene in *Curfew*, 'cos there was nothing to write about. We'd lost the Jericho Tavern and were about to lose the Venue as it was then, in a short space of time.' Despite Radiohead and Supergrass sailing up the charts, the infrastructure of Oxford seemed to be collapsing.

Newton: 'The carpet had been pulled from under our feet. The reason the Venue closed was because Nick and Adrian wanted to take it over. They pulled the PA out, which basically meant that no bands could play there. So the landlords had to sell the lease. Nick [Moorbath] was playing keyboards for Ride on the album and tour in 1994 and 1995. He came to us to ask if he could borrow the money. He said, "We'd give you a great interest rate." I said no to that, but we'll invest in it, because I thought it was really important that the Venue existed. Because when Ride started, they needed the Co-op Hall as it was then. They headlined the Jericho Tavern on 15 June 1989. It was all sold out – so where could you go to from there? I think it was May of that year that the Co-op Hall was opened, and that was our new venue with a bigger capacity. Playing the Venue became a real fixture for any kind of local celebrity. The ceiling got lifted. So the ability to keep that momentum going expanded. I said no to lending the money, but we were interested in raising money through shareholders. I agreed to look at it. It was fairly fundamental, everyone thought, that Oxford had a venue of that size. It was a fairly big part of what made Oxford what it was. I didn't hear anything more.'

Events then moved out of Newton's hands. 'I happened to see Chris Hufford one day, and I found out they'd offered Radiohead and Supergrass shares. After some apologizing, we ended up putting together a deal that raised about £60,000. There were thirteen shareholders. Andy [Bell] from Ride didn't want to put anything in. So Steve, Mark, Lawrence of Ride and myself, plus three of Supergrass, five of Radiohead and Tim [Greaves], their tour manager, were the shareholders. The deal enabled Nick and Adrian to buy back the shares at an agreed price. It was like funding, but it gave everyone a share in the whole place.' Of the members of Radiohead, only Ed – the economics graduate – has sold back his shares.

The Zodiac is now the linchpin of the local music scene. Newton: 'I can't imagine life without it. Years ago, we had the Poly, but that lost its licence in about 1986. But now we've got plenty of bands and plenty of venues. We've got venues of 200 capacity [the Point], one of 500 capacity [Zodiac], we've got Brookes University at 1,100 and the Apollo at 1,500. You've got to have a selection for local bands that evolve with it. And you've got to have places where touring bands can play, or you become too isolated. There are a lot of places around the country where people have great local bands, but they don't really shape up. In their own context, they're better than everything else around them. But they evolve in isolation. But here, as has been the case for about seven or eight years, most touring bands come through Oxford at some point. If you're in a band you get the chance to see what it's like outside of that cosseted local scene. Even if it just makes them realize that they're not very good despite being on the cover of the *NME* last week – even that's quite important. And you need venues of decent size to do it.'

You also need supporting literature and promotion. Andy Smith: 'Without *Curfew* and *Nightshift*, there wouldn't have been the Oxford indie scene. It's the one thing that kept it going. When we had no venues, *Nightshift* kept it going and was always there as a focus point.' Amelia Fletcher pays tribute to the three individuals who, collectively, have supported and nurtured the Oxford music scene. 'We [Talulah Gosh] were probably important, Ride were definitely important. But the really important people were Dave Newton, Ronan and Mac. Those three stayed involved all the way through, and I think that's really admirable.' Mac has a simpler explanation: 'We're just fucking lazy bastards. We're too lazy to get proper jobs so we do this and keep it going.'

Newton believes the Oxford music scene has benefited enormously from the breakthrough of bands like Radiohead and Supergrass. 'One thing that has changed from a local perspective is the knock-on effect that there's an awful lot of people now who are working within the music industry. Almost everyone a few years ago was doing it as an aside. A bit of promoting or writing, this or that. Something as simple as Radiohead's road crew – they're largely locally based. [Radiohead continue to employ the same road crew as they used on their very first tours.] That's the same with Ride and Supergrass. We've now got record companies coming out of our ears. None of that was in place, there were just a few local bands before. Because these bands have evolved and taken on a national following, they've dragged a lot of other people along with them. As quickly as they've had to learn how to handle moving from being a local pop star to a national one, the guys supporting them have made that conversion too, evolving at the same pace. So when a new band comes through now, there are the resources available. There couldn't be a better time to be in a band. Basically, if you're in a band and you're local, and you're good, you'll get noticed. If Radiohead formed now, it wouldn't take anything like the time it took to get noticed first time round.'

Ronan, Dave and Mac are still out there, working for Oxford's local music scene. They're all proud of Radiohead, but that's only a small part of their commitment. Mac: 'I'm really proud of all the bands from Oxford that I've helped at their first gig or first step. I'm proud of what I do. I'll talk to people if they want to write books, but I don't introduce myself at parties as the man who gave Radiohead their first gig. I'd rather be the man who gave the Panda Gang their first gig *now*. They're my current favourites. See what I mean?' Mac has at least one trophy from the On A Friday gigs, however – a video of Radiohead running through covers including 'Rhinestone Cowboy', the Beatles' 'Money' and an instrumental medley, 'Hooked On Classics', taped at the Jericho in October 1992. He's proudest of the fact that Colin can be seen wearing an Arthur Turner's Lovechild T-shirt. ATL, named after the former Oxford United manager, are the group that Mac still regularly convenes to this day.

-four-

a band called radiohead: the ridgefield road massacre

Ed, Phil and Colin had all graduated by 1990. On A Friday had remained active throughout the late eighties, retaining the female horn section and still encoring with Elvis Costello's 'Pump It Up'. Phil had his desk editor's job, and Ed worked as a barman and assistant to a photographer. Colin also returned to Oxford and took a post at Our Price. On return visits to Cambridge, he is remembered as being very bullish and animated about his new band – according to Martin Keady, he was now convinced that On A Friday were going places.

Thom finished his degree in the summer of 1991. Despite being repeatedly told by his tutors that he had no ability, he secured a 2:1, and the group reassembled in Oxford. They decided they would have to take the whole thing more seriously, and as a result, the horn section had to go. Jonny: 'It was getting more and more difficult to write parts for them.' Unsurprisingly, the post-graduation On A Friday decided to base themselves amid the Cowley Road milieu. They found a house at 5 Ridgefield Road (off Magdalen Road). 'Which of us was the father figure? No patriarchs! We were all mothers,' noted Colin. However, they could have done with some domestic-science classes. They quickly turned a nicely appointed semi-detached into a run-down boys' dormitory; the wallpaper ripped off when they moved the Hammond organ in, the living room (where

Thom slept) dominated by a communal record collection. Colin: 'We all lived there in the course of the year but people would drift in and out. Technically speaking, Phil had a room there but most of the time he couldn't bear to come round. I felt sorry for the landlord because he could never work out who was living there. We'd get angry phone calls saying, "The rent is overdue!" And we'd say, "Sorry, call Phil..."'

The home's magisterial centrepiece was the mound of 'crap records' bought by Thom to facilitate his ongoing career as a DJ. Colin: 'I was working at Our Price, and in the evenings all I wanted to do was sit round and listen to the Pale Saints. But Thom would stick on this horrendous techno music. He got pretty short shrift from the rest of us.' Jonny soon joined them, thereby completing the band (Colin: 'He never did the washing up') and switched from keyboards to guitar. Jonny's committing to On A Friday was practically the last straw for the Greenwoods' mum, who even in the mid-nineties was still asking when 'all this hideous nonsense is going to stop'. In fact, when the band were first signed, she refused to inform their grandfather for fear it would 'finish him off'.

Thom's fascination with techno and dance music eventually faded, in a manner that recalls the disillusionment documented by Jarvis Cocker in Pulp's 'Sorted For Es and Whizz'. 'It was a period of acute embarrassment. I kept trying to go to raves and stuff. Then I thought: "Fuck this, I'm not standing in a field getting the fear at five in the morning." I understand some of the music, I was pretty into it at college. But I couldn't afford any synthesizers and it wasn't the stuff I'd grown up on. It just didn't have the same emotional appeal.'

It was only now that Jonny picked up electric guitar (he had previously played jazz guitar), and was soon playing 'like Brian May, the bastard', according to Thom, tutoring himself on Lou Reed's *New York* album, which was essential listening for the band over that summer. Jonny's commitment to the band was a mixed blessing for Ed, however, who was now somewhat marginalized as just one of three guitarists in the band. 'There were times when we've been competitive,' he says, 'but we've got this really nice situation where if one guitarist doesn't play in a song, we're OK with it. We can really chill out and enjoy it.' Jonny's obvious flair gave the band's sound too much momentum to be ignored. His compositional skills were equally self-evident, and he and Thom began to work on four-track demos together, often busking the resulting songs in Oxford. However, the only way to turn a coin, apparently, was to play R.E.M. covers *ad infinitum*. The members of local hotshots Ride once stopped to listen and claimed they enjoyed the duo.

Ride had first featured in a major music paper news article in the spring of 1989. The feature in *Sounds* was read by Colin, who bought their debut EP. All the members of On A Friday were aware of Ride's existence, and of the Candyskins and Swervedriver. However, they had no personal contact with Oxford's new superstars. Colin: 'We didn't really know them, because Ride all met at art school, they dropped out of art college to be in a band. We all met at school, did our A levels, stopped doing the band to go to university, and then got back together after. I think that shows the same level of commitment. When you're at college, you're going to change. You can become even more individual. You're going to have different experiences, rather than if you start doing the band at the age of eighteen. I'm very glad we did that.'

Jonny and Thom's influences were drawn from further afield. The 'Boston scene' of the late eighties/early nineties, with the Pixies, Throwing Muses, Dinosaur Jr and Buffalo Tom, was in full swing. Thom, like many others, admired the hard edge of these records, many of which were produced by the Fort Apache Studios team of Paul Q. Kolderie and Sean Slade. He also remained drawn, however, to strong narrative writers such as Elvis Costello, Lou Reed and Tom Waits, considering the vast majority of contemporary songwriters charlatans. 'I find it very disturbing that there are thousands and thousands of these wonderful love songs which aren't really wonderful at all, and it's evident that the people who were writing them have never even been close to anything resembling the emotions they represent. Love songs have been killed by mainstream music, and to actually write a love song is a kind of peculiar thing to do these days.'

In Sutton Courtenay, a village close to Abingdon overshadowed by a huge power plant, a studio enterprise entitled Courtyard Studios was falling apart. Chris Hufford (guitar, bass and vocals) and Bryce

Edge (keyboards) had formerly been members of Aerial FX, who had recorded a couple of independent singles ('So Hard' and 'Instant Feelings') in the early eighties and once supported Spandau Ballet. In 1987, in their mid-thirties, they formed a partnership to run a complex of business units with matching houses in an ambitious attempt to bring twenty-first-century living to Oxfordshire. The core resource was a recording studio. By 1990 the whole project was in dire financial straits and they were forced to sell up.

Hufford and Bryce managed to persuade the new owners to rent them back the studio space. They used this studio time to book in the Oxford band Slowdive, who recorded their 1991 singles 'Morning-Rise' and 'Holding Our Breath' there. The album *Just For a Day* followed, with Hufford acting as producer and engineer. Slowdive were one of a clutch of southern bands who relied on effects pedals and atmosphere rather than conventional rock dynamics. Like most of their peers, they were heavily indebted to My Bloody Valentine's *Isn't Anything*. Two largely derogatory terms defined this emerging genre. The first, 'shoe-gazing', was coined by Andy Ross of Food Records to characterize a lack of movement or stage presence. A second label, 'the scene that celebrates itself', denoted what some perceived as an overly cosy support network, centred around pubs and venues like London's Underworld and the Borderline, where band members would meet, drink and talk shop.

Slowdive's success ensured the studio's short-term survival. At the beginning of 1991, John Butcher, a friend of Hufford's assistant and both Thom Yorke and Colin Greenwood, brought a demo tape to Courtyard Studios. Recorded at Union Street Studios in Oxford, it featured On A Friday's entire output to date, fifteen songs' worth, little of which impressed Hufford. 'You couldn't hear any one band on it. There were some good tunes but it was all obviously ripped off mercilessly.' But the very final track interested him. 'It was a weird looped-up dance thing which was completely mental but had something about it that was very different. I asked if they had anything else. After about six months John brought in another tape with "Stop Whispering" and "What Is That You Say?" on it. These were great songs. Now they had an identity.'

55

The tape Hufford refers to, which cost the band £300 to record, was a three-track effort recorded in April 1991. Additionally it featured 'Give It Up' – a truly horrible slice of pseudo-funk which recalled A Certain Ratio or an emaciated Higsons, with some hilarious vocal affectations from Thom. Hufford and Bryce were most impressed by 'Stop Whispering', acknowledged by the band as their Pixies tribute. At this stage it included background vocals repeating the line 'Dear Sir, I have a complaint' and an incongruous finale that ended in a squealing organ rush. Hufford and Bryce agreed to see the band in performance at the earliest opportunity.

Meanwhile Thom's songbook expanded, though the myriad styles of composition suggested he was still struggling to find a direction. His early efforts included 'Rattlesnake' (a drum-loop-based track featuring hip hop scratching), 'The Chains' (an attempt to sound like the Waterboys and requiring Jonny's viola skills) and 'What Is That You Say?', which employed heavy, Jesus & Mary Chain-esque feedback. Songs that survived to appear in On A Friday's live set included 'I Can't', an affecting, simple song amplifying Thom's lack of confidence, and 'Nothing Touches Me', 'based on an artist who was imprisoned for abusing children and spent the rest of his life in a cell, painting [Adolf Wolfli again]. But the song is about isolating yourself so much that one day you realize you haven't got any friends any more and no one talks to you.' 'Jerusalem' and 'Everybody Lies Through Their Teeth' were putdowns of life in Oxford.

On 22 July 1991 On A Friday played their first post-graduation gig at the Hollybush (now known as Walter Mitty's) in Osney, Oxford, in front of just six people. Venue manager Barry Beadle, who eventually relocated the Hollybush in nearby Witney, recalls Thom's performance: 'I remember his veins used to stand out on stage, he really went for it, but when he wasn't on stage he was quite passive. There was a major contrast between the two characters.' Meanwhile Jonny was preparing to begin his short-lived studies at Oxford Polytechnic – a choice of locale that would enable him to continue his involvement with the band and earn some money by busking with Thom.

On A Friday secured a prestige slot at the Jericho Tavern in August 1991 and invites were sent to journalists on the band's own letterheads. Predictably, the only taker was local scene magazine *Curfew*. The other important attendee was Chris Hufford. 'I was completely and utterly blown away. Brilliant songs with the amazing power of the three guitars. I made a complete buffoon of myself, bursting backstage saying, "I've got to work with you!" I was so excited by them. They had fantastic energy. I could see it on a world level, even then.'

The November issue of *Curfew* gave On A Friday their first cover feature. Ronan Munro: 'I decided after that first Jericho gig I'd give them a front cover. The reason they didn't get one till November was because of the backlog of other local bands we had to cover. From an Oxford point of view, they were starting to get good reviews. They had a big following, too. Word was spreading because a lot of other bands they played with were saying, "You've got to see this band."'

The interview took place at the group's house in Ridgefield Road. Ronan: 'They were absolutely terrified of the interview, I heard later. Only Colin had ever spoken to me before. I myself never got over my fear before interviewing bands, and they were even worse than me. But they were very, very determined, more than anyone I'd interviewed before in the paper. It wasn't like: "Oh, we just want to play our music, and if anyone else likes it…" They were aiming much higher than that.'

In the feature, Colin recalled Hufford's reaction to their Jericho gig. 'Afterwards he was almost shaking. He said we were the best group he'd seen in three years and invited us to record with him at the Courtyard. We see it as an investment.' As a result, Hufford struck a deal with the band – which, given his enthusiasm, seemed cautious but was probably prompted by his own delicate financial position – that he would allow the band to record professional demos for £100 each. Thom: 'It's a good studio… We recorded "Prove Yourself" and a couple of tracks for the album there, and we were really pleased with the results. Before that, we used to go around doing demos for between £200 and £400 a go, and that can be a severe dent in your pocket. If you're a live band, it isn't that cheap. If you're using sequencers, you can programme it all beforehand, and all you need is a bloody DAT machine, but with a rock band, you need a big space to do it, and you need all the right mics and so on.'

Hufford and Bryce approached Ride's manager Dave Newton for advice on what to do with their new charges. Newton: 'I remember speaking to him [Hufford] just after he'd taken on On A Friday. They went to demo at Courtyard and he was really knocked out by the results. He said, "Well, what do you do? How do you do it?" I said, "I don't know, just do it." I couldn't really offer much help to him at all. He was looking for a major label and an approach that was almost the other side of the coin to what happened with Ride.'

Still, most people on the local scene remained less convinced of On A Friday's potential. Amelia Fletcher: 'They surprised me. About the time they started going, Oxford was being looked at quite a lot as a potential breeding ground for new bands. There were quite a lot of new bands, but they were quite boring, they sounded stereotypically indie. I saw On A Friday twice and I thought they were very much like that, I didn't like them at all. I really regret it now, because I now think they're really good.' Andy Bell of Ride holds similar views. 'Although I think Radiohead are great, I got into them after most of America had already bought their albums.'

This first result of the deal with Hufford and Bryce was a further demo tape. Released in October 1991, and known as the 'Manic Hedgehog demos' after the local record store where it was sold, it comprised 'I Can't', 'Nothing Touches Me', 'Thinking About You', 'Phillipa Chicken' and 'You'. The price was £3. Although Colin wasn't allowed to sell the tape at the neighbouring Our Price, his position there did serve to the band's advantage. It was while working in the shop that he met Keith Wozencroft, a sales rep for EMI, who soon moved to a new position in A&R. When Colin learned of this, he pressed a copy of On A Friday's demo tape into his hands. Wozencroft: 'He gave me a tape and that tape had some really odd old stuff on it, but also a rough demo of "Stop Whispering".' Wozencroft promised he would try to catch the band live, and kept his word when he came to a poorly attended open-air show at Oxford Park which was watched principally by two of the band's girlfriends. He left word with the sound engineer that he had to go but had enjoyed the show and would keep in touch.

Another ally came on board in the shape of Jan Brown, who booked shows at Bath's Mole Club. She sent a copy of the tape Colin had given to Wozencroft to Charlie Myatt at the influential ITB booking agency in London, who agreed to book gigs for the band. At one of the first gigs that resulted, they were supported by Money For Jam, whose bass player, Hannah Griffiths, recalled to *Mojo*: 'They had to use our drum kit, because theirs was in such a state. It was strange to see so many people turn up to see them. You could sense something was happening. Thom was like a little kid, having tantrums all over the stage. We shared the door money – we got about £30 each.'

The immediate problem for the band was their name. The cursory On A Friday was inappropriate, particularly if the band were performing on any other day of the week. Several alternative names were considered. Colin told friends that one name they briefly deliberated was Free Beer, so they'd be the ultimate support band ('Such and such plus free beer'). Thom went for Music, which the others considered horrible. Equally pretentious was Jude, after Thomas Hardy's novel *Jude the Obscure*, with its Oxford setting. They toyed with Dearest and Shindig, and came close to choosing Gravitate, but in the end they decided to persevere with On A Friday for the time being.

Progress was slow. Typical gigs included a set at Banbury where, as Jonny recalls, by the end of the performance only one man was left standing: 'in a slouch hat, coat and cigarette holder. He said to Thom: "You were wonderful, darling. You played that guitar like it was your penis."' In others they excited less fervent praise. Mark Sargeant: 'They were just one of those local indie bands that no one was that bothered by. They were a bit boring, really. But they seemed to have one or two songs that stood out.'

Another gig at the Jericho was booked in October. Wozencroft dutifully turned up, and was once again impressed by the intensity of the band's performance and their developing songcraft. Wozencroft's boss, A&R director Nick Gatfield (formerly saxophonist for Dexy's Midnight Runners), also saw the potential in the group's demo, and was introduced to the band when Wozencroft invited them to EMI's offices in London. (Wozencroft would also subsequently sign Supergrass to the label, on the recommendation of Hufford.)

In November On A Friday played a second gig at the Jericho Tavern, which coincided with the publication of their first interview with *Curfew* fanzine. This time it was sold out, the A&R grapevine having gone into hyperdrive about the Oxford quintet. Quite why a band who had been around the circuit for several years were suddenly the subject of such giddy excitement is a question only the concerned A&R departments can answer, but rumours had evidently been leaking out of their growing Oxford fanbase. Island Records had joined the hunt after obtaining a copy of the band's demo. With the guest list filling up, the A&R staff took the unprecedented decision to pay for entry. The promoter, Mac, was taken by surprise, but he quickly turned the situation to his advantage. 'It was obvious Radiohead were going to get signed. To be honest, the Jericho was still fairly young in its existence at the time. We hadn't dealt with a lot of A&R men, we didn't know how to play that game. We do now. A bloke would phone up and say he was from Spunk Monkey Records and you'd go, "Fuck me! A record company!" On A Friday was the first A&R stampede we'd had. We didn't know anything about them at all. We learned quick. Probably by the end of that night, I'd realized how easy it is to get a drink out of an A&R man, which is the first step. We very quickly installed a receipt service in the bar upstairs.'

Andy Smith of The Bigger The God was also there. 'Me and David [Cowles-Hamar, The Bigger The God's vocalist] were out flyposting that night. That could be a pretty nefarious activity – you didn't want to get caught, or you could face a £400 fine. We were doing the wall of the Jericho when a weird bloke in a leather jacket came and said, "You're The Bigger The God." It was Colin. Typical Radiohead thing – principles, generosity. He said, "We have all these A&R men coming down, come along and bring some tapes." Colin had seen us at a gig before, that's why he recognized us. Ed showed us a list of A&R men that filled a piece of A4 paper, thirty or forty people. We legged it off our flyposting circuit, came back with some tapes.'

Unfortunately, none of the assembled A&R staff showed much interest in anything but On A Friday. Instead, the members of The Bigger The God stood at the back, watching the band. 'Both me and David thought they were great songs. They had a crowd down the front, but they weren't packing the place out. I remember the songs sounding very much like the Pixies, with alternately very loud/very quiet bits. After that we pestered Mac [the promoter] and then Thom to let us support them at the next gig at the Jericho.' Wozencroft was also in attendance. 'I had gone with the director of A&R and everyone was down there. That gig was really funny. Parlophone loved it, and we did the deal. Chris and Bryce came in, they really liked what we were saying and it was all very quick.'

Among those attending the Jericho Tavern that famed evening was EMI director Rupert Perry, now the company's CEO, who had been impressed by 'Phillipa Chicken' from the demo tape (a strange, likeable song with a comical, bird's-eye view of retribution – with lines announcing Thom's possession of both 'ammo' and 'plans' for the future – which, ironically, the group had now dropped from their live set). A meeting was arranged shortly thereafter. EMI made a formal offer of a recording contract, and Hufford and Bryce were engaged as the group's managers. Although they had never overseen a band before, and considered rock-band managers as a species to be 'complete tossers', they agreed to give it a go, so convinced were they of On A Friday's potential. John Harris describes Chris Hufford as a 'fantastic' find for the band. 'A very genial, likeable fella, there's none of that corporate big hitter about him. Bryce has a bit more of that.'

The deal with EMI was clinched on 21 December 1991, after On A Friday travelled to London to complete the formalities. Halfway through the negotiations, Rupert Perry poked his head round the door, saying, 'You'll never see me again until you sell 500,000 units and then we'll shake hands and take a photo. By the way, I really like that song "Phillipa Chicken".' Afterwards the band celebrated in typically understated fashion. Wozencroft: 'We went to this restaurant and then we went to a bar and got pissed and then they caught the bus back to Oxford. [Nick] Gatfield put a good offer in straight away and it was fine, we didn't mess around.' They intended to meet up again to discuss the ramifications over a pint in an Oxfordshire pub, but lost track of each other and went home instead. The advance was immediately deposited in an interest-bearing account ('So if we're dropped, we'll have enough money to put out another album on our own label,' Ed declared at the time. 'We're quite tight with the old purse strings.').

They declined EMI's kind offer to place them on a faux-indie subsidiary, electing to work on the 'classic' Parlophone imprint. This meant the band had the full weight of EMI's resources behind them. John Harris, writing for *Melody Maker*, was contacted by the band's new PR representatives, Hall Or Nothing. 'Philip Hall, God rest his soul, he used to ring me up quite a lot. Even though all I was doing was little reviews for the papers, he used to use me as a sounding board. He said, "Come and see this band On A Friday." I said, "I've got letters off them." "No," he said, "they're really good. They've signed to Parlophone." But Nick Gatfield believed in going the way of the independent press, he wasn't that confident in the ability of Parlophone to break them, which seems strange now. The point was at that time there was such indie snobbery. People thought this was a really salient question – why did you sign straight to Parlophone?'

There were good reasons for this. Thom: 'We never wanted to be the most exciting band in our ghetto. The idea was to cut straight through all that "paying your dues" bit and get the whole world to see us. That was part of the attraction that our record deal offered us. The contract signed us to Parlophone "all around the world and in the known and unknown universe". I liked that breadth of vision.' Thom may be horrified to learn that such clauses – relating to a company's ability to exploit their investment on Mars should they discover life there – is actually a standard feature of music industry contracts.

Still, they were delighted at the turn of events. Thom: 'We all went home for Christmas to get our heads together. I sat down and thought: "You have just been signed by EMI, who signed the Beatles and David Bowie... RIGHT!"' This realization was repeated on numerous occasions elsewhere, not least in a later interview with *Curfew* magazine. Thom: 'We're NOT an indie band. We write pop songs but some people can't see that.' That sentiment was echoed by Ed. 'When we first signed, someone said, "What agenda do you have?" With British bands, there was this whole thing about having something to say. But, maybe naively, we said, "It's about music." And that's what it's about.'

Despite his protestations, a series of lyrics emerged demonstrating that Thom was well aware of the pitfalls of joining the corporate music industry. 'There's no question we got lucky in the beginning,' he conceded, 'and that was the primary reason why the London music press didn't like us. It was ridiculous; the record companies were making outrageous offers and we had only maybe five songs and this show that was exciting but sometimes haphazard as well.'

At the close of 1992 the hottest ticket around London was Brett Anderson's Suede, a group seemingly intent to base their whole career on a small portion of David Bowie's recorded output. They were nevertheless fêted by the press, the *NME* featuring them on their cover before they'd released a single. But as On A Friday later noted in their second interview with *Curfew* magazine: 'We were completely ignored for a whole year before we started getting reviews. We're not a Suede. We don't have that kind of angle for the press to grab on to. People have to really dig to get an angle on us.'

For the Oxford music scene, On A Friday's signing was seen as a communal victory. Andy Smith: 'There was a definite buzz about the Oxford scene. When you're a young, unsigned band, you think the whole thing about being successful is getting signed. When Ride got signed, that showed people that they could do it. There was a sense that you weren't locked into Oxford, you could build an escape route. You weren't just a local band banging around the same venues for ever. But this is also an indication of how On A Friday/Radiohead were perceived of as nice blokes – when most bands get signed, there is an element of resentment. With Radiohead, nobody ever felt that. There was always a good feeling about them. Everyone on the scene was one hundred per cent behind them all the way. No one thought: "They don't deserve it" – they all thought: "They deserve it, but so do I."'

That the band can still co-exist in relative harmony with their surroundings (the members continue to live within a stone's throw of Cowley Road) speaks of both their lack of pretence and the protective nature of many of their friends and peers. Being in Oxford also kept the group away from the in-fighting and backbiting so prevalent in the capital. In 1995 Thom complained to a journalist: 'The British music scene is so insular, so petty and so fucking bitchy. I just don't want to have any contact with it. That's why we've never moved to London. If we did, that would be it. We'd last a month and then split up.' However, the band's attitudes have changed over the years. Thom is now depressed by the pollution that envelops Oxford, which he claims makes him and his girlfriend ill.

The record deal afforded the band some security and their parents a little peace of mind. It also enabled On A Friday to expand their sound. The Thames Valley scene (Ride, Slowdive) was still a big influence, as were Boston and the Pixies, and now the equipment to replicate some of those sounds was within their financial reach. Andy Smith: 'Slowdive had been produced by Chris [Hufford], so we were hearing them lots. The first thing that struck me about seeing Radiohead was the songs, they had tunes. But when they got signed, they started experimenting more. For instance, the guitar sound on "Blow Out" is very reminiscent of Slowdive. That whole experimentation with sound seemed to start happening when they had the money to buy effects pedals, which came after they signed.'

The band's optimism at the beginning of 1992 was tangible. They were planning the release of their debut EP, and earned their first favourable review from *Melody Maker*'s John Harris for their February gig supporting the Candyskins at The Venue. However, Harris concluded his review by pointing out that On A Friday's name was more 'apt for beer-gutted pub rockers'. Harris: 'They came on and played for about half an hour. Ed had his white Rickenbacker, and bits of it made me think it sounded like the Jam. Maybe it's because I'm an old Mod, and seeing Ed with a white Rickenbacker, I thought: "I haven't seen that for a while." They played "Nothing Touches Me", which they never released, but the best bit was "Stop Whispering". Even then they were doing that bit where it drops out and it goes, "Doesn't matter anyway". Thom had a shaved head and he looked about four foot tall. He didn't have a guitar on, and he was just reeling around. I thought: "This is great." They didn't look great. But it was obvious, it was very intense, very frenetic, and he [Thom] was very compelling. Like all the great frontmen, he got lost in the music.' What appealed most to Harris was that the band sounded completely out of step with the rest of the music scene. 'The context at that time was all shoe-gazing and fraggle [a term denoting low-charisma pop-punk bands] – so a band who wrote songs like "Stop Whispering", compared to Slowdive or Mega City Four, sounded like the work of God.' Headliners the Candyskins were similarly impressed, even humbled. Nick Burton: 'Even from the earlier gigs, I had the sneaking suspicion they were a better band than we were. But now the word was out about them.'

Long dissatisfied with their name, all parties now agreed that their new campaign should be spearheaded under a new banner. Harris: 'I don't know whether Parlophone had been nudging them in that direction, and I think they probably had, and the review was the last straw.' That's confirmed by Wozencroft. 'It wasn't a great name and when we did the deal we said, "It's up to the band, but it's not a great name." Their managers said, "No, it's OK." And then they had their first review in *Melody Maker* and it was a favourable review, but it said something like "[the] band are different to what their beer-swilling Friday night moniker might suggest". And when the band read that, they realized that it wasn't such a good name and at the same time they came up with a name they liked.'

In March 1992 On A Friday became Radiohead – a name adopted from the track 'Radio Head' on the Talking Heads' 1986 album *True Stories*, a song which was also issued as a single in 1987. Thom: 'Radiohead was cool and it is still cool because it just sums up all these things about receiving stuff... All these people in America have these teeth you can pick up radio on. They have this sort of metal in their teeth and some of them can pick up radio with it. I think that is very cool. And now of course they can implant things into your head that they can work and sort of observe your brain patterns. Radiohead is sort of ... it's brilliant.'

With the change of name, Jonny left college to pledge his full-time allegiance to the band. The Greenwoods' mater was not impressed. According to Colin, she considered the group's manager 'the son of Satan' for allowing this situation to pass. Jonny claimed in interview he had been encouraged to leave by his tutor – a man who had formerly spent time in a New York punk band. The head of Brookes University's music department, Dai Griffiths, recalls Jonny only attended classes for about three weeks, though he adds: 'Radiohead – top band, of course.'

The group's first major London gig came on 27 March 1992 at the Venue in New Cross, south London, supporting the Catherine Wheel and God Machine. According to friends from Cambridge, Colin was desperate for the London media to see his band, and everyone was invited to a subsequent gig in May at the Islington Powerhaus. It was completely packed, with several music celebrities there to check the band out, including Miles Hunt of the Wonderstuff, who was said to be 'blown away'. Or, as Martin Keady remembers, 'he could see his career going up in smoke'. As Radiohead recorded their debut EP, Parlophone, having applauded the band's decision to change names, tried to convince them to wear better clothes. A stylist was appointed, only to see Thom blow his personal budget on charity-shop detritus. Colin, sensibly, bought a suit that would see him through job interviews if the band didn't work out.

The EP, 'Drill', was recorded with the help of Hufford and Bryce, a pairing which proved instantly counterproductive. Thom was suspicious of Hufford's involvement, a situation aggravated by Hufford's admission that he is 'quite overbearing and opinionated in the studio'. In the end they retreated to previous recordings for two of the songs. 'Drill' was released on 5 May 1992. Its running order featured a reprise of two tracks from the 'Manic Hedgehog demos'. 'You' and 'Thinking About You' were present in unaltered form. The guitar intro to 'You' was heavily reminiscent of the Icicle Works – a band On A Friday had supported in 1988 at the 'Exeter Event' at Exeter College in Turl Street, Oxford. 'Thinking About You', Thom's homage to nocturnal emissions, possessed a much harsher, rockier edge than the version which eventually appeared on the first album.

The new songs were 'Prove Yourself' and 'Stupid Car'. 'Prove Yourself', undoubtedly the standout track, teetered between shoulder-shrugging resignation and the vocabulary of a suicide note – Thom lamenting the life-sapping inertia of the couch potato, weaned on a cathode ray nipple. The sharp twists from becalmed quiet to invigorating noise were the result of what Ed describes as being 'in hock to the Pixies and Dinosaur Jr up to our eyeballs'. Eventually re-

recorded in a superior version for the group's debut album, it was the first Radiohead stage favourite – and the first, but not last, to be misinterpreted. For several years to come Thom was burdened with the prospect of his audience singing the line 'I'm better off dead' straight back in his face. 'Stupid Car' was the only one of the four songs that didn't make the first album. It is the first of Thom's transport paranoia epics – inspired by the accident he suffered in 1987 when he crashed his car and gave his then girlfriend whiplash.

Any band sees their first release as a justification and a coming of age, and Radiohead were no exception. Andy Smith recalls dropping in at the house in Ridgefield Road to be greeted by Colin in ebullient mood, clutching the band's first single. Yet there was still parental pressure to get a proper job. Colin: '[My mother] couldn't believe I spent nine months after I graduated working at Our Price in Oxford. Even the fucking bank manager at NatWest gave me a lecture about having a degree from Cambridge and selling records, and I stupidly said, "Well, I'm going to be in a band", and he was like, "Come on, get real and wise up, boy." So when our first record came out it was a nice "fuck you" to all those people, though not to my mother, obviously. She was more upset about my younger brother Jonny joining the band because he dropped out of Oxford [Poly].'

However, there were problems with 'Drill' that made the EP largely unrepresentative of the band. The recordings were rough mixes by major-label standards. EMI chose fashionable design house Icon to provide cover artwork, at enormous expense, considering that the EP was released in an issue of only 3,000 copies in each format of CD, cassette and vinyl. Of those, one batch of CDs was misplaced at EMI's warehouse (which at today's market value adds up to about £150,000), and as a result the CD had to be repressed. Promotional versions mailed out to the press included a CD by Joe Cocker rather than Radiohead. On top of that, the accompanying photo session (by Tim Paton) saw Thom giving the snapper the finger in a most unappealing way – his short crop making him look like a relic of the 'Oi! wars' of the early eighties.

The reviews, when they came, were mixed. Several focused on the fact that Radiohead had been 'snapped up' by EMI within weeks of their careers starting – which could not have been further from the truth. Thom found the criticism of his songs hard to bear, as did the rest of the band. On tour in Nottingham, they shamelessly tried to purchase copies of the record themselves in order to hype its chart position. Imagine the size of their collective bottom lip when they were told by the record shop that, as they'd been given the EPs by EMI and simply couldn't sell them, they could have them free.

The clouds were lifted slightly when they earned their first feature in *Melody Maker* courtesy of John Harris in May. In it, Thom Yorke professed his desire to make a single as arresting as Nirvana's 'Smells Like Teen Spirit' in its intensity: 'When it came on the radio, you had no choice but to listen to it.' However, this remark backfired on the band. Harris: 'At the time, it was very trendy, and they themselves were massive fans of American college rock. They were really into Throwing Muses, and liking the Pixies was *de rigueur* – this was around the time the Pixies headlined Reading in 1991. Immediately it was obvious they were in thrall to all that. They said that they wanted their music to have the same visceral impact as "Smells Like Teen Spirit". I think Thom got quite cross when he saw that in print, it made them look like they wanted to sound like Nirvana. That wasn't their point, it was more about having that sort of impact.'

Otherwise it was a fairly typical music press piece on a new band. 'They didn't have much to say. I remember Jonny walked in with a bag from Chelsea Girl, because he used to wear women's scoop-necked blouses, and he'd just bought a new one. Jonny is quite camp. He looks quite androgynous. I thought: "This is interesting" – I hadn't noticed him that much before. Ed, Thom and Colin looked fairly blokey. Then in walked this fella who looked like a woman.' The group were also featured on Gary Davies's weekend breakfast show on Radio 1, where the DJ made 'Prove Yourself' his 'happening track of the week'.

To promote the single the group toured with the Catherine Wheel, Phil borrowing the headliners' drum kit for the whole tour, apart from their debut at the Marquee, when he had to employ a kit they'd found dumped outside. They also played several dates with the Sultans Of Ping – a novelty indie band from Ireland briefly famed for their hit 'Where's Me Jumper?' Thom: 'When we first signed we hadn't a clue what we were about. So we went out on the road, and I shaved all my hair off and got really drunk every night, smoked too much, we had to cancel loads of gigs. I hit the self-destruct button pretty quickly.'

The music press remained suspicious. To all intents and purposes, Radiohead appeared to have come from nowhere and coasted to a fat major-label deal. They had played a grand total of eight gigs in the year that they were signed. Though they had actually slogged around the live circuit for aeons, it was only people in or around Oxford who knew of that. The fact that they had attended public school did not escape their critics, either. Unlike some, they never sought to hide this fact, though it was a point on which they were naturally defensive. Thom: 'The middle-class thing has never been relevant... The thing that winds me up about the middle-class question is the presumption that a middle-class upbringing is a balanced environment, when, in fact, domestic situations are not relevant to class. A bad domestic situation is a bad domestic situation. It's just such a fucking warped perspective on things.' Perhaps class is irrelevant to pop music in terms of aesthetic criteria. But most working-class schoolkids are lucky to get the chance to play the triangle in the nativity play. They never enjoy the privilege of well-equipped, soundproofed music rooms to hone their skills in.

Others had legitimate concerns about the group's originality. According to John Harris, there was one central reason why Radiohead were initially considered inauthentic – and it wasn't to do with preconceptions about their background. 'If you have a look at the artistic outlook of the people making these decisions, they have no problem with middle-class people at all. I think the residual impression was: there's Nirvana, the Pixies and all that, and they did it properly, and Radiohead were some failed imitation. That was the point. They were like Cliff Richard was to Elvis.'

-five-

i don't belong here:
'creep' and the
heroically wrong hacks

Managers Hufford and Bryce had decided that if the band were to progress, they needed proper production help. Nick Gatfield suggested Paul Q. Kolderie and Sean Slade, Yale graduates now based in Cambridge, Massachusetts. The Fort Apache team behind so many of the successful Boston bands beloved of Radiohead (Throwing Muses, the Pixies, Buffalo Tom, the Lemonheads) have always regarded themselves as 'facilitators' rather than producers, often using the French term 'réalisateur'. Kolderie: 'We like to work with a group and realize their songs – make a song, which might exist only as humming in the air, into something real, something people can buy and play on the radio. That's our job.' They also share production duties while working – on a given track Slade will engineer and Kolderie produce, then the roles will be swapped. Fresh from the success of Buffalo Tom's *Let Me Come Over* album, they agreed to record Radiohead's next single after hearing the demo version of 'Stop Whispering'. The band themselves were delighted to be hooked up with the producers of some of their favourite records.

Sessions were convened at Chipping Norton in Oxfordshire, originally for what was slated to be a double A-side featuring 'Inside My Head' and 'Million $ Question'. Both songs were said to concern Thom's doubts about signing to a major label. 'Inside My Head' is

70

also, coincidentally, another line from the Talking Heads song that gave the band their name. The pay-off line in 'Million $ Question' saw Thom wonder aloud whether he was making a 'big mistake'. The song also announced Thom's desire to find a car and ram-raid his old employers, Cult Clothing. 'I just wanted to do that so badly,' he revealed. However, neither song came across as well in the studio as it had in a live context, and the producers were left scratching their heads as to what to do with the band. In fact, Kolderie later conceded: 'It even occurred to us that maybe they were trying to see what we could do with the weaker material.'

Kolderie's first impression was that the band was desperately inexperienced. 'We didn't like these songs Parlophone had chosen, and I don't think the band liked them much either. "Inside My Head" was not very melodic, didn't have any of the stuff we thought the others had, so we were rather disappointed.' It was only when the producers caught the band playing around with a new song they'd broken in during the tour with Catherine Wheel that their interest was reignited. Kolderie: 'When they finished it, Thom mumbled something like, "That's our Scott Walker song." Except I thought he said, "That's *a* Scott Walker song." Now, I was pretty familiar with Scott Walker, but jeez, there's a lot of albums and I could have missed something! We walked out of the rehearsal that night and Sean said, "Too bad their best song's a cover."'

The sessions ground on without much sign of a breakthrough. Chris Hufford described the results of the initial recordings as 'overblown, bombastic rock'. It was only when Kolderie suggested the group run through their 'Scott Walker' song that light appeared at the end of the tunnel. The group obliged, offering the song in its entirety. Kolderie: 'Everyone in the place was silent for a moment and then they burst into applause. I'd never had that happen before. I called Keith [Wozencroft] and said, maybe you should come down. So he drove to Oxford that night, listened to it three times, and said, "Hmmm…" And a couple of weeks later he called me and told us to work on it some more.'

The lyrics also had to change, however. Kolderie: 'The original words weren't too happening, something about a "leg of lamb". I remember saying to Thom, "You've got to try it again, it's just not that strong." At first he said, "No, no, it's too late. I can't change it now." So I said, "You really should if this is the single." Then he got this weird look on his face and went away for about twenty minutes. Then he had it.'

'Creep', originally written on campus at Exeter in the middle of a drink binge, was a shotgun marriage of Thom's self-disgusted lyrics with the clever dynamism of the music's sustained four-chord progression. It concerned an infatuation he'd had while at the university (he will only admit that the song's subject 'knows who she is'). sHack: '"Creep" came a little after Thom had left Exeter and was still in the habit of coming back for the odd weekend. The first time I heard it I was sitting in John [Matthias]'s dingy front room and Thom just sat and played it on an acoustic guitar. We were mesmerized.'

Alienation, as enacted by bookish post-adolescents, is one of rock's most over-explored and underwhelming themes. Yet 'Creep' gave everyone who heard it a visceral thrill. The quiet minor chords at the beginning of the song turn to major chords during the chorus, emphasizing the astonishing final release of energy which diffuses the downcast lyrics into something triumphant, lending the song the properties of a manic depressive's mood swing. Musicologist James Doheny was invited to analyse the song for *Select* and declared it to be 'very Brian May, actually' – ironic, given Thom's early infatuation with Queen.

The song turned on Jonny's contribution. The harsh, thuggish guitar strokes – which echoed the emotionally stunted words of the song – were adapted from a tuning technique he had developed (if the 'clunk' sounded right, then everything was as intended), and arose from his impatience with the song as it stood. 'I didn't like it. It stayed quiet. So I hit the guitar hard – really hard.' Thom: 'That nervous twitch he does, that's just his way of checking that the guitar is working, that it's loud enough. And he ended up doing it while we were recording. And whilst we were listening to it, it was like, "Hey, what the fuck was that? Keep that! Do that!"' The song also borrows from the Hollies' 'The Air That I Breathe'. Jonny admitted in an early interview that 'What happened was, we wrote "Creep" and the middle eight just had my guitar playing a tune. And Ed stopped and said, "This is the same chord sequence as that Hollies song" and then sang it. So Thom copied it. It was funny to us in a way.' The group immediately knew they had something, and so did Slade and Kolderie. The latter recalls: 'At the end of the few days, we listened back to it and Thom turned to Jonny, asking, "What do you think?" Jonny just said, "I think it's the best thing we've done in ages." I remember thinking: "Well, when did you do something better than this?"'

Among the bands working at Sutton Courtenay were The Bigger The God, whose Andy Smith notes: 'It was quite a futuristic, Scandinavian-looking, glass-fronted place. It was twenty-four-track, so that was luxurious for us. We did some demos there, as well as our first single. Then Chris [Hufford] played us "Creep". We listened politely through the first two verses – we couldn't see anything. Then the guitar came in, we went, "Wow, yeah!"' There was a similar reaction when Ed played the track to members of the Candyskins on a car stereo. Nick Burton: 'He said, 'This is what we've just done, we're not sure about it." We were like, "Fucking hell! This is amazing." But I suspect they secretly knew it was good. They just wanted confirmation.'

On 22 June, Radiohead's first BBC session for Mark Goodier was broadcast. Recorded nine days earlier, it featured 'Prove Yourself', the first-ever transmission of 'Creep', 'I Can't' and 'Nothing Touches Me', a survivor from the Manic Hedgehog demos. 'Creep' got its official release three months later, backed by 'Million $ Question', 'Inside My Head' and a new song about a relationship that had soured, 'Lurgee' – a survivor's guide to love propelled by a jangly Rickenbacker sound rooted in early R.E.M. This time the print run was 6,000 copies in each format, but Radio 1 effectively ignored 'Creep', playing it just twice, thereby relegating it to a best showing of number seventy-eight on the UK singles chart. Reviewers were generally enthusiastic. As John Robb notes: 'That song transcended all the reservations journalists had about Radiohead.' A video was shot to accompany it – the band's first – set at Oxford's the Venue. Two hundred and fifty local fans provided the crowd seen in the video. Unfortunately, it received as few broadcast airings as the song had on radio.

The single was promoted via a series of support slots with various groups (or 'everyone who's no one') through August. Among them were Kingmaker, with whom Radiohead were invited to play at an EMI bunfight at the company's UK conference in September. Radiohead were briefed to play well, win friends and influence people, thereby encouraging the reps to work harder on their behalf. Carol Baxter headed EMI's international office, responsible for promoting the group's British signings overseas. 'I know nothing about instruments or drum riffs, or what have you, but this funny little band come on and they obviously had something. This was a hideous record-company do but Thom gave it everything.' Up until that point Baxter had been considering leaving her post. 'I sat there thinking: "I'm not going to leave: I want Radiohead on my roster!" I bumped into Colin and Thom in the corridor after their performance and I thought they were junkies. Bloody druggies sitting there in the corridor looking so pale. I asked Thom if he was all right. He said he was. So I asked if they wanted a drink and all they wanted was a glass of Coca-Cola. I bought that for them and we got talking, and I found out they were from Abingdon...' Born in Abingdon herself, Baxter thereafter took a personal interest in the band's fortunes, and played a pivotal role in bringing their initial American success.

Also at that EMI conference was John Harris, who had now joined the *NME*. 'In the *NME* Simon Williams and Steve Lamacq did an ON piece around "Drill". The general impression was that Radiohead were a good thing, which wasn't a commonly shared opinion at the *NME*, certainly not after Steve Sutherland took over. It was in Manchester, an EMI sales convention. EMF, Kingmaker, Radiohead – they were the first band on. We went back to the Britannia Hotel and had pizza and I interviewed them. I remember Thom talking at length about how he would never be happy. He was quite prone to self-loathing. They all laughed when I asked if they'd ever be happy. Nigel Powell was doing the lights. He burst out laughing when I said, "Do you think you'll ever be happy?" Thom boldly stared into his pizza and said ... "No."'

On 21 October the 'Creep' tour proper began, as support to Kingmaker. This included the ignominy for Radiohead of playing third on the bill to a juggler. The band conceded to *Curfew* that these were the least enjoyable support slots so far: 'Not because they were horrible or anything, it's just that we never got a soundcheck because they had such a terrible production.' Despite this, both Kingmaker and their other touring colleagues, the Frank And Walters, voted Radiohead their favourite new group of the year. And Thom was able to continue writing new songs. In a car driving to one of the gigs, he played Ed a tape of '(Nice Dream)' for the first time, though the song would be earmarked for the band's second album. 'The Bends' was also written during this period.

EMI were disappointed with the showing of 'Creep' on radio, but were convinced that in Kolderie and Slade they'd found the right team. The duo again joined Radiohead at Chipping Norton to embark on sessions for Radiohead's debut album. The problem was the timescale – the group were given only three weeks to record it. As Kolderie relates, overcoming their naivety was the main stumbling block: 'It was a bit of a struggle. It was their first record and they wanted to be the Beatles, and the mic had to have no reverb, and they had all the ideas they'd ever come up with in twenty years of listening to records. But we managed to get it done.' The group's insistence on a reverb-free sound was in keeping with the vogue for 'dry' production, which Kolderie and Slade had helped to pioneer. There is no doubt that for Radiohead clarity of sound was as much a philosophical distinction as an acoustic one.

The band's relationship with the press cooled sharply after the good reviews which greeted 'Creep'. At a headlining appearance at the Smashed Club in London, the *NME*'s Keith Cameron declared Radiohead '...a pitiful, lily-livered excuse for a rock 'n' roll group'. John Harris: 'There was a big change round at the *NME* and John Mulvey took over [as features editor]. And he said something to the effect of – Radiohead would be in the *NME* over his dead body. And Phil Hall wrote a letter to Steve Sutherland complaining. There were some terribly damning things said about Radiohead and their chances of ever progressing to other pages of the *NME*. That all crystallized around the live review that Keith Cameron wrote at the Islington Powerhaus. Not only that, but the photos weren't any good. So they inserted four pictures of Thom. And when you perform, you pull faces. And each picture was captioned "Uglee – oh yeah! Radiohead Thom gurns his living". I know for a fact that Thom was very cut up about that and I don't blame him. And that's why he rarely speaks to the music press.'

John Mulvey at the *NME* puts the paper's doubts over Radiohead into context. 'When they started I was features editor and my professional position is that I've always tried to be opinionated but be pragmatic in editorial decisions. I've always tried to see the bigger picture. There were some things I liked: they had intelligence and ambition and seriousness, and 'Creep' was a good song. But in retrospect I thought *Pablo Honey* was a terrible record. Whilst I can see why people think *The Bends* and *OK Computer* are good records, they're not for me. I genuinely thought the first album was poor and they were one-hit wonders. I was patently, heroically wrong, and I don't mind going on record saying that. It's a weekly paper, and you try to see a broad perspective, but sometimes you get it wrong.'

Thom was reportedly so upset by the Cameron review that he went out and bought a box of plasters to stick copies of the review all over his flat. He quickly reassessed his relationship with the media. John Harris: 'The story is that Michael Stipe advised Thom that he didn't have to talk to the weeklies. The monthlies were OK, but one's sense of mystique and artistic whatever declines slightly if you talk to the weeklies. If you read *NME* stuff about R.E.M., it was only ever Peter Buck.' Thom confirmed that in an interview in June 1996. 'I admire the way he [Stipe] dealt with that whole period of his life around *Automatic For The People*, with the AIDS rumours. He just wasn't gonna answer and they did give up eventually. Elvis Costello was the same. He just walked away from it all.'

The band still lacked a title for their debut album. Inspiration came from manager Hufford. He had acquired a tape of American telephone pranksters the Jerky Boys from Chapterhouse, who had just returned from America. On one of the sketches a man is rung up by Jerky Boy Frank Rizzo, who opens the conversation by saying, 'Pablo, Honey', before pretending to be his mother and inviting the bemused man out to Florida. As Thom confessed to David Cavanagh, 'Pablo

Honey was appropriate for us because we're all mothers' boys.' Ironically, Cavanagh's piece continues: '[the Jerky Boys tapes contain] telephone pranks so abusive, nasty and malicious that they make Victor Lewis-Smith seem like the smug public school under-achiever he really is.' He was evidently unaware of Radiohead's own background.

Yet Radiohead, unlike Joe Strummer, Shane McGowan and other rebel rockers of the past, never made any attempt to hide their public-school background. Further, it was something about which they didn't even feel defensive. Ed: 'Look at the history of British bands. Most are from the middle class, with the stress on higher education. The young people turn to music as a reaction to the middle-class treadmill. They form their own little gangs.'

As 1993 dawned, Radiohead were touring furiously once more. Having completed well over one hundred engagements in the previous year, they now faced an itinerary stretching from 13 January to the start of March. While on the final lap of the thirty-four-date stint at London's Camden Underworld, Australian raconteur Clive James tried to get in on the guest list.

The latest stint of gigs promoted the February 1993 release of the 'Anyone Can Play Guitar' EP. One of Thom's most self-conscious songs, featuring a self-deprecating line about wanting to be Jim Morrison, it was a gift for the music press. The lyric was inspired by Oliver Stone's biopic *The Doors* and was written the day after Thom saw the film. 'I just ranted that verse the day after I saw the film. It really wound me up, really upset me. It was like [Morrison] was some sort of Arthurian legend or something.' As well as the reference to the Doors' singer in the lyrics, the chorus echoes some familiar images (the Clash's 'London's Burning', while 'Standing on the Beach' is a line from the Cure's 'Killing An Arab'). One journalist also complained that the single was derivative of Carter the Unstoppable Sex Machine's 'Do-Re-Mi'. Among those who were more supportive was Radio 1 DJ Steve Lamacq, then writing for *Select*. Indeed he travelled with Radiohead and Kingmaker for several dates, at which Radiohead would hand out flyers for their new releases before the main act came on stage.

The song's sentiment seemed to be one of amazement that anyone would still want to belong to a conventional guitar band – the lyrics decrying the fact that most of those taking up the instrument did so to gain social cachet. In an interview with *Indiecator*, Thom noted: 'I was reading something the other week where someone said that joining a band now is like when people used to run away to join the circus. You want to get away from everything, have a good time, travel, lead a glamorous life. It's come to something when the only way to be happy is to go and join a band.' Everyone around the studio, however, seemed to be doing just that, as Kolderie recalls: 'We had everyone in the place come in and play a track. Even the lady who was cooking the meals and the studio owner came in and played what they wanted. Some people just played feedback. Thom played a guitar with a coin. Everybody tried to do something wild and we mixed it together into a big collage.' The closing guitar effects on 'Anyone Can Play Guitar' were produced by Jonny running a paintbrush up and down his fretboard. The accompanying video was shot by Tom Sheehan, the well-known music photographer who had also contributed stills to *Pablo Honey*'s cover.

The B-side tracks, 'Faithless, the Wonder Boy' and 'Coke Babies', were produced by Chris Hufford with James Warren. The songs themselves were written while the band were on sundry support slots during 1992. 'Faithless, the Wonder Boy' offered some disaffected views on the subject of grunge's thrift-store chic, Thom's wry lyric even included a cheeky reference to slacker youth's 'ripped and torn' fashion motif. The allusions to intravenous drug use – 'I can't put the needle in' – was an ambivalent metaphor. 'That phrase is more about trying to get back at people, get nasty,' Thom retorted. 'Coke Babies' was equally ill-judged – a My Bloody Valentine-style effects marathon. The humming at its end came from Colin, who was unaware the tape was still running in the studio and had presumably got as bored, by the song's close, as everyone else who has heard it.

The single brought Radiohead their first Top Forty success, after entering the charts at number thirty-two. *Melody Maker* made it single of the week, as did industry journal *Music Week*. Unsurprisingly, they were also featured, for a second time, as cover stars in *Curfew*. As with their first interview, the band's responses revealed much about their determination and ambition: 'We haven't really achieved that much yet. There's still a lot of hard work to do. We're always thinking about the next stage. We're on a roll now, but we haven't let it go to our heads. As we said last time, we're very ambitious but it takes work.'

On 20 February Radiohead played a homecoming gig at Oxford's Venue, supported by The Bigger The God, whom they described in the *Curfew* interview as 'the best band in Oxford'. Andy Smith: 'That was nice. I don't remember too much about the gig, though. But I do remember noticing that suddenly the crowd had changed. You know, something was happening. There were people at gigs who don't go to gigs – rather than the same group of people who will seek out new stuff. That was a noticeable change for me.' The group's first foreign date followed at the end of February in Paris, a performance broadcast live on radio as the 'Black Sessions'. The forty-five-minute set included the band's reading of Glen Campbell's 'Rhinestone Cowboy' – prompted by Ed's devotion to the star of country cheese.

Pablo Honey, Radiohead's debut album, was officially released on 22 February 1993, after further mixing by Kolderie and Slade back in Boston. Chris Hufford was also credited as co-producer for 'I Can't' and 'Lurgee'. The album was housed in what, in retrospect, seems an inelegant sleeve – a baby, which Thom thought looked like him, enveloped by a flower. The image on the reverse of the sleeve is Christ's body projected over a scene from Las Vegas, provided by Lisa Bunny Jones, a 'mad woman' of Colin's acquaintance. The album reached twenty-five in the UK charts on its week of release, eventually earning BPI (British Phonographic Institute) gold certification.

The reviews were not unkind. *Q* commented: 'Despite the attempted uplift of "Ripcord", "Creep", "Prove Yourself" and "Anyone Can Play Guitar", the way lyricist Thom Yorke sings it, British teenagerhood has never been grumpier. Grumpiness enlivened by the odd shaft of self-mockery, is not an easy mood to curl up with of an evening. The vigour of Radiohead live loses a great deal of fun in translation to plastic, but the best bits rival Nirvana, Dinosaur Jr and even the mighty Sugar.'

The band acknowledged the American influence – they were still regarded as faux-grunge in some circles – but played down its importance. 'That whole Boston thing came and went with the Pixies and the Muses. We're a British band and the album doesn't sound like it came from Boston, like everyone's expecting. We're an English pop band,' Thom insisted. Nevertheless, the choice of Slade and Kolderie as producers reinforced the impression that Radiohead were trading on their influences rather than expanding on them.

There was also, despite the occasional abrasiveness of the three guitars, something timid and unworldly about the album, which sounded like its protagonists were only tentatively establishing their identities. Probably the most insightful comments came from Caren Myers in *Details*, who described the album as 'wimp rock with teeth, a tinny English clatter saved by an amateurish exuberance... For melancholy boys who shrank from the rippling torsos of bands like the Chili Peppers, Radiohead provided a chance to feel worthless on an equal basis. Here, after all, were five boys with no torsos at all.'

Others considered the album derivative of U2 – Thom's vocals on 'Stop Whispering', in particular, echoed what Bono might have achieved with similar material. It was a track that proved hard to pin down in the studio. The producers tinkered laboriously to find the perfect arrangement, but the five-minute-plus version which made *Pablo Honey* was not the ideal solution.

The main problem was that Thom lacked an identifiable personality throughout the album – the hysteria of 'You', for example, is as overarching as its opening line, which cloyingly compared its subject to the sun, the moon and stars. Pitched into a UK musical firmament hooked on the *nouveau* glamour of Suede, the songs had no real seam; they were more a ragbag collection of current indie sounds. 'I Can't', with a melody reminiscent of the House Of Love's 'Beatles And The Stones', was among the worst offenders, despite its amusing line in self-deprecation – Thom pleading to be excused for the 'strange and creeping doubt' that speaks out of turn and unannounced in his place. Kolderie: 'That was a real nightmare. We could never get it the right speed. I wanted it to be faster and everyone kept wanting it to be slower, we went back and forth. I had high hopes for that one and I don't really feel like it panned out that well.' So much so that the Kolderie/Slade version was abandoned in favour of the original Hufford-produced demo for the album's final cut.

The references to 'playing with myself' in 'Thinking About You' add it to the noble canon of rock 'n' roll masturbation songs, but the tune itself, recorded in a new acoustic format, did nothing to develop the sense of humility in the lyric. Thom: 'I remember we didn't like the way it ended originally and scrapped it and it became the basics of "Planet Telex", or "Planet Xerox" as it was originally gonna be called before Xerox threatened to sue us. Anyway, I always preferred the demo I did on a four-track but that wasn't "worthy" enough.'

The most miserable, trite effort is 'How Do You?', which featured a sample from the Jerky Boys' 'Pablo Honey' sketch point-lessly inserted into the guitar solo. Kolderie: 'They got pilloried in the press for that one. I never saw that coming. I figured it was just a quick little punky thing for the album, but the critics picked on it in a big way.' 'Ripcord', at least, had a little more vitality and a highly alluring guitar riff, which made it an instant live favourite, contrasting with some excellent harmonies. It's another of Thom's 'what have I done?' lyrics written after committing to EMI. He later observed on stage at a Swedish show in Gothenburg in 1993 that the song concerned '...signing, having lots of money and absolutely no idea what the fuck to do with your life'. Later, when supporting Belly at London's Town and Country Club in 1993, the verses were childishly amended to 'They can kiss my ass!'

'Vegetable' was another song to benefit from an engagingly spite-ful lyric, though this time it was unclear who the target was. The album concludes with 'Blow Out', an effects-driven meditation on anxiety and self-doubt doused in Latin and jazz flourishes (it employed borrowed guitars from friends the Candyskins). Serving as a showcase for Phil's drumming, the guitar-generated wind tunnel noises were created by scratching a coin up and down a guitar neck.

Though it was kindly treated at the time (*Rolling Stone* wrote: 'If they don't implode from attitude overload, Radiohead warrant watch-ing') derivative songs and empty rock posturing made *Pablo Honey* an inessential purchase – 'Creep' aside. The lyrics are, in retrospect, far too personal and self-obsessed. Thom: '*Pablo Honey* is really extreme because I was deliberately projecting all these things personally on to me, but only to give it extra meaning. It could be completely calculated but it was just personal bits of me and I thought the best place to put it was in a song.' Another of the problems is the sequencing of the songs, which crash into each other without much thought for the overall impact. It is one of the reasons the band would spend so long toying with the running order of subsequent releases. A more reflective Yorke later acknowledged the album's shortcomings in an interview with *The Big Takeover*: 'A lot of it was posturing, I think, which was fine in the context of what we were about at that point.' He went on record elsewhere to state that the band preferred the demo versions of some of the songs they'd worked on with Hufford over the finished product.

Ronan's review of the album for *Curfew* was hugely enthusiastic: '*Pablo Honey* isn't a masterpiece or in any way perfect, but it shows off a band emerging as one of the most potent songwriting units in pop. The shifts not only in tempo but in mood within and between songs is startling. Sometimes Radiohead sound like they want to crawl into a corner and cry quietly to themselves. At other times they are so wired they could tear themselves apart. Often there are only milliseconds between these extremes. Radiohead are subtle and sensitive, equally they are petulant, belligerent and insolent.' He still feels the (mostly retrospective) denigration of the album is unfair. 'I think you can pick faults with it when you compare it with *The Bends* and *OK Computer*. The imagination and production and everything on those albums are things it would be difficult to compare anything to. *The Bends* has possibly some of the greatest songs ever written on it. But I can still listen to *Pablo Honey* and think: "This is a great album."'

The press backlash, when it came, focused on 'Creep'. Many compared it to Nirvana's 'Smells Like Teen Spirit', the anthemic song of two years earlier, and nailed Radiohead as Home Counties grunge – possibly the result of Thom's comments in the band's first interview with John Harris on coming home to roost. Thom countered to *Mojo*'s Pat Reid: 'At least their album sounded like "Teen Spirit" all the way through. And ours didn't. They had a formula with which to work, and we didn't.' The truth was that the album was rushed. It contained at least a couple of songs that should never have been recorded but were committed to tape in haste, and others that would have been greatly improved given a less punishing schedule. But Radiohead were nothing if not quick learners, and it was a mistake they were not to repeat.

At the end of March the group began a minor tour of Israel, unaware of their growing popularity in that country, where 'Creep' had reached number one. Colin attributed its success to a local cult figure, Yohaf Kutner, a kind of Hebrew John Peel. 'He lost his memory in an avalanche in his twenties and he rebuilt his memory through music. Now he's in his forties and he just loves us. He really promoted the singles. The audiences we got at the gigs were quite big. The first two we got 700 and at the third there were about 1,200. Thom was actually mobbed by 300 screaming girls when he left his dressing room before the gig.'

Keith Wozencroft relates one funny story about the band's arrival. 'They got to customs and they said, "You're Radiohead!" And they had the whole lot of them, managers and band, everybody, sing "Creep". They said that they wouldn't let them through otherwise. That was quite weird for Thom, for all of them, because I don't think they'd ever thought about the star thing.' Their success in Israel actually did much to bolster the band's confidence. Jonny: 'While we were all down in the dumps we heard from Israel that it was high in their charts, so we went there and it kind of proved that it could be a successful song as long as people got to hear it.' It was on that tour that Jonny met his girlfriend and later wife.

On returning to England the band released the 'Pop Is Dead' EP on 22 May. The title song was originally intended for inclusion on their debut album. Peaking at forty-two in the charts, it was issued at the band's insistence, amid record company efforts to get them to put out something else from the album. (In retrospect, Parlophone might have been right.) Thom described the song as 'vitriolic'.

At the time there were rumours that EMI were having doubts about the band and were perhaps even considering dropping them.

The unconvincing 'Pop Is Dead', subsequently referred to by Ed as 'bollocks', did little to help bolster confidence in the group. The song was written in response to mainstream assertions that pop music had run its course, and as 'an epitaph to 1992'. Contrived and smug, it impressed no one. John Mulvey at the *NME* states: 'It seemed like confirmation of all the reservations we'd had about Radiohead. We thought that was it, career over.' For once, *Melody Maker* was no more sympathetic. 'Lyrical genii Radiohead are not. I was too convulsed by laughter to be able to listen further. Doubtless my elder colleagues would have it that Radiohead can "write" "songs". If this is what's known as "songwriting", give me fucking incompetent incontinent musical illiterates any day. I had previously gotten Radiohead pinned down as the indie U2 but even that comparison's too grand for them. They're the indie Kingmaker.'

These were dark days for Radiohead. Thom made a foolish effort to whip up some controversy in the British press, attacking current media darlings Suede. 'There's nothing that riles me about Suede. That's the whole point. It's not so much that they're manufactured, which they are, but that the product that's been manufactured isn't a particularly interesting one. There are adverts on the television that challenge me more than any song I've heard this year. There's more art in the Tango and Pot Noodle adverts than there is in "Animal Nitrate" or anything by Bikini Kill or Cornershop.' In the light of the hugely disappointing 'Pop Is Dead', such comments were justifiably considered sour grapes.

There was also some carping from the press at the inclusion on the EP of a live version of 'Creep', recorded at the Town and Country Club on 14 March. As well as another live B-side, 'Ripcord', taped at the same gig, the release also included a superior new song, 'Banana Co.', seemingly an indictment of Western imperialism, and taken from an acoustic radio session Thom had recorded. However, the mood of journalists from the national press was out of step with that of their regional colleagues, who had seen first hand how powerful a reaction Radiohead's live shows drew. Several of these clubbed together in an effort to petition Radio 1 for greater airplay.

-six-

america loves us: dumbo and the angstonauts

American radio stations, notably San Francisco's KITS Live 105 (notable for 'breaking' A Flock Of Seagulls to American audiences) and K-ROQ in Los Angeles, were picking up on 'Creep'. Clark Staub, who was Capitol Records' vice-president of marketing in America, recalls: 'Live 105 had a UK copy of "Creep", and they started playing it on the air and there was a huge response and we took our lead from that.' Station reps contacted Capitol about the possibility of removing the words 'so fucking special' for radio play. By March, 'Creep' had been re-edited for the American market, and it began to achieve heavy exposure, eventually topping Live 105's annual singles' poll.

Back home, the band caught a welter of flak for the decision to edit the swearing. Their justification was that Sonic Youth and Dinosaur Jr had both done much the same thing with their singles. Ironically, once the album was released several fans wrote in complaining about swearing on the album version of 'Creep', which was not edited out. *Pablo Honey* was released by Capitol in America in April 1993. It was not immediately apparent that it was going to enjoy the huge success there that it eventually did. However, the affection for 'Creep', issued as a single in June, gave it new momentum.

All the band were well aware of what would be required of them to cement the breakthrough in America. Ed: 'I remember, like, '87 through about '91, you didn't have anyone from England coming over. The Manchester scene in '89, '90, kind of revitalized that, but because they became so huge in Britain very quickly, bands like the Stone Roses and Happy Mondays came over to America with completely the wrong attitude. You have to keep touring [America]. They didn't... Echo and the Bunnymen, the Smiths or U2 ... came over for a year. They came over from this enormous adulation in their own home country to playing clubs, and they didn't like it that much. They weren't willing to do the work.' Radiohead, on the other hand, were diligent to the point of exhaustion in terms of tour support of their records and 'cracking' America. After frenetic touring of Denmark, Sweden, Holland and France, they boarded the plane for the States.

According to Thom, the US tour allowed the band some respite. 'After the EP came out and the slagging started, it made me so paranoid I wasn't able to write. Everything I did seemed contrived because, true or not, I was anxious to avoid the criticisms. I froze, couldn't write a thing, so when we were offered a North American tour, we jumped on it, because it was a great relief to get out of the UK. That first trip over there gave us a chance to start over, to develop confidence in our music without being subjected to the intense scrutiny we had at home.'

Their American debut came on 23 June at the Venus De Milo in Boston. Thom: 'My first memory of America was waking up on a coach in Boston. I walked into the hotel at about seven o'clock in the morning, switched on the television, and there was "Creep".' It was a portent of things to come. The group also recorded their first television appearance, on the *Arsenio Hall Show*. Jonny: '[It] was our first live TV show and we were very, very scared. Thom was so nervous that he was actually shaking.' The *Arsenio Hall* experience was chronicled in London's *Evening Standard* under the headline 'British nobodies rock the USA'. The article was later read out on Radio 1 by DJ Steve Wright.

Further gigs followed in Philadelphia and New York (CBGB's and the Academy; at the second they supported PJ Harvey). If the band were unaware of the dangers of being labelled one-hit wonders, there were plenty of journalists on hand to emphasize the point.

Melody Maker's Jon Wiederhorn, one of several hacks who would revise their opinion of Radiohead after *The Bends*, reviewed the Academy show, expressing concern about the group's ability to transcend 'Creep'. In the audience for the following show at Washington's 9:30 Club on 28 June was expatriate British music fan Fiona Conway. 'There had been a lot of airplay for "Creep", which everyone loved, but they played much better than we expected. Thom was amazing. The whole set had so much energy, and I'd never seen a frontman like Thom Yorke before – this was after bands like Blur and the Charlatans had come through the 9:30 Club. I was completely blown away. I talked to Jonny afterwards and he just seemed very shy, but very polite, and surprised to find an Englishwoman talking to him.'

In Chicago two nights later their show at the Cabaret Metro was broadcast on JBTV. They also heard for the first time the new Chris Sheldon remix of 'Stop Whispering', edited down to four minutes and complete with string section. However, they told their label they'd prefer to develop the twenty or thirty songs they'd written since *Pablo Honey* rather than release another song from their debut album. As Carol Baxter remembers, the pressures on the band on that first tour were extraordinary. 'Eight a.m. – breakfast with this executive; one p.m. – lunch with fifty-five retailers, solid press interviews between; seven p.m. – dinner with this many journalists and, by the way, can you do a live radio phone-in at two a.m.? It was a sixteen-to-eighteen-hour day with no breaks. I couldn't handle that. But they managed it. I was sitting there going grey thinking: "I'll never make my bands do this again."'

The group spent time in LA's Hyatt Hotel – where *Spinal Tap* was filmed – and were driven about in limousines by their indulging record label. Their penance was having to deal with up to sixteen hours of questioning in any one 'press day'. By August, *Pablo Honey* had reached its US chart peak at thirty-two. It eventually chalked up sales of over two million worldwide, mostly in America, and mostly due to the success of 'Creep'. The snowball began at K-ROQ and accelerated via its heavy rotation as an MTV Buzz Clip in the summer. The group were welcomed with open arms by college radio and independent publications, while *Rolling Stone* described 'Creep' as 'the most auda-cious pop move since the Police scored a number-one single with a song more or less about stalking ["Every Breath You Take"]'.

More chillingly, the song also earned the band fans on death row. Thom started to receive mail from convicted killers who felt 'connected' to him via the lyrics of 'Creep'. One, in particular, suggested the murderer was the creep in the song, and it was the words in his head that made him kill. Thom: 'That really fucking scares the hell out of me.' Jonny acknowledged that the band do meet a lot of people 'who aren't very articulate'. Despite their always having believed in the potential of the song, it quickly became some-thing of an albatross. Thom: 'The one thing I regret about that song is people identifying me as the creep. Everyone sets me up to be Mr Serious Of Rock, which is ridiculous.' However, he concedes that 'I used to take myself very seriously, so I suppose I asked for it.'

The band survived the rigours of the promotional tour by amusing themselves with Smashey and Nicey impersonations – all of which were lost on American radio DJs. Yet the exhaustive promo-tional campaign seemed to be paying off. Backed by non-stop MTV exposure, 'Creep' had become an anthem for America's 'slacker' youth. MTV's pixelated losers *Beavis and Butt-head*, were fans, evidently to the group's pleasure. Thom: 'It's so cool to get on a programme like *Beavis and Butt-head*. That was great. My favourite bit is where Beavis goes, "If they didn't have a bit of the song that sucked, then the other bit wouldn't be so great." Yes! ... Wonderful. He should write for the music press.' At one gig Michael O'Neil, an MTV production assistant and the voice behind Beavis, was overheard enthusing: 'Radiohead rock, man! They've got attitude. They're alter-native crossover! They're like Jim Morrison-meets-Jimi Hendrix.' Others to admire 'Creep' included everyone from Blur to Jon Bon Jovi, who claimed he wished he'd written it. If that wasn't perversity enough, Arnold Schwarzenegger apparently requested it be included in his next film.

There was a clear danger that Radiohead were becoming one-trick ponies, for ever associated with a song that they had long claimed was unrepresentative. Thom: 'You start to realize that you're

The brothers Greenwood in action;
Oxford, early 1992.

Radiohead at the Jericho Tavern,
the spiritual home of Oxford music.

Above: Another
early Jericho
Tavern set, another
lacklustre sartorial
performance.

Left: Thom adjusts
himself onstage.
Live at the Garage,
Glasgow, in 1994.

'There is irony, there's implied irony, and there was my hair.' Thankfully, the Los Angeles influence never extended beyond Thom's mullet.

Thom, still wearing entrance bracelet, at the Lowlands Festival in Holland in August 1995.

Above: Drummer
Phil 'Mad Dog' Selway,
as unflinchingly
photogenic as ever.

Left: Colin Greenwood,
Phil's rhythm partner,
as usual hiding his
light under a bushel,
or a Marshall stack
at least.

Right: Ed O'Brien, Radiohead's rhythm guitarist, diplomat and sex symbol.

Below: Jonny Greenwood, the most inventive guitarist of his generation. Note presence of fabled armguard.

Above:
Radiohead
onstage at
Manchester's
Nynex Arena
on the 17th of
November 1997.

Left: 'Today, we
will mostly be
wearing black.'
Radiohead in
Amsterdam
in 1995.

Left: Thom onstage at the Tibet Freedom Concert. 'Buddhism was really everything that was missing from my life.' That and a shave.

Below: A tense moment as Thom risks the displeasure of his bandmates by flirting with a smile.

Left: Thom Yorke
in New York in
1996.

Below: 'Anyone
mentions bridge
again and we'll
****ing have you.'

only really spending 40 minutes of your day as a musician, and even those 40 minutes can get a bit jukebox-like. The rest of the time you're answering questions on how it feels to be a one-hit wonder. It's not the best existence in the world.' The one-hit wonder status caused the band and its management serious anxiety. The fact that Capitol Records commissioned 'I'm A Creep' contests and decorated Radiohead product with the legend 'Beavis and Butt-head Say They Don't Suck' merely exacerbated matters.

The American trek was draining enough in terms of performance itinerary, but the additional weight, and inanity, of promotional duties wearied everyone in the band. Jonny: 'I got this fax saying: "Please record the following message: 'Hi, I'm Jonny from Radiohead. You're listening to those crazy heads on the radio and, hey, we're creeps.'"' Jonny also bemoaned a K-ROQ phone-in, *Love Lines*, that they were forced to participate in. 'We were in town there and that's what bands are asked to do there. Its very embarrassing, it's kind of shit. We were told it would be a joke kind of evening with people phoning in with false stories. What actually happened was that real people were phoning up and saying: "My boyfriend's started hitting me, should I stay with him?" So what can you do? You can't give advice to that, so it was very embarrassing and we sat there saying nothing.'

MTV earned the band's ire by asking them to play at an MTV *Beach Party* show, where they ran through a number of songs only to watch the station isolate 'Creep' as a new live performance video. Thom: 'Schedules. That was my whole life. Things were being thrown at us all the time. Like, "You're doing the *Arsenio Hall Show* tomorrow." And no one tells you why. But it all went sour because we couldn't … get rid of the song. We had to milk it. And the album was never given a chance.' Other crimes against the soul followed. They were featured in *Sassy* magazine under the headline 'Cute Boys, Loud Guitars'. Capitol believed they'd hit paydirt with the band, with their label manager Bruce Kirkland crowing to *Billboard* magazine about 'keeping them on the road'. Capitol subsequently organized a meet-and-greet at their Los Angeles HQ, where the band found that everyone in the building had been specially instructed to wear a Radiohead T-shirt.

Many surprises accompanied the North American tour, not least their show at Canada's Edgefest in Toronto in July, which involved them performing on a revolving stage. Thom: 'I remember that gig well. They told us we'd be playing on this stage that went around. For some silly reason, the fact that people would be able to see our bums put us into fits of laughter. It was OK once we were on, but then I had to go and cut my head open with my guitar. Oh, it wasn't any intense guitar solo or anything. I was just trying to take the bloody thing off and succeeded in whacking my head open.' They were supporting Ned's Atomic Dustbin. Colin: 'It was like Disneyworld. It was this glass amphitheatre with a stage that revolves very slowly as you're playing. Every time you looked up the audience was completely different. Utterly bizarre. Occasionally you'd see Dumbo fly by...'

These comments were recorded in another interview with John Harris, this time for CD booklet/magazine *Volume*. 'I remember seeing them play at the Highbury Garage [in London, on 1 September] when they got back from America and "Creep" had hit, and they looked quite "LA". I don't think Thom had had his hair extensions, but they looked like a totally different band. In the pictures [in *Volume*], they've all got pendants and stuff. Their hair had got longer, and Thom especially was starting to look pretty good. At the Garage, I was thinking: "Why aren't they on the *NME*'s cover?"'

The band's low profile in Britain wasn't helped by their non-appearance at the Reading Festival in August, the cancellation being attributed to Thom's throat problems. He later admitted to Stuart Bailie of the *NME*: 'The morning of the Reading gig I couldn't say anything and Rachel, my girlfriend, was on the phone ringing up our manager saying, "He can't speak!" I'm fully aware that the reason a lot of people though we didn't do Reading was that I was too shit-scared. And I'm sure that part of it was that I was so scared that my voice just collapsed. I went to see a Harley Street specialist the next week and he felt my neck and it was just like concrete.' He told others that he'd refused to take the steroids recommended by his Harley Street doctor because of the long-term damage it might do to his voice. Despite this, the incident provided further evidence to some that Radiohead were an unhealthily neurotic concern.

The Bigger The God were the support band for the Garage show. Andy Smith: 'The thing I remember was going to soundcheck and Radiohead being there, and for the first time seeing them as a proper band with a full crew, soundchecking, then going off to get something to eat. Up till now that was unheard of – actually having people to take care of things, not having to pack up your gear yourself. There were a few celebs there, including Sean Hughes. It was rumoured that Kate Moss was apparently refused entry backstage.' Mark Lamarr was also in attendance. His later antipathy towards Radiohead may have been triggered by the audience member who confronted him, saying, 'Shaky! I've got all your records!' For Smith, securing the support proved once again how nobly Radiohead greeted their success. 'It was the generosity thing, they were prepared to waste time on their mate's band because they thought we were good.' That Petrol Emotion's frontman Steve Mack was at the gig, and noted of Thom: 'He's great, but what *is* his problem?'

By 4 September, 'Creep' had reached thirty-two in the *Billboard* charts. It was therefore credited with being the first Top Forty US single by a 'new' English band since KLF charted at thirty-nine in 1991. With *Pablo Honey* still riding high in the charts, Capitol were keen to organize a quick return trip to America. However, the label's suggestion that Radiohead perform as the opening band for Duran Duran's tour was given a terse response by the band (and more importantly Hufford, who faced down the suits at EMI). Instead they chose to fulfil previous obligations to join the Belly tour from September to mid-November. They had first encountered Belly, then a hugely fashionable outfit on the 4AD label, after lead singer (and former Throwing Muses member) Tanya Donelly invited them to support her at Belly's Town and Country Club gig. Like so many others, she'd been impressed by 'Creep'.

While the band toured America relentlessly, 'Creep' was re-released in the UK. Colin defended this decision to *Vox*. 'We did all originally agree not to re-release "Creep", but after doing so well in America, there was tremendous pressure from radio people, the press, the record company, even our fans, to put it out again.' The new B-side, 'Yes I Am', documented a group increasingly ill at ease with the rock 'n' roll circus and its banality and intrusiveness (the lyrics saw Thom run off a list of things he resented about it, not least his lack of choice in the process). The group also complained about the BBC's unwillingness to play their records, as this prevented them re-creating their US success in the UK. The fact that they were unloved in their own country was still an obvious source of discomfort. The decision to edit out the 'so fucking special' line in 'Creep' for airplay in the UK (as had been done for American radio) was berated by *NME* guest reviewer Sean Hughes, who said it would otherwise have been his single of the week. On 18 September, the day after the start of the Belly tour, 'Creep' finally became the hit everyone believed it should have been, peaking at number seven on its reissue in the British charts.

The Belly tour was a largely unhappy experience. Thom: 'We'd really had enough and didn't want to go on any more. We were being plugged in every day like a jukebox.' He confessed to one reporter that the whole experience was spoiling Radiohead as a live band. 'We reached a point where we stopped communicating, me especially. I just decided that it wasn't true. I decided that live Radiohead wasn't some fantastic combination. I said to myself, "This is not working, it's falling apart" and we actually sat down and had it out. We went back into rehearsals and we are quite musically attuned to each other but we all had the power of veto over things and that led to more conflict.'

The problem was that *Pablo Honey* was breaking in different parts of the world at different times, and the tour to promote it, playing songs the band were growing sick of, just kept rolling on before their eyes. They were beginning to lose it – Thom appeared in a magazine advert for Iceberg jeans, fixed himself up with hair extensions and appeared in a fashion spread in *Interview* magazine. All of which, he soon came to admit, was a big mistake. Meanwhile Jonny had become introverted, consoling himself by listening to BBC talking books on his Walkman and avoiding human contact as much as possible. 'I do wish I had my friends around to enjoy this sometimes,' he said, 'but even that's gone wrong because they've all gone to different universities as well and they're all graduating now. I think, I could be there doing that.' When he did speak to the rest of the band, his conversation was apparently littered with quotes from the Sherlock Holmes stories he was ingesting. With Colin spending most of his time in rapt conversation with the road crew, it was a toss-up as to which Greenwood was mislaying his marbles fastest, as Belly came fully equipped with their own fun-loving, unhinged Greenwood – bass player Gail.

As a result of his growing dissatisfaction, Thom wrote 'My Iron Lung', a song dismissing the promotional demands on a touring band as 'a total waste of time', to which Jonny added a John McGeogh (Banshees, Magazine, etc.) type intro, and then another mesmerizing guitar break. The McGeogh reference is one which crops up repeatedly in descriptions of Jonny's style, and is something that he puts down to subconscious early influences. 'It's very weird, because I didn't listen to any bands really when I was learning to play guitar. I only had one album until I was sixteen, it was Talking Heads, I think, and that was all. Quite tragic, really. As a result I wasn't interested in guitar players as names. But a couple of years ago our sound man said, "Have you heard of Magazine?" and I said, "I think my older sister used to play me Magazine." So he lent me a CD and of course, not only did I remember every note, but all the words and everything. And this was from when I was seven or eight. It was quite scary how I'd been ripping off and copying John McGeogh even though I hadn't started playing guitar until I was thirteen. So, basically, thanks a lot. Thank God my sister wasn't playing me AC/DC.'

There were some highpoints in the Belly tour, however, including the show at New York's Roseland, where Thom joined Tanya Donelly, who had convinced the starstruck Colin that girls pee lemonade, on stage for an acoustic version of Belly's 'Untogether'. They were also, by the month's end, able to celebrate a platinum disc from the RIAA (Record Industry Association of America) for sales of *Pablo Honey*. Suede, still considered by the press to be British rock's best hope of cracking America, sent them a telegram offering congratulations – quite magnanimous given Thom's earlier attacks on the band. Later in the tour, an open-air show was booked in Athens, Georgia. They turned up to see the projected stage disappearing into the mud, with no generator in sight. Instead they switched venues to play at the 40 Watt Club, where they met R.E.M. for the first time.

However, the constant touring, increasingly idiotic grillings by the press corps and the sheer boredom took their toll. Thom put his back out, frequently complained of feeling unwell and at one stage simply collapsed after getting off a bus in San Francisco. The punishing schedule was also making it impossible to write and rehearse new material, which all members of the band considered to be their prime directive and rationale for being in a band. The impression that Radiohead were losing rather than gaining ground was compounded when their next single, 'Stop Whispering', released in America only in October, proved a commercial misfire. Chris Sheldon's remix, with its incongruous strings, entered at twenty-four before quickly falling off the chart.

The nadir came when the group were 'told' to support Tears For Fears in Las Vegas at the Aladdin Theater, a billing and venue which would have horrified much more careerist bands than Radiohead. Practically no one was in the audience when they took the stage, and Tears For Fears treated them like lepers and refused them a soundcheck. Thom reacted, petulantly but understandably, by making sure all the stage lights were kicked in before the Tears For Fears' set. Colin: 'We flew right across America to do this one gig, cancelled a load of other things to do it, were told it was really, really important. Turned up and got told we'd be on at seven o'clock when there'd be nobody there. We got fucked over big time. No soundcheck, moved about on the bill so we were opening, and we were assured we weren't going to. And they were all complete wankers.' Bizarrely, Tears For Fears encored that night with 'Creep'. Colin: 'He has to pay money for it, so that's cool. It was the ultimate irony.'

Thom was finding things particularly difficult, and later admitted in an *NME* interview that he considered leaving the band. 'I thought I could go it alone. I thought I didn't need anybody, but I fucking do. It's so easy to think like that. It's such an easy frame of mind to lock yourself into and never get out of. As soon as you get any success, you disappear up your own arse and you lose it for ever.'

As soon as the tour was completed with a handful of dates in Canada, the band were forced to fly to Germany to begin a new round of shows in support of James in November. 'They were finding the process very stressful and alien and not what they were in it for,' their agent, Charlie Myatt, recalled. 'The main crisis was coming off the Belly tour. They were supposed to go straight on to a tour of Europe with James, and there was a lot of soul-searching about why they were in a group at all.' Another setback was the death of popular publicist Philip Hall, to whom the band dedicated their set at the Brixton Academy leg of the tour on 9 December.

Relationships within the band were at a very low point. An emergency meeting was called, and arguments flared after too much drink was consumed. Nothing consequential was determined, though things were patched up enough for the tour to continue. It concluded when Radiohead supported James at their homecoming gig at G-Mex, with the Mancunians at the height of their fame thanks to 'Sit Down'. Colin: 'It was a huge, frightening place and we were supporting James in their home town. Did we think "big time"? No – "Are we gonna get off alive?" is what I was thinking.'

Exhaustion was replaced by disorientation on their return home. Jonny: 'We got back to Oxford after touring … and it was really sad. We all got home, and I phoned up one or two people that we knew, who were away, and then we ended up sort of phoning each other up again.' Thom: 'When I got back to Oxford I was unbearable. You start to believe that you are this sensitive artist who has to be alone and you have to become this melodramatic, tortured person in order to create wonderful music. The absolute opposite is true, I think now.' Thom's 'madness' included a Jericho Tavern gig he attended where he and a member of the Candyskins were to be found rolling around on the floor, screaming, 'I'm a fucking degenerate, I am.' The story was picked up by the *NME*.

Instead of returning to the basement flat in Oxford he'd had for the past couple of years, Thom invested in a house. 'I christened it The House That 'Creep' Built, 'cos I wouldn't have been able to buy it without the royalties. I didn't pay in cash, though, 'cos I decided it might be the only money I ever make. I've got a nice little mortgage, twenty-five years, fixed rate, easy repayments. I didn't fancy the endowment mortgage. The guy took half an hour to explain it and I didn't understand it at all.'

-seven-

phase two:
the bends and beyond

In January 1994 the band converted a fruit farm in the isolated Oxfordshire village of Cumnor into a rehearsal space. Jonny: 'The idea of coming to London to a big rehearsal studio is a nightmare to us because we all live in Oxford. So we wanted a room that was completely ours, and also a room that wasn't like a rehearsal room. So basically we hired this old kind of shed on a fruit farm for five weeks, soundproofed it and put in a vocal PA and it was our space. It was great.' Christened Canned Applause, it became the band's headquarters for the next few years, the place where they would rehearse new material after returning from touring. It was here that they began to write songs for their second album. Jonny: 'Our creative process is more driven by disappointment with past work we've done, and realizing what kind of shelf life a recording has after it's out. You've got to get it right the first time, so you don't regret anything.' They were initially pleased with the new songs they'd worked on in isolation.

John Leckie, famed for his work with the Stone Roses, Magazine, XTC and many others, was drafted in as producer. Both Colin and Jonny were big fans of XTC. Thom liked the fact that Leckie had not only produced for the Fall (including their best eighties' album, *This Nation's Saving Grace*) but had actually *survived* working with them relatively intact. Both he and the Greenwood brothers were also big fans of Magazine's *Real Life* album. Only later did the band learn of his engineering work on

96

various Beatles solo projects and Pink Floyd's *Dark Side Of The Moon* and *Wish You Were Here*.

It was another Oxford connection which teamed Leckie with Radiohead. He was working with Ride in 1993 when he was passed a copy of *Pablo Honey* and some demos Radiohead had subsequently recorded. Both parties were interested in working together, but put the project on hold because of their schedules. When the band slotted the opening months of 1994 to record their second album, Leckie was able to come on board. He later told *Melody Maker*: 'I'd listened to *Pablo Honey* and thought it was a bit noisy for me, but we met up and they were not what I'd expected at all.' Sessions began at RAK Studios in London's St John's Wood on 28 February. Strangely, the one album that all five members of Radiohead were listening to before recording began was John Lennon's debut solo offering, *The Plastic Ono Band*. The first day they entered the studio, it was the record Leckie put on (he had been the tape operator, under Phil Spector's supervision, for the album).

However, the band were still reeling from the disillusionment and exhaustion that had emerged during their extended North American tour and was exacerbated by the support dates with James. In fact, rather than subside, the self-doubts had flourished, leaving the band both listless and apprehensive. Thom: 'I could tell we'd held everything in because there wasn't enough energy there. We were all crawling around the studio, not walking around. We were really scared of our instruments. That might sound over-dramatic, but that's how it felt. It must have been tortuous to watch. I know it was very hard on our producer John Leckie, who didn't know what the fuck was going on.' Leckie was powerless to pull the band out of its nosedive, described by Jonny as 'insidious and depressing'. Having just spent a fruitless four years – without a retainer – trying to capture the Stone Roses' much-anticipated second album, Leckie had learned to be patient.

However, Radiohead were soon engaging in erratic behaviour redolent of Leckie's previous charges. They were fed up and emotionally exhausted with each other, the artificial peace that had been achieved on the remaining dates with James now crumbling. All of the band except for Thom wanted to take a break and delay the sessions for a while to catch some breathing space. The tapes they eventually brought out of RAK were overblown and pompous, with the initial version of 'Fake Plastic Trees' even said to sound like Guns N' Roses. Rumours of a split began to circulate. Phil: 'I think if you speak to anybody in the band, at some points when things get particularly stressful, everybody toys with the idea of just stomping out and being a big drama queen about everything. But I don't think we ever seriously contemplated splitting the band.' Thom is more ambivalent on this point. 'Was I freaked out? I couldn't have been more freaked out. If we hadn't have pulled this record off, I would have given it all up. It has got to be the hardest thing I've ever, ever done.'

For Wozencroft, one of the causes of the band's anxiety was their adherence to unnatural time constraints. 'There were pressures on deadline, but accidentally. We'd all sat round saying, "In an ideal world what would be good?" Setting a rough agenda. But being a young band they took that seriously; they were very keen to achieve the best scenario.'

At the same time, their record company was insisting that the second album should yield a minimum of four workable singles. Leckie: 'The record company wanted a single and we ended up trying to record four number-one records on our first session together. The band were shitting themselves and we spent two months exploring every possibility, then getting feedback from the management and America, like "make it shorter" or "it sounds too dark".' Jonny: 'What happened was because of schedules – that dreaded word – it was suggested we record certain songs in a certain order so we'd have what people thought would be the singles recorded first. It was a very bad idea because it set the album on a really wrong track. The songs were sounding very good when we were rehearsing them but as soon as we'd work on a song for two weeks and then go back to one of the other songs, we'd forgotten it. So we ended up overrunning what was initially going to be two weeks and then we had to go on tour, and of course when we came back we ended up doing them all again.'

The band attempted to placate their record company with attempts at 'The Bends', 'Killer Cars', '(Nice Dream)' and 'Sulk', none of which the band were happy with. Indeed, 'Killer Cars',

Thom's latest treatise on our precarious relationship with the auto-mobile, written in ten minutes first thing in the morning, was dropped from the album altogether – though its swaggering hook would have made it a perfect Stateside single (it had already appeared in live form on the B-side to the 'Creep' twelve-inch reissue). All they had at the moment was a seven-minute version of 'Just', which Thom once described as 'a competition by me and Jonny to get as many chords as possible into a song.'

Record company pressure also affected Leckie, who recalls being hounded by Parlophone to give Jonny a 'special' guitar sound. For all the good it did him, he contended that Jonny already had an innately individual acoustic fingerprint. A great deal of time was wasted hiring amplifiers and guitars. Leckie then took the recorded versions of the four projected singles to remix at Abbey Road Studios. He describes the original versions of those songs as '...all a bit manic. The original version of "The Bends" was more overpowering than it is on record – it was a bit too much to take. The vocals were screaming more, and things were cranked up more.' The band was left to develop new material – namely 'Black Star'. Jonny: 'John Leckie was at a wedding – there was a real "teacher's away" larkiness to that day, hence the ace raggedness of the playing.' On their own they ran through this new song, and within an hour had recorded it, in the company of Leckie's engineer, Nigel Godrich. 'Black Star' would be the only band-produced composition on the album. Godrich remembers the tension around the recording sessions: 'I had a great time, but I know they felt under pressure. Remember, they were still relatively inexperienced in the studio and Thom, especially, found the studio environment difficult, not the best place for being creative in the way he is. But the tension can lead to things happening. It's an interesting process but it can be quite a painful one.'

'It was horrible,' concedes Ed. 'At one stage everyone was trying to find their get-out clauses. The worst thing was that our friendship was being altered simply because we were questioning everything too much, questioning the fundamentals of what we were doing. It was horrible but I think that's the problem with a university education. You just end up thinking too much.' Some of the pressure was also coming from the band's management, particularly Chris Hufford. 'That was certainly the lowest point I've had in my relationship with Thom and I'm sure vice versa. Thom became totally confused about what he wanted to do, what he was doing in a band and in his life, and that turned into a mistrust of everybody else. I came very close to saying, "I can't be fucked with this any more. I can't be doing with all this hassle; it's just not worth it." Thankfully, just prior to me – and Thom – really snapping, it suddenly turned around.'

Rumours were flying around that Capitol weren't intending to renew their option on the band. Ronan Munro remembers speaking to Hufford around the time of the sessions. 'He was saying, basically, "six months". I was thinking, this is awful, because it was a local band that I really liked. I didn't look beyond that context. But now you look back and think, all those bands who aren't even getting six months and are getting dumped. If "Creep" hadn't been a big hit in America, there might have been no *OK Computer* or *The Bends*. It's symptomatic of short-term profits from the record companies destroying artists.' Hufford retrospectively admitted to *Q*: 'I was shitting myself, to be honest. Me and my partner started shopping around for another group to manage because they really didn't look like they'd make it. I'm glad they proved us wrong.'

'I'm not really sure what the crisis was,' Thom explained to *The Big Takeover*. 'That was probably part of the problem. The principal thing was people at the label telling us what they expected us to do, and not having complete artistic freedom. Until I started running around the studio disconnecting the phones and telling people in reception that no one was allowed in the studio. That was when we actually started to work. It was that bad.' Phil: 'We were sort of trapped in the studio, recording and re-recording. It didn't seem like the songs could really grow on us until we started playing them live for people.'

It was Capitol in America, who had enjoyed most success with the band, who exacerbated the pressures. Jonny: 'We were just kind of discounting America pretty much, because they had us down as a pop act. Now we have record company bigwigs ringing us up and telling us how we should be doing things, which is worse, in a way.'

Some of the travesties the band would have to endure included being told by an executive that the group must use a Bob Clearmountain remix of 'Fake Plastic Trees' – which, according to Thom, gutted the keyboard sounds and strings which make the track so alluring. The pressure was on for Thom to come up with anthemic, bombastic rock songs for the American market, when what he really wanted to write was more understated material – one of many contrasts between *Pablo Honey* and *The Bends* is the latter's extensive use of quiet passages and silences.

Some valuable breathing space came at the end of March 1994, when the record company postponed plans to release a single from the album. Leckie: 'We all had a meeting and it was finally decided that they weren't going to release a single after all. So from there on in, there was an air of relief to the sessions. In the second month we did nearly all the tracks really, with overdubs and everything, and then the band went off on tour in May.' With some of the pressure off, the songs began to grow, Leckie working in his established manner – guitar parts laid down first, then guide vocals. Among the songs that took shape was '(Nice Dream)', which dated from 1992 and had already been through several transformations. It was inspired by Kurt Vonnegut's novel *Cat's Cradle*, the main action of which takes place on an island called San Lorenzo, a poor country whose inhabitants keep themselves happy by filling their lives with false totems and beliefs. Thom's lyrics, depicting an illusory, fleeting sense of belonging, also expanded. Leckie decided to add some effects from a tape of Arctic sounds he'd acquired at the Vancouver Aquarium. 'What you can hear are whales under the ice, but it sounds like someone playing strange noises on a Moog.'

The nine-week sessions were interrupted by long-held touring commitments, including shows in England, the Far East and Australia. The 'world tour' began in May and included dates in Spain, Italy, Switzerland, Germany, Hong Kong, Japan, Australia and New Zealand. However, while playing 'Anyone Can Play Guitar' at the group's tour opener at Manchester University on 25 May, Thom endured a greenstick fracture of his ankle. He played on through to the band's date at London's Astoria two days later, which was videotaped for MTV and video release later in the year. *Live At The Astoria* is an engaging document of a band at a crossroads – of the *Pablo Honey* material, only 'Ripcord', with its distinctive riff, and 'Creep' sound convincing. Old favourites 'You' and 'Stop Whispering' sound anaemic in comparison with new songs 'The Bends', 'Fake Plastic Trees' and 'Street Spirit (Fade Out)'.

Leckie set up recording equipment to document the event. He and the band had been frustrated in their attempts to record a workable version of 'My Iron Lung' in the studio. The Astoria performance of the song was duly appended to *The Bends*, with Thom overdubbing the vocals. The song featured his most esoteric lyric yet. Fans came to cherish the distorted lines which, when transcribed, suggested that the 'headshrinkers' wanted to rob Thom of everything, including his 'Belisha beacon'. Belisha beacons, the spherical yellow lights on black and white poles at pedestrian crossings, were named after Leslie Hore-Belisha (1893–1957), who instituted their widespread introduction. Ironically, given Thom's automobile fixation, Hore-Belisha was also responsible for bringing driving tests to Britain. 'Headshrinkers' may refer to the African art of shrinking skulls to produce war trophies, as exhibited in Oxford's Pitt-Rivers Museum. The collection, put together by a Victorian anthropological enthusiast, is worth seeing if you never fancy sleeping again. The dense textures of 'My Iron Lung' submerge and overlap Jonny's centrepiece John McGeogh-style guitar break, as the song builds to some thrashy bloodletting reminiscent of Nirvana's 'Heart-Shaped Box'. But unlike many of the tracks on *Pablo Honey*, it was demonstrably more than the sum of whatever influences informed it.

Next came Japan, always a receptive audience for Western rock acts, seemingly regardless of quality or originality. These engagements were well attended, whereas subsequent shows in Australia and New Zealand were played to half-empty auditoria. The Antipodean shows at least provided the chance to break in new material. But the band dynamic remained fractious. Thom confessed that he was suffering from disorientation: 'You're either completely unable to talk to any kind of strangers or you're utterly overt and demand to meet them the next day. I go between the two extremes, there's no middle ground.' He also felt compromised by his position, the benefits it conferred sullied by the demands of the music industry. 'We were in New Zealand. We were taken to one of the most beautiful places I've ever seen in my life, the place where they filmed *The Piano*. And there I was, thinking: "This is wonderful. I don't think I've ever seen scenery to spectacular." And suddenly it occurred to me that the only reason we were there was because ... I can't put my finger on it, but something to do with the industry, a lot to do with MTV. And whenever you see MTV, there is a Coca-Cola machine right next to it. And I just felt like we were a part of it all. And all at once, the view lost all meaning.'

They returned home to play on the closing day of the Glastonbury Festival at Worthy Farm, Somerset, on 26 June – their first appearance at a British festival. In an interview with *Select* Thom recalled: 'Glastonbury was a bit of a shock to us. I've never really understood the appeal of standing in a field not being able to hear the band, but I could after that. There was just such an amazing atmosphere. We've played a lot of festivals in Europe but they tend to be rather ragged, depressive affairs, and Glastonbury was such a mellow place.' Music writer John Harris: 'They were on in the afternoon. It was Colin's birthday, and they played "Happy Birthday", and they played these three songs no one had heard – and "My Iron Lung" especially – wow!' Yet there was some sniping from the critics, and Ian Gittens's review for *Melody Maker* got it spectacularly wrong: 'I'd love Radiohead to surprise me and produce a wealth of turbulent, towering new songs to prove their rumoured greatness, but I'm not holding my breath.'

On 2 July the band appeared at Denmark's long-running Roskilde Festival. Jonny nearly didn't make it after losing his passport, missing his flight from Heathrow and then having to wait for a cancellation. Once in Denmark, he had to hitch a ride with the Mary Black Band's van, which broke down twice. He got there moments before the band took the stage. To Thom's great pleasure, he was able to watch Elvis Costello play directly after Radiohead's set.

Afterwards the band resumed their recording commitments with Leckie, relocating to the Manor in Shipton-on-Cherwell in

Oxfordshire from 16 to 30 June. The Manor, bought by Richard Branson in 1971 for £30,000, was famously the incubator of Mike Oldfield's *Tubular Bells*, which effectively established the Virgin brand name. The two weeks Radiohead spent at the studio saw the album redefine itself. After several weeks on tour the songs had developed, whereas the existing versions of the tracks committed to tape had not fully explored their potential. Leckie: 'We finished nearly everything in our time there. I think it helped that they'd been on tour because they had confidence in a lot of the songs again, which I think they'd maybe lost during that lengthy recording period. At one point, Thom was thinking about scrapping some of the songs and writing more.' They began to rework the existing versions of 'Bones' and 'The Bends'. Leckie disapproved of the new, guitar-driven version of the latter song, thinking it overblown and over-recorded. Nevertheless, it became the first track on the album.

Other tracks that saw progress included the delicate, frigid 'Bullet Proof ... I Wish I Was' – at the time Thom's favourite song. It featured some refined brushwork from Phil. 'Naturally you don't want to blare away with four-on-the-floor, with big tree trunks of sticks. I suppose I draw my drum parts mainly from Thom; he's got a very good sense of rhythm.' After Colin and Phil laid down the bass and drum track for 'Bullet Proof', Ed and Jonny were at a loss as to what to add. So Leckie isolated them in soundproof booths to see what they could come up with. Thom: 'We thought it was a bit slow and timid at first. Then we taped the guitarists without them knowing where they were on the track and they came up with these weird noises at just the right moments. It was completely indulgent but it sounded great, like a lot of trains going past.'

After the Manor sessions Leckie returned to Abbey Road for further mixing, with the intention of completing those songs required for the band's upcoming 'My Iron Lung' EP. Convinced that in 'My Iron Lung' they had written a song big enough to satisfy expectations of the band, the pressure was off for the B-side tracks. Leckie: 'Being B-sides, of course, you don't want them to be too good. So we went from trying to make a big hit to trying to make something not too great when what we really wanted to do was the album. That caused a lot of, "What the fuck are we doing here?" kind of thoughts.'

In spite of the limited enthusiasm with which their efforts were being greeted in America, the band were determinedly moving towards the completion of an album that registered few concessions to that market. Among the most affecting songs to find a place on *The Bends* was 'Fake Plastic Trees' – a rare third-person narrative using singular vocabulary (fake, plastic, rubber, polystyrene). The conclusion reached by most observers was that the words detailed Yorke's agonizing over becoming a commodity, though, as usual, the truth is less literal. Thom described the song as 'the product of a joke that wasn't really a joke and a very lonely drunken evening and, well, a breakdown of sorts'. While maintaining the fragility and brittle edge of earlier songs, its movement away from self-emphasizing narcissism unearthed new possibilities and allowed the music's keynote of resignation to strike home more keenly. Later, Thom revealed a little more about the inspiration behind it. 'I had a week in Los Angeles which is the longest time I've spent there – one of the things I discovered was that most of the women in Hollywood are desperate to find the perfect man, and most of the men are desperate to shag around and bugger off. Then occasionally you catch glimpses of these really lonely people, especially the women. The men are just screwing around and it was really sad.' The song included one of Phil's favourite lyrics: '"Gravity always wins" – what a line.' Thom also noted: 'For me it wasn't about any of the words that I wrote but about the melody. The words were treated very much as noise, except perhaps the last verse which means something to me. The rest is gibberish, not relevant.'

The band made numerous attempts to commit this to tape, with little success. They were still playing around with it as the sessions neared completion at Abbey Road in August. At Leckie's suggestion, they took time off to catch Jeff Buckley in concert. Leckie: '[Thom] realized that you could sing like he did, in falsetto, without sounding drippy.' The stark emotional directness and simplicity of the late singer-songwriter's delivery made an immediate impression, but on the band's return to the Manor the atmosphere remained muted. Thom: 'That was one of the worst days for me. I spent the first five or six hours at the studio just throwing a wobbly. I shouted at every-one and then John Leckie sent everybody else away. He sat me down and I did a guide vocal on "Fake Plastic Trees".' Colin: 'We went back to the studio and tried an acoustic version of "Fake Plastic Trees". Thom sat down and played it in three takes, then burst into tears afterwards. And that's what we used for the record.'

The finished song saw Jonny employ the studio's Hammond organ, formerly used by John Lennon. Orchestral backing, to be provided by Thom's old Exeter friend John Matthias and Peter Gabriel accompanist Caroline Lavelle, was booked in for the follow-ing day. Leckie: 'I said to Jonny, "We'd better have something for them to play." So he just sat down there and then and scored it.' The original version of the song employed strings throughout, in the style of twentieth-century American composer Samuel Barber. However, in the final version the strings only surfaced at the song's finale.

The standout track for many was 'Street Spirit (Fade Out)', a song so quietly compelling it left the band speechless after they'd recorded it. Built around a complex, repetitive arpeggio composed by Ed O'Brien, like 'My Iron Lung' it had been written in the summer of 1993. Its lyric was inspired by Thom getting off the bus and observing a row of dead baby sparrows lying on the pavement (using images such as 'cracked eggs', 'dead birds', and the 'beady eyes' of death – a kind of unhappy, fatalistic bookend to the more optimistic 'Phillipa Chicken'). It featured another superb vocal performance from Thom, whose emotional reach as a singer was growing all the time. Though there was talk subsequently that the band were not entirely happy with Leckie's production, or more specifically, his mixing skills, the one thing he was able to do was locate Thom's voice in the right context – a factor sorely lacking in *Pablo Honey*. Leckie: 'Vocals are important in the way they sit in the mix. Sometimes I'll do a mix and someone says, "Can you turn the vocal up?" And I'll say, "No, you can't," because the mix is built around that balance, and turning the vocal up throws the whole thing out of balance.'

Thom and Jonny were learning a great deal about the recording process through Leckie, who tutored them in the use of mixing desks, tape operation, engineering and patching in effects. More importantly

Leckie, a noted eccentric, had provided some emotional ballast throughout the album's troubled creation. As Thom told *The Big Takeover*: 'He was very calm. I don't think anybody else would have stayed in the atmosphere that was there at the beginning of the album.'

With a lull in proceedings, Radiohead returned to touring yet again (though Phil did manage to get married and honeymoon in Lyme Regis). Among the notable engagements over the summer of 1994 were a Polish festival and an emotional set on the second day of the Reading Festival on 27 August – at which they played a rare cover version, Tim Buckley's 'Sing a Song for You'. It was widely reported that the band's attempts to concentrate on their new material alienated the crowd, though a glance at the set list confirms the presence of at least four first-album-era songs.

On 23 September the group returned to Abingdon to support Oxfam's Rwandan refugee campaign. A series of four gigs were staged at the town's Old Gaol, a former Victorian prison, with Ride, Radiohead, Carter the Unstoppable Sex Machine and Supergrass each headlining one night. The concerts, organized by the Unbelievable Truth's manager Dave Holt and Warwick Sayce, were completely sold out. Mark Sargeant attended all four nights and remembers Radiohead's set as one of the best 'local' gigs he'd ever seen. 'Radiohead played for about an hour, and "Creep" turned into a karaoke session, with everyone singing along. Thom was going to the edge of the stage and reaching out, touching the audience. Which isn't something you normally associate with him. It was heaving, and in terms of atmosphere, it was phenomenal. Being Abingdon, there were lots of underage kids there, and by the end of the night condensation was just pouring down the walls.'

Three days later the 'My Iron Lung' EP was released. The most abrasive, disconcerting song the group had written stalled at twenty-four in the charts. Keith Wozencroft: 'Isolated, without hearing its place within the album, I don't think people got it.' The song also proved unpopular with the group's American representatives. Clark Staub: 'Chris and Bryce came over to the States with "My Iron Lung" and played it for the Capitol staff and of course, everyone's first reaction was "It doesn't sound anything like 'Creep'." I made the suggestion that we test out the band's US fan base because my suspicion was that there was no fan base and so we put out "My Iron Lung" and even though we topped the college radio charts, which we'd never done with *Pablo Honey*, it didn't sell a tremendous amount of records. It sold about 20,000 EPs.'

At the time, Thom considered it the best lyric he had written. Chillingly evocative of confinement tempered by the need for sustenance, the song was inspired by a picture of an ill child caged by the giant lung machine in the fifties, which Thom had first seen at college – he's said to have used the picture extensively in his college work. Once again the band were frustrated by Radio 1's decision not to playlist the song, which was deemed 'too raucous'. Thom: 'I actually saw reviews of "My Iron Lung" which said it was just like "Creep". When you're up against things like that, it's like, "Fuck you". These people are never going to listen.' However, in truth the record company never pursued radio exposure, considering the EP an article of faith for fans – with different track listings appearing all around the world.

Of the B-sides, the standout was 'Punchdrunk Lovesick Singalong', with its hints of Tim Buckley and Thom's much-quoted observation that a beautiful girl can turn your world 'into dust'. The band rarely played it live because Colin kept forgetting the bass line. 'The Trickster' was the most orthodox track, an impenetrable lyric stapled to a recurrent rhythm-guitar base that recalled late-seventies' new wave. The title of 'Lozenge of Love' came from Philip Larkin's poem 'Sad Steps', about encroaching old age, and featured some impossibly operatic vocals even by Thom's standards. The lyrics were radically amended from their original form in the recording that eventually made the EP.

'Lewis (mistreated)' may or may not concern the misbegotten sidekick of Oxford's TV detective Inspector Morse. In this precursor to the sentiments of 'No Surprises', Thom once again empathizes with the little man. 'Permanent Daylight' was the first song to be produced solely by Nigel Godrich, the engineer who deputized for Leckie when he was busy mixing. A regular in live sets from 1993, it was originally offered for a film soundtrack but rejected. It is a largely uneventful effort, notable mainly for Jonny's jazz-inflected guitar work. 'You Never Wash Up After Yourself' was taped in one take at the Cumnor studio with Jim Warren. Rather than a reference to Jonny's slovenly habits while the group roomed together off the Cowley Road, it was inspired by the lethargy Thom felt after returning from touring in 1993 – the fish he kept at the bottom of the garden died because he didn't have the common sense or pragmatism to knock a hole in the ice. 'My girlfriend's allergic to all fur, so we can't have anything except goldfish. We had some really exotic Oriental fish in this pond in our garden. Over Christmas, they died. It was down to me being completely vacant, because you have to keep a hole in the ice to keep them from suffocating. That was my only encounter ever with pets and it didn't work out very well.' About halfway through the song Phil can be heard downing drumsticks and walking out – he thought it was only a rehearsal.

Radiohead were on their travels again either side of the EP's release. Their ten-date UK tour began at the Plaza, Glasgow, the final date coming at London's Shepherd's Bush Empire on 8 October. Dates followed in Thailand, with Colin dashing home to catch a rare set by his latest hero, Mark Eitzel and his American Music Club, in Birmingham. The notoriously contrary Eitzel refused to sign his CD. Radiohead were also reinvigorated by an eight-date tour of Mexico, including shows in the capital and Guadalajara, which completed October's itinerary. Thom: 'The first show we did was in a really dirty club. There were three tiny wooden tables that were used as a barricade. The only way off stage in the back was through a little window. We had just finished this large tour with James in Europe, and it was about as different an experience from that as humanly possible.' Colin: 'We were four days into the Mexican tour, on the Mexican sleeping bus from hell. There were thirteen of us and six bunks. We arrived and everyone was pretty despondent. And the venue was this old theatre with no ceiling above the stage, one electrical socket and pigeon shit everywhere. And against all the odds, it was very cool. Phil hated it 'cos there was five or six guys who refused to leave the stage who claimed to be the guys who'd put up the lights. They just stood behind him, watching him drumming all night.'

At the same time as they were beginning to try out the new material live, Radiohead were also exploring relationships within the band. The Mexican experience brought a new rash of temper tantrums, arguments, heightened emotions and the airing of previously guarded feelings. In an interview with Mark Richardson for the *NME* in December, Thom revealed how pivotal the experience had been. 'It just all came out. All the stuff that we'd always been fighting and, I think, when we started our little band, when we were kids at school, it was never really about being friends or anything. We were playing our instruments in our bedrooms and wanted to play them with someone. Years and years of tension and not saying anything to each other, and basically all the things that had built up since we'd met each other, all came out in one day. We were spitting and fighting and crying and saying all the things that you don't want to talk about and I think if we hadn't ever done that... I think that completely changed what we did and we all went back and did the album and it all made sense.'

The cleansing and refocusing of the group, which had begun with the aborted sessions for *The Bends*, was now complete. They felt renewed, their relationships re-cemented by a common purpose. Jim Irvin at *Mojo* notes: 'Chris Hufford once jokingly told me that whenever Radiohead were having problems in the studio, he'd pack them off on tour. Seemed to do the trick. They'd always come back vibed up and ready for it.'

After the Mexican tour Jonny and Thom travelled on to America to play a couple of acoustic sets in New York and Los Angeles, a chance to try out new material. Then it was back to England to complete the album.

Final revisions to the unfinished tracks now took place, alongside Leckie's jackdaw discovery of an old song. He'd chanced upon a track from the group's 1993 demo tape that he thought could be resurrected: 'High & Dry', which was originally written during Thom's time at Exeter. Leckie suggested that it would fit *The Bends* perfectly, but the band resisted, having earmarked it for use on their next album. However, his protestations prevailed and they reconsidered. Thom decided he liked the lyric's naive charm, and the rest of the band relearned their parts and added 'High & Dry' to the running order.

Thom was also labouring with the lyrics to 'Sulk', a song origi-nally written in response to the Hungerford slayings committed by Michael Ryan in the late eighties. It was the track Capitol wanted as a single, but it ended up being the band's least favourite on the album. Colin, in particular, disliked it intensely. In the light of Kurt Cobain's suicide in April, Thom elected to replace the last line – 'Just shoot your gun' – to 'You'll never change'. 'Sulk' was the final song to be completed and the first song from *The Bends* to be dropped from the band's live set.

The Bends was practically complete. Opener 'Planet Telex', later acknowledged as a band homage to Can's 1971 album *Tago Mago*, was written entirely within the studio. It was originally titled 'Planet Xerox' before the trademark implications dawned on the band. Jonny and Thom had worked out a chorus, but the band went out for a boozy meal at a Greek restaurant in Camden (the studio chef had the night off) before committing the track to tape. Leckie: '"Killer Cars" had this funky drum bit at the end, which wasn't quite working. We'd had quite a few bottles of wine – they don't do all that sort of thing too much, generally – and came up with the idea of looping this track. After the meal, we steamed back to the studio.' There the band started to reassemble the song, using three drum loops spliced together to provide an anchor for the stuttering guitar chords. Thom recorded the vocal while still heavily under the influence in the early hours of the morning, at Leckie's insistence. Leckie also helped work out the piano arrangement with Thom, Jonny having retired to bed. Ed provided the slow-burn chords dominating the chorus. Thom had to sing it with his head on the floor because of the evening's excesses. It's a confused, distressing narrative, founded on the observation that, everything, and everyone, is 'broken'. The manner of its recording and the group's new-found spontaneity predicted the scope of the whole album.

The fine tuning continued. 'Bones' had its original outro, which was Jonny's nod to the Fall, curtailed. '(Nice Dream)' featured all the band members playing acoustic guitars on the grass outside the studio. The lyrics were taken from an alcohol-fuelled dream and explored the group's relationship with the outside world. 'Just' featured another amazing guitar part by Jonny – described by Thom at that time as the most exciting thing he'd heard Radiohead put on tape. 'Black Star', too, featured an extraordinary Greenwood guitar motif, though everyone apart from Thom and its author wanted it to be re-recorded.

The title track was another old song, conceived before the release of *Pablo Honey*, and featured Jonny returning to his first instrument, the recorder. The unusual sound effects are drawn from a scene witnessed and recorded by Thom outside an American hotel room – a man tutoring a group of children in various musical instruments. 'The bends' is a condition experienced by divers resurfacing too quickly from deep water; the expressive term is thought to have been coined because the resulting pain forces sufferers to double up in agony. High pressure in deep water produces an excess of nitrogen, which dissolves in the bloodstream. If a diver resurfaces too quickly, the body cannot fully adjust, causing the nitrogen to form air bubbles. The song's central analogy uses this 'decompression sickness' as a metaphor for emotional pain. However, many critics took its sour lyrics to be a meditation on the band's success. Others kept quoting the line 'I wish it was the 60s' at the band. 'We wrote that line as a joke,' deflected Thom. 'We were taking the mickey. We all found that song hilarious.' Later he admitted that the words were formed from an unconnected selection of phrases running around his head. Nevertheless, Thom's striking metaphors - he washes to hide the 'dirt and pain', but becomes frightened that he'll discover there's 'nothing underneath' – conjured up some chilling images.

'Fake Plastic Trees' is a perfectly sarcastic look at human inadequacy and greed fuelled by media escapism. It may also be seen as another sour reflection on the false dawns offered to artist and consumer alike by the dehumanizing touch of celebrity. Thom: 'The day we recorded that song was a complete nightmare – I had a complete meltdown, so everyone left the studio. It was just me and my acoustic guitar, but there was something chilling hanging around in the air. We'd been there for a month, and that was the first time I felt any connection with what Radiohead's about. The funny thing is, it took bloody months to get everything else on top of it to sound natural.' All the bizarre keyboard noises were done at Abbey Road using an old Hammond organ that Paul McCartney had used on *Magical Mystery Tour*. 'We had it plugged into all the guitar amplifiers, every single effect, all the knobs and switches going. It was deafeningly loud, filling up the whole studio. That song could have easily sounded like Guns N' Roses. We wanted it to sound like Phil Spector.'

In many ways 'Fake Plastic Trees' is the keynote track of the album, a fact which Thom conceded to *The Big Takeover*: 'It was certainly the most important when we were making it, because it was the hardest one to make. And I think for us, especially for me, it was a real breakthrough, because up until that point in the recording I wasn't really happy with anything we had done. It seems that the way we operate is through a series of crisis points. That's the way that we exist creatively and in other ways as well, and "Fake Plastic Trees" was one of the biggest ever. So I agree in that sense it was important, because it wasn't meant to mean anything. It was really what it doesn't say which was important to me, and what lay behind it which was really important to me, and whether people sort of took it as ironic... I didn't really care about the interpretation, I just cared about the act of making the song itself.'

The intimacy of the lyrics throughout *The Bends* was a revelation. More than simply shorthand for Thom's psyche, the tone was open, honest and less mannered than conventional confessional approaches. 'If I'm happy I don't usually write. I'm happy *after* I write. There's an enormous sense of release. But I don't feel that we have to carry on churning out songs that are all about desperate human beings at the end of their tether la-la-la. That's all a bit old and boring now. It's a fine line between writing something with genuine emotional impact and turning into little idiots feeling sorry for ourselves and playing stadium rock.'

As a piece of self-analysis, Thom's argument is demonstrably coherent. Too many of his earlier lyrics had dealt, in almost excruciating detail, with failure. A whole raft of songs such as 'Prove Yourself' ('I'm better off dead'), 'You' ('Why should I believe myself'), 'Stupid Car' ('I failed in life'), 'Thinking About You' ('All the other men are far, far better'), 'Faithless, the Wonder Boy' ('All my friends said bye-bye'), 'Blow Out' ('Everything I touch turns to stone') and 'Creep' (practically the whole lyric) tackled problems in an affecting but one-dimensional way. Even on the title track to *The Bends*, Thom was declaring 'we don't have any real friends', or wondering why he 'can't get the stink off' in 'Just'. Yet the singer was clearly outgrowing this vein of exaggerated, morose introspection. Significantly, he elected to print the lyrics on the sleeve in an effort to demystify the songs.

Despite his advancing skill and technique as a songwriter, Thom insisted he had to continually arm-wrestle his muse into submission before accomplishing anything worthwhile. 'I can never do it all at once. If I know that I've got to do it, I won't do it. I have to do it whenever I'm doing something else, whenever I'm driving or on a train or on a plane – the washing up, or whatever. Some days, everything means a lot and you write it all down in your notebook, extremely profound, and then you go two months and nothing will mean anything. You can't really go and look for it, so I have to keep notebooks. The only valid thing I learned from art college is keeping notebooks all the time.'

Current Poet Laureate Andrew Motion recently asserted that pop lyrics are 'repetitive and banal'. While this holds true for many artists, music's ability to connect on a direct emotional level lends good songwriters an edge. Dissecting Thom's lyrics bereft of their musical context is a more fruitless exercise than most. Unlike those of, say, Morrissey or Motion's hero, Bob Dylan, most of his lyrics would not prosper from being read in isolation. But he understands the dynamic tension between words, imagery and sound better than any other artist in his field: 'I think the music makes it feel more powerful as well, which means I don't have to give so much in words. I think you need to be able to take a step back from what you're doing anyway. I took a step back from what I was writing in words. I just sort of treated that as another instrument rather than this is me personally giving you all, everything in my soul. You do that once, and you never, ever want to do that again.'

As much as the band enjoyed working with Leckie, they weren't entirely confident of his mixing skills. This meant that several tracks on the completed version of *The Bends* were finalized by Kolderie and Slade at Fort Apache Studios. Leckie: 'When it came to mixing the album, no one came! Then they started asking for copies of the multi-tracks and I realized they probably had someone else mixing the album as well and it turned out it was the same team who mixed the first album. The record company had been going on about trying to get an American sound for the record from the minute I got involved. The annoying thing for me, a little bit, was that there are things on there that they'd told me not to do originally – like using big reverbs on the voice or certain tones that were forbidden – that the Americans did. I found it quite funny. There's a lot to be said for other people mixing stuff because sometimes you get so into it that it's a good idea to have a fresh outlook on it with a total stranger. The finished product is a lot harder. I don't think I could have got it sounding quite as blasting as that.'

Work on the album was completed in November. The band were triumphant, Thom believing, on hearing the first test pressing, that they had finally laid to rest the ghost of 'Creep'. 'I thought, this is it. This is what it was all about in the first place. We've come out of all this more alive than we ever were when we went in.' Parlophone were less convinced of its commercial viability, though they did agree to release it. In America, Capitol's executives were even more reluctant to endorse the record. Thom and Jonny were asked to come out and play a handful of promotional dates, which involved flying coast to coast. All they found were audiences still chanting for 'Creep'.

-eight-

thin english boys and influential friends

Nineteen ninety-five began with a secret warm-up gig at the Lomax club in Liverpool, before a sold-out showcase at Oxford's Apollo with support from the Candyskins and Supergrass – the latter now managed by Chris Hufford. The venue was derided by the band for previously playing host to John Inman's *Mother Goose* and Little and Large's production of *Aladdin*. It was also the venue where, in December 1958 as the New Theatre, Lonnie Donegan recorded his immortal 'Does Your Chewing Gum Lose Its Flavour On The Bedpost Overnight?' Some seventy journalists were in attendance to witness Radiohead's homecoming. *Melody Maker*'s review observed a set of 'gloriously good songs by thin English boys'. According to John Harris, the music industry was some way short of embracing Radiohead, but perceptions were changing. 'There was a big do for all the record company people at the Randolph Hotel, just before *The Bends* came out. The only thing anyone had heard was the twelve-inch of "Planet Telex" and "High & Dry". And they were just frightened by it, it was so brilliant. I remember writing, this is it – Radiohead – this is it. It was just so obvious, even then. It got described in the *NME* as the best indie rock album of the year, and I was thinking: "It's bigger than that!"'

Mark Sargeant watched the Apollo performance. 'It was a good gig, musically, but the Apollo has a house policy of bringing in their own security to stop people standing up and having a good time. It's not a good place to go and enjoy yourself at a gig, and that tainted it for me. So the crowd reaction wasn't at its best. I remember the photo pit was like a bunfight, though, absolutely packed out, people from all over the world falling over themselves to take pictures.' Sargeant could tell that Radiohead had arrived because 'Lots of guys with Scouse accents were outside selling posters, the first time I'd been to an Oxford gig with Oxford bands with bootleggers on site, doing their bit.'

At the Randolph, Thom defended himself against accusations that he was merely an angst-peddler. 'I love life, I really do,' he began. (Contrast this with his famed 'If I was happy, I'd be in a fucking car advert' mantra.) 'But there's so much shit to deal with. Like, I have friends who are artists, maybe even great artists. But they're at the end of their tethers. What with the dole, the poverty, they just don't have the energy to carry on. When we started this thing, I really did believe the good will out, the best rise to the top. But I no longer believe that. People are continuously overlooked and ignored. You only have to watch the news to know that. It's not just artists. It's everybody.'

Radiohead were misguidedly construed by some to be part of the Britpop phenomenon. *The Bends* was recorded at the time Blur and Oasis were squaring up for their tilt at the top of the charts. Jonny: 'The Britpop movement was wrong for us because it was so awash with this knowing irony. In some ways, it wasn't about being in a band and being serious about being in a band, which we hate and which was an anathema to us.' As Melvyn Bragg has noted, in the late eighties the 'passion for the ironic' was 'collapsing into the moronic'. He was speaking about British TV, but the observation equally applies to the knowing archness of the domestic music scene of the mid-nineties. Musical influences, too, had become shackled to endless rewrites of the Beatles and Kinks, ring-fenced by notions of the three-minute pop song and an unswerving deification of the decade that most current musicians had been born in, the sixties. Radiohead were the only band within the credible mainstream who were consciously striving for something removed from that.

The first single from the album was the double A-side 'High & Dry'/'Planet Telex', released on 11 March. Pairing together two of the most compelling songs on *The Bends*, it debuted at seventeen in the charts. The British press was far too busy hyping Britpop to notice. Those that did again compared the band to U2, a response as inaccurate as it was deeply unimaginative. 'High & Dry' was an elegant, almost balletic piece of modern rock, albeit an unusually traditional-sounding one for Radiohead. Its most distinctive feature is Thom's skyscraping falsetto and a lyric about those – the band used the analogy of Evil Knievel – who will do anything for fame. Tucked away as a bonus track on the first of two CD versions was 'Maquiladora' – a term denoting the trade agreement between the US and Mexico which has seen the proliferation of sweatshops just below the border, serving American corporate interests. It was previously titled 'Interstate 5', and is notable for its inclusion of one of Thom's most self-deprecating lines: 'Useless rockers from England'.

A week after the release of 'High & Dry', *The Bends* entered the UK charts at number six. The cover image was of a dummy used for practising mouth-to-mouth resuscitation that Thom and Stanley Donwood (aka Dan Rickwood) had found in Oxford's John Radcliffe Hospital while they were shooting video material. Donwood: 'We were careful not to film any of the patients. Well, not living ones – it's an invasion of privacy, isn't it? And we ended up in this room where they stored all their dummies, we chose this resuscitation dummy...' Donwood had become Thom's best friend at Exeter University, when he was likewise studying art and English. He had been living for a year on income support in Cornwall, creating community murals, when Thom called him and asked him to design the cover for Radiohead's second album – after admitting the artwork on the first was 'stupid'. The sleeve dedication was to recently deceased American comedian Bill Hicks.

Where the response to *Pablo Honey* was begrudging, critics fell over themselves to salute *The Bends*. Thom, rather than rejoicing, offered his usual pithy contrariness: 'Nothing sensible was written about the album. All journalists picked their brains to come up with the weirdest superlatives. Well, that's a bit over the top. *The Bends* is a nice album, but you don't have to shove it down people's throats. If they like it, they'll buy it, you don't need all that sucking up to the press stuff.'

Colin was less disturbed by the turnaround in the group's relationship with the press, but he too downplayed the music papers' importance in what Radiohead had achieved. 'We're incredibly proud that the record is doing so well. We've only had one *NME* cover, which is ridiculous for a band who've sold three million records, but it proves that people are buying the album because they've heard through word of mouth that it's good.' Ed's friends convinced him of its worth: 'For me, the biggest high I got from reactions to *The Bends* was, I've got friends who do not listen to bands with guitars. They're just into dance music. And universally, they would say they'd come back from a rave or whatever and would stick on *The Bends* to chill out ... even though they weren't into that kind of music, it was the only guitar album of '95/'96 that they really loved. That was very, very cool.'

The press were right: it was a stunning album which punched a hole straight through critical resistance to a bunch of Oxfordshire public schoolboys with guitars. It also convinced some music writers that Radiohead really were a band worth investing in, as Perry Watts-Russell, Capitol's vice-president of A&R, noted. 'I went to see the band play in Paris and was less than impressed. But when I heard *The Bends* and saw them play it live, I realized they had blossomed into one of the most vital rock bands in the world.'

Thom was suffering from a painful physical disorder caused by the contradictions of his lifestyle – manic stage performances on tour followed by periods of almost total inactivity. 'My whole body was aching like an old man,' he told Steve Malins of *Vox* in April 1995. Jonny admitted: 'It's a real medical album for me. Thom went into a hospital to take pictures for the cover artwork, and it struck me the other day how much it's all about illness and doctors. It kind of makes sense, because we've been on a cycle of illness. I've been run down with gastro-somethings, horrible things with Latin names that are attached to my lower intestines... There's also that feeling of revulsion about your own body: that resentment that you're so reliant on it.' In the same interview, Thom countered long-held criticisms of Radiohead as middle-class rebels with no rock 'n' roll heart, going into embarrassing and unnecessary detail about his drinking binges and how 'We put together a lot of this album when we were stoned.' It's arguably the most un-Radiohead quote to ever appear in print, and given the stature of the album he'd just produced, doubly hard to fathom.

The Bends contained far more complexity, yet has more compositional clarity and focus, and better production, than its forerunner. Thom told *The Big Takeover*: 'I think a lot of that comes from just really growing up. I think it's every musician's dream to get to the point where they can be themselves within the medium they're working in. Every artist dreams of that, and it's a really difficult and painful thing. If it's any good it's usually fairly difficult and painful to discover why or what you want to say and you can't do it consciously, it just sort of happens. But it's what you're aiming at. I think that making *The Bends* was us discovering a lot of that quicker than I think we expected we would. I don't understand where the leap came from, and it's a leap for us in terms of who we are as a band, it's not a leap commercially. We have to swallow that.'

The highlight of the album was Thom's singing – which deftly invoked a range of moods from fragility and tenderness to snarling misanthropy. The reliance on falsetto, as brilliantly as it was executed, was becoming as inescapable a trademark as was the Pixies'/Nirvana's stop-start song dynamic of earlier years. Similarly, perceptions of the band shifted from one pigeonhole to another. The songs on *The Bends* evoked isolation and terror in a manner unrealized (but much attempted) since Joy Division's late-seventies' peak. That led the press to cite the album, alongside the Manic Street Preachers' *Holy Bible* and Nirvana's *In Utero*, as a calling card for a new 'culture of despair'.

The theme was picked up by the Stud Brothers in a Radiohead cover story for *Melody Maker* that particularly galled Thom. But it wasn't just the music press. For a while in 1995 you couldn't turn on the TV or read a newspaper without the phrase cropping up. The only despair Thom would acknowledge came from the pigeonholing of his records. 'For Christ's sake, I did not write this album for people to slash their fucking wrists to,' he told Caitlin Moran. Later he elaborated: 'I have a theory that all good music is uplifting, whether it be chirpy acoustic guitars and stuff about "taking the weather with you", or whether it sounds like Joy Division with lyrics about your dog dying in a well.'

The next step was to take the songs out on the road. *The Bends* tour began on 9 March with a performance at the Aston Villa Leisure Centre. On stage, Thom responded to earlier critical barbs against the band, flippantly claiming: 'We aren't the new U2. U2 are the new Radiohead.' Reviewer Sean McManus of *Making Music* missed the point spectacularly by concluding: 'That's as may be, there's no one more likely to write the *Rattle And Hum* of the 90s.' The U2 comparisons stuck with Radiohead for some time, and there are superficial similarities between the bands. They are both backed by powerful management teams, have endured periods of hostility from the *NME*, and possess highly distinctive guitarists and vocalists. Thom and Bono's favourite film is *Jacob's Ladder*, Adrian Lyne's Vietnam vet saga, and both make extensive use of falsetto for emotional impact. Yet U2 were always a far more traditional rock band, with an internationalism that Radiohead never replicated or aspired to. U2 always wanted to be rock stars, and acted accordingly. On the few occasions Radiohead have displayed flashes of ego, it has been in advocacy of their music rather than personal agendas.

Dave Sinclair of *The Times* concurred, having watched Radiohead on *The Bends* tour. 'They display little enthusiasm for the stereotyped role-playing that tends to go with being a rock band on the road, save for one intriguing detail. They are doing the entire tour, which takes them from Truro to Aberdeen and most points in between, without staying at hotels. This entails sleeping, indeed living, on the tour bus for two weeks, which is far from standard practice for a band at this level (even the support group, Marion, are staying in hotels).' The tour concluded with a show at the Kentish Town Forum on 24 March that was recorded, several songs later appearing on various international B-sides.

The band were understandably anxious about how the quieter, subdued strains of *The Bends* might be received by audiences, but were pleased with the reaction. Thom: 'We're a good enough band that we can actually translate a song from an album into a live context and just do it in a slightly different way, and what the fuck, not worry about it. We did this British tour and it was just amazing for the whole tour to be sold out, and for people to stop and not say anything during quiet songs like "Fake Plastic Trees" and "Bullet Proof". To just stand there and listen at a Radiohead gig, and not jump up and down and not mosh. This is great. It was a real revelation for us.'

However, on subsequent engagements in America through April and May – two separate tours that sandwiched further European dates – they faced much greater difficulty in convincing audiences to embrace their new material. In Boston, Thom lost his rag with the audience, scowling and telling them: 'This is for all the people bumping in to each other down the front. I hope you all break your necks.' Later he explained his position to *The Big Takeover*. 'Last night it was really out of control. A lot of people getting hurt. I don't understand it, playing "Fake Plastic Trees". In the back of my head, I always knew it was going to be like this. I'd be singing with my guitar, the bit where it goes down. It's always embarrassing and always quite awkward to sing that part, and the video was again embarrassing and awkward. I get off on it, because I think that's what good art is about. Good creativity is basically embarrassing to the creator. It's like pulling your pants down in public. And you do it for ever more. But in the back of my mind I was always aware that you were just getting these fucking morons who were just pounding up and down on each other. They should go listen to the Offspring instead. I think we were always aware when recording "Fake Plastic Trees" that we would get people moshing all the way through it, and the comedy of that, and how ridiculous that would seem, and not caring. We finished the song thinking: 'Why do we have to pander to that?' There's a sense of complete freedom of sorts. This isn't about supply and demand.'

Radiohead's refusal to tread the path of least resistance combined with a low boredom threshold to produce different takes on different songs in any given evening on this tour. That was especially true of Jonny's parts, which were becoming progressively more freewheeling and improvisational. 'Have I ever fallen flat on my arse?' he mused. 'Oh yeah, definitely. But as long as the hit rate is over seventy per cent, I'll carry on playing like that.'

Yet resistance to anything the band had to offer outside of

'Creep' continued in America. Released on 4 April 1995, *The Bends* peaked at eighty-eight in the *Billboard* charts before disappearing. That was despite radio station WXRK giving away free packets of condoms with the album's artwork embossed on one side, alongside the legend 'Our listeners come first'. Paul Kolderie believes that the American public couldn't get a grip on it because '*The Bends* was neither an English album nor an American album. It's an album made in the void of touring and travelling. It really had that feeling of, "We don't live anywhere and we don't belong anywhere."'

On 27 May the group appeared on BBC2's *Later With Jools Holland*, performing 'High & Dry' and 'The Bends', a set filmed before their departure for the second leg of their US tour. Also on the bill were Elvis Costello, Chris Isaak and James Burton. Burton, rockabilly's premier guitarist and a veteran of recording sessions with Elvis Presley and Gram Parsons was overheard saying to Steve Nieve of the Attractions: 'What's he doing now?' after clocking Jonny Greenwood's guitar style. He later said that Jonny's playing reminded him of the time when he cared enough to 'give a fuck about playing music'. Thom was introduced to Costello, who proved convivial and complimentary about Radiohead. The frontman's performances, Costello said, reminded him of his own, adding: 'Thom Yorke's mentioned my name a few times. Of the people who are around at the moment you couldn't have anyone more talented than him paying you a compliment.'

The second single from the album, 'Fake Plastic Trees', became a UK Top Twenty hit on 3 June, though this ostensibly quiet, reflective effort was hardly conducive to airplay (hence Capitol's interest in a Bob Clearmountain remix for America). Thom was aghast at his US label's attempts to mould the song to fit FM radio schedules. 'Capitol remixed it. But it isn't as good as the original. The record company want us to release the remix, because they say it would suit American radio better. But that's a line we can't cross. I mean, it's a beautiful song as it stands. If it doesn't get on the radio the way it is now, then I don't think it's going to get on the radio at all. There's nothing anyone can do to it. And that really scares the shit out of me. I mean, if there's one reason why I'd give up this business, it's because people will try to fuck with your stuff to fit a formula. People say it won't work on the radio, but I have no fucking idea what they mean.'

On release in America, 'Fake Plastic Trees' did help to reignite interest in the band. Clark Staub: 'If anything, "Fake Plastic Trees" was such a left turn from where the last big commercial exposure to Radiohead was in the US, that it really caught people off guard and made them take notice of Radiohead, because even though we only sold 35,000 records, the fact that we were all over MTV with a very visually stunning video and a beautiful song for that matter, sort of threw people off. From there the band started touring and during that time they really matured, and as a live band, they exploded.'

'Fake Plastic Trees' was later used in the vile teen flick *Clueless*, in which Alicia Silverstone's character asks why so many American students listen to 'complaint rock' – which seems, frighteningly, to have become an officially sanctioned genre in US rock. Thom deflected accusations of Radiohead being, to use the film's vernacular, 'cry-baby music'. 'Cool! I mean, I suppose it does piss me off, but I am a moaning cry-baby from hell, really. Besides, the characters in that film aren't the kind of people I'd want to like Radiohead. They're just average, two-dimensional Beverly Hills kids, and the person who is actually listening to us in the film is the only three-dimensional character. So the answer is: "Fuck you, we're for 3D people!" Some famous pop star told me to lighten up. And I felt really proud of myself. I felt really good because I haven't lightened up. I have absolutely no intention of lightening up because when I do, I really will turn into Jim Kerr.'

Two new tracks were recorded for the B-side. 'India Rubber' and 'How Can You Be Sure' offered contrasting views on the band's development. The former was a homage to the apocalyptic drum sound of DJ Shadow, predating *OK Computer*'s 'Airbag' experiment. The latter was a return to wistful relationship anxiety (the song dated from at least two years before), with female backing vocals courtesy of Dianne Swann. The lyrics were a throwback to the self-derision exhibited on earlier records, the theme being: if you *really* knew me, you wouldn't really like me.

'Fake Plastic Trees' was promoted via the first of a series of highly imaginative, slickly produced videos employed by the band. This one, directed by Jake Scott (son of film-maker Ridley Scott, who directed *Blade Runner*), captured the band being pushed round a supermarket in shopping trolleys. It was released in America and Canada before Europe, and one of the many to see it and love it was Michael Stipe of R.E.M., who subsequently went out to buy the album it promoted. He then offered to take Radiohead on tour as R.E.M.'s support band. Jonny: 'It was an invitation from them, and we assumed there was going to be another Radiohead from Alabama or something that were going to turn up at the first concert.' With most of the band long-term fans of Athens, Georgia's most famous export, they agreed.

After their American tour ended in mid-June came dates in Japan, where, in Osaka, Phil learned of the presence of the 'Phil Is Great' club. Jonny, a fan of Japanese designer labels, became so fascinated with Oriental culture he attempted to pick up a little of the language. 'In press conferences and on TV I used some Japanese phrases, so the next day there were piles of "learning Japanese" books waiting for me in the lobby.' He'd also tried to learn a bit of Hebrew for the Israeli tours. Typically for the band, Radiohead made an effort to engage with the culture and not treat the Japanese as the uncritical sycophants characterized by other Western bands. Jonny: 'We found them very well researched and well written. Did you know that the *Oxford English Dictionary* sells more copies in Japan than in America annually? They're really perceptive; not the faceless mass everyone makes them out to be.' Members of the band would often greet the fans waiting for them in hotel lobbies and ask them to recommend good local restaurants, 'breaking bread' with them. However, one anomaly occurred to Jonny – rarely would the same young female faces reappear after each tour. 'I'll ask them, for example, "Where's Keiko?" and they'll say, "Oh, Keiko doesn't hang around with bands any more." It's a little sad.' A short club tour of North America, with intimate dates in Arizona, North Carolina and Ontario followed.

The promised dates with R.E.M. began on 30 July at a two-day festival in Milton Keynes, alongside Blur and the Cranberries. Thom recorded the experience in a diary written for *Q* magazine. Of particular satisfaction was the way Michael Stipe introduced himself to the band before the gig as 'a very big fan'. Despite never believing in hero worship, Thom concedes he had to fight for breath.

The end of July brought the start of the video shoot for 'Just', directed by Jamie Thraves. He had simply sent in a treatment on a sheet of A4 paper. Filmed over three days, the video depicted the band thrashing away in an apartment while outside a man lies down on the pavement. As a series of interlopers try to discover his reason for lying there, he pleads with them to leave him alone. Subtitles replace the soundtrack for the conversation. Eventually a crowd builds, desperate to know the rationale for his outlandish behaviour. He eventually tells them. The closing shot pans across all his interrogators lying alongside him on the ground, but what he says is not revealed. The video was filmed in two other formats – one with just the band performing, the second with the pavement scene played out on its own. Just what the man says has become the most frequently asked question on most Radiohead Web sites. The answer was scripted, but Radiohead have been reluctant to reveal it, though Jonny has stated it includes a number.

In August they rejoined the R.E.M. tour for a show at the Berlin sports stadium that was built for the 1936 Olympics. Afterwards Thom recalled in his *Q* diary a bizarre after-show party thrown in R.E.M.'s honour: 'I'm shocked. It seems you have to be nice to people for ever. I may as well get used to my cracked smile now.' The next day, on the plane to Oslo, he was shown a letter from Bill Clinton offering his sympathy to R.E.M. bassist Mike Mills over his recent stomach complaint. Also during the flight, Radiohead taught the Georgians the basics of cricket.

Peter Buck told Nick Johnstone why they'd invited Radiohead to support them. '*The Bends* was probably my favourite record of that year [1995]. And Michael had a copy and I'd had a copy earlier and we were playing it and we thought, this is great, we should get them to open for us. And you never know what musicians can be like, and generally they're nice people, but I've had some bad experiences. So we booked them for basically eight or nine shows and we just had a great time and they were really nice people. They're all really well educated, they're smart and talk about different subjects. You know, you could talk about books and paintings and stuff. Then we tried to drag them around America which was a good experience. They've kind of re-invented the guitar hero. I mean, Jonny doesn't actually use his fingers all the time, if you see him, he's playing with his elbow and all that but he was coming out with some amazingly invigorating sounds. I watched them do twenty-five shows and there wasn't a bad one ever.'

Later it emerged that Radiohead had turned down a support slot with the Rolling Stones in order to remain on the R.E.M. tour. On the day of the Oslo gig, and as noted in his diary for *Q*, Thom saw Kurt Cobain's suicide note for the first time on the back of a T-shirt, following the girl wearing it around in an attempt to read it in full. After the show he played the band a new song he'd written, at this point entitled 'No Surprises, Please'. Colin, in particular, loved it.

After a date in Stockholm the tour moved on to Sicily, where the band were once again paired with Elvis Costello. In Tel Aviv, Thom was embarrassed by an autograph hunter who approached a table he was sharing with R.E.M. and requested his signature rather than theirs – Radiohead were huge pop stars in Israel, though this time there was no problem with crowds of fans as they passed through customs. It was at that night's gig that Michael Stipe made his famous on-stage remark: 'There aren't many things that scare me, but Radiohead are so good they scare me.' However, Radiohead's set was cut short owing to Colin's stomach ache.

'Just' was released on 7 August, peaking at nineteen in the UK charts at the beginning of September. A week later Radiohead rejoined R.E.M.'s *Monster* tour for a performance at the Miami Arena. The pairing seems to have proved a uniquely harmonious experience, R.E.M. allowing their support act a full half-hour warm-up, which after previous experiences with bands as lowly as Kingmaker, Radiohead greatly appreciated. Although big fans of R.E.M., in some early interviews the band had openly criticized them for releasing too many singles from *Automatic For The People*. Jonny had told a fanzine writer in 1994: 'I don't like R.E.M. any more. All their songs are too full of mandolins and ballady. They all play sitting down. They're sort of old men's rock 'n' roll.' However, the rest of the band were assuredly fans. Colin told Andrew Mueller: 'I can remember listening to R.E.M.'s first couple of albums on my Walkman on the way to school. They're one of the reasons I wanted to be in a band. This is still really strange.'

The influence of R.E.M. can be observed in many aspects of the English group's activity. On the *Monster* tour, Radiohead were introduced to some of the political and environmental movements that R.E.M. supported, including Greenpeace, Rock the Vote and the National Coalition to Abolish the Death Penalty. Thom, in particular, has been a more active spokesperson for such concerns since. In addition, the tour taught the band vital lessons about being a major mainstream act, and the level of expectation they could expect to encounter. 'The thing that's really freaked me out about doing a tour with a band as big as R.E.M.,' Thom told Andrew Mueller, 'is seeing how being so famous can change the way everybody, and I mean absolutely everybody, behaves towards you.'

Peter Buck analogized the fraternity between the bands to Nick Johnstone: 'The one thing I'm kind of proud of is that we were like the older guys in that relationship. You know, that tour we did, we were writing these songs at the soundcheck and then playing them that night at the show and I remember the Radiohead guys were really impressed with the fact that we had enough nerve to go out and play the songs that we'd only played once out in front of 20,000 people who'd never heard them. And I think that was maybe a little influential to them. I hope so, because next time I saw them, they had like five new songs in their set!'

Back in Britain in September, Radiohead returned to the studio to work alongside a host of high-profile British acts on the compilation *Help!*, an LP raising funds for the War Child charity, which aided victims of the war in Bosnia. Publicists Anton Brookes and Terry Hall, with Tony Crean, marketing manager of Go! Discs, planned to get the bands to record their tracks on Monday and have the album in shops by Saturday. Oasis, the Stone Roses, Massive Attack and Suede all agreed to be involved, and Radiohead earmarked for the project a new song they'd written, 'Lucky' – a number Thom wrote around a guitar effect Ed had stumbled on. Ed: 'We were in Japan – and putting together a different pedal order and actually hitting the strings above the nut on the headstock. The pedals that I did it with, and the delay that was going on – it was one of those moments – "Yeah, this is pretty cool."' The lyrics were edited down from a much longer draft. Thom: 'There's a lot of strength in just omitting a lot of things. "Lucky" was pages and pages of notes. It was all bollocks, trying to be really political. And in the end it wasn't. It was much better to say, "The head of state has called for me by name/But I don't have time for him." And that was it.'

However, there were some reservations about the project. Thom: 'We did it because we were asked to do it and because Ed studied the Balkans. We just felt it was a good idea to just make the gesture. We realized that there would be a lot of back-patting but we knew it wasn't going to end up like *Live Aid*. To be honest, we were really itching to record the song anyway, and we just didn't see why we shouldn't put it on this record. I'm not a big one for bands getting involved in charity but at the same time it was so close to home it just made sense to do it really. The other bands in it almost put us off, though.'

It wasn't the first time Radiohead had been involved in fundraising – alongside their benefit gig for Rwanda at Abingdon's Old Gaol, they had contributed a track, 'Banana Co.', to the *Criminal Justice! Axe the Act* benefit LP. The *Help!* sessions were recorded on 12 September, along with a good amount of video footage of the bands for press purposes (the videos from the recording were all lip-synched for the benefit of cameras). Brian Eno was the co-producer. 'Lucky' was easily the standout song on the album, a fact acknowledged by several other contributing artists. Thom himself admitted he cried when he first played the tape back at home. Excited by the possibility of grinding out songs in this pressurized atmosphere, the group returned to the studio to record two further tracks, 'Talk Show Host' (one of their most R.E.M.-like titles) and 'Bishop's Robes'. Nigel Godrich recalls the session as 'the best bit of recording we ever did'. 'Lucky' also allowed fans a tantalizing glimpse of what the band's third album might sound like.

Help! was officially released on 19 September. However, the album was controversially excluded from the main charts as a 'various artists' collection, though it hit number one in the compilation listings. Radio 1, suspicious of the recent glut of charity recordings, refused to playlist 'Lucky', which stalled outside the Top Fifty on release in October. The broadcaster's stance mystified the band. Thom said they were waiting 'for the karma police to come and sort it out.' Ed suggested the phrase be bookmarked for future use as a song title. The effective scuttling of 'Lucky' and the cause it represented was Thom's worst moment in 1995, he later confessed.

The *Monster* tour was completed in October, with the group trying out several new songs in their soundchecks, including 'Climbing Up The Walls' and 'Airbag'. The latter was another song inspired by Thom's anxieties about and fascination with modern car travel – its original title, 'An Airbag Saved My Life', was a play on the 1983 Indeep song 'Last Night a DJ Saved My Life'. Thom had been reading a promotional leaflet from the Automobile Association. 'I just think that people get up too early to leave houses where they don't want to live, to drive to jobs where they don't want to be, in one of the most dangerous forms of transport on earth. I've just never gotten used to that.'

As recounted in Andrew Mueller's book *Rock And Hard Places*, the band spent much of their time before the final official show (there was a secret gig the following night at the Mercury Lounge in New York) in the Meadows Music Theater, Hartford, Connecticut, pondering what tricks to play on their hosts. An avalanche of ping-pong balls and an *en masse* entrance via strung harnesses were considered, then the ideas abandoned. R.E.M. talked a big game about visiting some misfortune on their beloved support act but settled for Mike Mills interrupting Ed's guitar playing with a radio-controlled car. In the end the band evacuated the stage before the final note of 'Nobody Does It Better' (dedicated to R.E.M.) faded, only to find the headliners waiting for them with champagne flutes. Thom had long since perfected the trick of standing at the front of the crowd during R.E.M.'s sets and staring directly at Pete Buck, who so dislikes seeing anyone he knows in the audience, he's forced to look in another direction.

Thereafter the group joined Soul Asylum for further dates across America. Soul Asylum turned out to be friendly, regular guys, and agreeable touring companions, even if Radiohead harboured little enthusiasm for their music. On the first night of the tour in Denver, Radiohead had all their equipment stolen from their hotel room. Thom: 'I quite enjoyed that because everyone felt sorry for us all day. We went to this restaurant and got the best tables, free pizzas. I was walking down the street and this tramp says, "Sorry to hear about your gear."' The band had to cancel a series of shows and travelled to LA to acquire new equipment. The necessaries were purchased on 7 October, Thom's birthday. The band were less upset by the loss of their equipment than many would be, though Jonny did volunteer a pithy 'I hope their next shit is a porcupine' rejoinder to the miscreants. Not especially attached to any of the missing equipment, they treated its theft as an inconvenience more than anything else

The Soul Asylum tour was certainly a mismatch, as Clark Staub recounts: 'That Soul Asylum record [*Let Your Dim Light Shine*] was overwhelmingly rejected, but nobody knew this when Radiohead took the tour. Here was Soul Asylum who had sold four million copies of their last record and who now couldn't sell tickets for their shows and what happened was Radiohead were selling a lot of the tickets for these houses.'

The band made it to the end of the tour, though not before Thom's vocal chords had begun to suffer from the schedule. They returned to Britain for yet more dates, supported by firm friends Sparklehorse. In fact, Jonny operated the lighting for their set because they couldn't afford their own engineer – he was disguised with a hat so fans wouldn't figure out who he was. (Thom later contributed to phoned-in backing vocals to the band's cover of Pink Floyd's 'Wish You Were Here'.)

Radiohead's biggest domestic indoor gig so far came on 4 November at the Brixton Academy. Simon Berridge of support act Bromide witnessed 'the sort of screaming teenage adoration that recalled an early Beatles live TV audience,' yet the band felt underwhelmed by such adulation, as Thom later confessed to John Harris. 'I hated Brixton. It was bollocks. It really was. It just felt wrong.

Meeting people's expectations was not what we were into doing. Especially 'cos we'd just done five weeks, and we were all mentally and physically fucked. And there we were playing these gigs that we'd really looked forward to, and we weren't able to enjoy it. There was a big wall between us and the audience. Apparently, from their side, it was a one-way mirror – it was fine. But it felt like that to us.'

The tour closed on 7 November at the Southampton Guildhall – a triumphant two-hour gig attended by Queen's Roger Taylor, and marred only by Colin's *Spinal Tap*-esque inability to find the after-show party in the Guildhall's honeycomb of backstage corridors. 'You know, people are always saying that we're like U2,' he mused, 'but I'm sure this never fucking happens to Adam Clayton.'

European dates with Drugstore in Spain, France and Italy followed, but the toll on the band was heavy. Finally, after trying a series of prescription drugs to alleviate his throat problems, at a gig in Munich on 25 November Thom blacked out on stage after five songs. After the *NME* misrepresented what happened, under the headline 'Thom's Temper Tantrum', Thom was furious: 'As they put it, I threw a tantrum in Germany and left the stage and nobody could understand what had happened and everyone was really pissed off and the whole audience were really angry and wanted their money back or whatever. The article was run like that and it was sort of second- or third-hand. What actually happened on that night was that I'd been really, really ill for quite some time and I didn't know whether I would be able to do it or not and it's very difficult to tell but after a while, if you're doing a tour, there is a point where you have to just carry on. It doesn't matter how ill you are, you still have to get on stage, and that really fucking does something to your head after a while. When I tried the soundcheck I got really worried because I couldn't sing anything. And when the show came round, people had driven hundreds of miles to come and it was snowing and it was like three or four foot deep and I just thought: "There is no way I'm not doing the show because these people have travelled this far." So I got up on stage and I thought it would be alright, but after three songs I lost my voice completely and I was croaking and I just got really fucking freaked out. I got tunnel vision and I don't really know what happened. I threw stuff around and threw my amp around and drum kit and ended up with blood all over my face and things. I cried for about two hours afterwards. I want people to know what happened that night. I'm sure no one gives a fuck and I'm sure the *NME* don't give a fuck, but what they wrote in that piece hurt me more than anything else anyone has ever written about me.'

Yet the group pressed on with further dates. Somebody, some-where, should have been persuading Radiohead's lead singer that his voice deserved a break from the strain of touring, which had now continued for ten months unabated. Thom: 'What I think is fucking ridiculous is the way that you get to a certain point and people get extremely upset if you don't go and play in their country. I mean, extremely. And it's like blackmail, you know? So every time you do a record, you're blackmailed into going on tour for two years, which is bollocks ... it's probably a good thing for us. We have a lot of time to work on stuff. But I still don't really think we're in control. I don't think you can be. Everyone has to do it – you have to go and promote. And there actually aren't that many bands from Britain who tour like we do. Around the world touring. Having said that, I don't think there's anything worthy in going on tour for two years.'

Yet the band went straight back on the road, with dates in Sweden and Amsterdam and, in between, an incongruous appearance at the *Smash Hits* Poll Winners' Party on 3 December, at which they contributed 'My Iron Lung' to the consternation of the teenyboppers in attendance. The reaction was one of supreme discomfort, though the evening did bring the consolation of moral support from Take That's Mark Owen, who claimed to be a big fan (and later added a Radiohead song to his live show).

The tour with Drugstore ended on 5 December in Brussels. To mark the event, Drugstore's Isabel Monteiro unveiled a specially written tribute – 'My Radiohead' – which included references to all her favourite Radiohead songs. The night was also notable for the first appearance of 'True Love Waits', an acoustic number which remains unrecorded but has appeared on numerous bootleg tapes.

Two precious weeks off ended when, on 17 December, Radiohead played a brief set (which again included Carly Simon's hit

'Nobody Does It Better') at K-ROQ's *Almost Acoustic Christmas Show* at the Universal Amphitheater, alongside Oasis, Alanis Morissette, No Doubt and Porno For Pyros. Clark Staub: 'K-ROQ filled up a 3,500-seat amphitheatre here in LA, and they had a revolving stage and each band got exactly twenty minutes and then the stage turns and they had about fifteen bands play. And basically Radiohead came out and fucking slaughtered people. It was an absolutely incredible show and since K-ROQ is one of the leading radio stations in the US and they're very tied to MTV, it was great that Radiohead came out and completely blew people's minds. I was standing in about the eighth row and there was this row of fourteen-year-old girls and they were pulling their faces and screaming for Thom. There was quiet awe during the first song and by the fifth and final song everyone was going berserk, and I think that was a really key stepping stone in the States.'

At the end of the year *The Bends* appeared in every major critical poll, including the Top Tens of magazines including *People*, *Melody Maker*, *New Musical Express*, *Musician*, *Billboard* and *Options*. *Mojo* called it the best album of the year. At home in Oxford, Thom attempted to get his feet back on the ground. 'The most important thing in my life at the moment is establishing something outside of this. It's almost like a frantic desperation thing,' he noted. 'At Christmas I tried to do it by shopping, by spending money on household appliances, taking them home and presenting them to my girlfriend and the other girl who lives in the house and saying, "Here you go." The house is scattered with stuff, in boxes mostly, that I bought to try and claim my life back.'

Meanwhile 'Creep', the song that wouldn't die, had suddenly become a huge hit all over again – this time in France. Holly Diener of the band's French record company recalled to Nick Johnstone: 'It became a hit because it was included on a soundtrack to a Franco-Vietnamese film called *Cyclo* [produced and directed by Tran Anh Hung]. It was presented at the Venice Film Festival and was a successful arty film in France and "Creep" figured really prominently in the soundtrack to the film and three years later radio decided that "Creep" was a fantastic track and had to be played and so we found ourselves in a hit single situation except the hit single was off the previous album.'

The timing of the release of 'Street Spirit (Fade Out)' has been ascribed to Parlophone managing director Tony Wadsworth, who wanted to utilize all the good press the band had received at the end of the year but not release a single that would be lost in the traditional Christmas rush. Wadsworth: 'We spotted an opportunity just before Christmas. The media as a whole identified the album as one of the best of the year and it figured very prominently in nearly all the end-of-year polls. The effect could not be capitalized on before Christmas, because the shops were full of high-volume product. It's very hard for quality material to shine through with all the seasonal stuff around.'

So 'Street Spirit' was released on 22 January 1996. Despite the expected absence of Radio 1 airplay – the song was deemed 'too sombre' – it reached number five in the UK charts. The B-sides included the superb 'Talk Show Host', 'Bishop's Robes', 'Banana Co.' and a new song called 'Molasses', a puzzling composition notable for the dominance of Colin's bass and the double-tracked take on Thom's vocal line.

The video for 'Street Spirit', directed by Jonathan Glazer, was stunning. Thom had talked of creating visual space, in order to let viewers build their own interpretations. Glazer, inspired by Surrealist photography, responded by juxtaposing band members, barking dogs and dancers in real time and slow-motion footage. The key reference point is photographer Philippe Halsman's abstract portrait of Salvador Dali, 'Dali Atomicus'. The primarily black-and-white shoot was completed with state-of-the-art technology (the Photosonics ultra-slow-motion camera). The dislocation between action and effect this produced became the video's motif. Not only did it fit the song perfectly, it also gave it additional texture and resonance.

-nine-

we have the
technology:
ok computer

The members of Radiohead had endured enough touring for a while, and felt it was time to embark on new recordings. They returned to Oxford and their rehearsal space Canned Applause. It could equally have been called Canned Austerity, as it had no toilet and stood near a field full of abattoir-bound cows. EMI told the band they could take as long as they wanted with the next album, which they proceeded to do. Tony Wadsworth: 'I've learned not to expect anything with Radiohead, and that way you are constantly surprised. They had been playing a lot of the songs live over the previous year, so we were starting to get an idea of the sort of album it could be, but a lot of the songs they played live they didn't put on the album. So we left them to it, and checked in now and again to make sure they were going the right way.'

They toyed with the estimated $140,000 worth of musical equipment they'd bought in Los Angeles to replace their stolen gear, and also brought in Nigel Godrich, whose recordings of 'Lucky', 'Talk Show Host' and 'Bishop's Robes' had so pleased them all. Colin: 'We recorded about thirty-five per cent of the album in our rehearsal space. Which is built like a storage shed. You had to piss around the corner because there were no toilets or running water. It was in the middle of the countryside. You had to drive to town to find something to eat.'

Godrich helped furnish Canned Applause. Thom: 'Nigel is a very positive and emotionally engaging person, and that's what we needed. We needed someone who was passionate and shared our taste in music. He also works incredibly fast and is our best mate; it's that simple. We rang him and said, "We want to build a studio so write a wish list." So he went away and bought all this dream gear he would want to record with.' However, Godrich, as important an adjunct as he was, was not Radiohead's new producer as such. The band felt confident enough of their own abilities – the hunches they'd tested on *The Bends* having been proved correct – that they wanted creative control themselves. Godrich: 'They hadn't really enjoyed recording previously, so they figured if we could make an environment where everybody feels comfortable, it would be a real bonus. I had a free rein in what equipment I wanted to buy, and apparently I was imposing more spending limits than I had to. They have a rehearsal space in the countryside in Oxfordshire, and we set it up there and did about half the album.' They also wanted root-and-branch change in their sound. Thom: 'We weren't listening to guitar bands, we were thoroughly ashamed of being a guitar band. So we bought loads of keyboards and learned how to use them, and when we got bored we went back to guitars.'

On 19 February the band attended the increasingly vile Brit Awards at London's Earls Court. Thom: 'A complete and utter disgusting charade. Yes, of course it pissed me off that Oasis got loads of awards [best group, best album, best video] and we got none. But it was worse than that, 'cos I realized for the first time what kind of business the music industry is. I was sitting there in a world of ugly men in suits, who were accompanied by women that weren't their wives and who were wearing a cocktail dress that didn't fit properly. All the bands were so far gone that they didn't have a clue as to what they were saying. Very humiliating.' Oasis's surly acceptance speech included references to the assembled music-industry types as 'corporate pigs'.

Thom and co-producer Brian Eno were in reluctant attendance to collect the Freddie Mercury Award for *Help!* The group as a whole also lent their support to the 'Rock the Vote' campaign, intended to encourage young people to use their vote. An accompanying compilation album was released in early 1996 which included the 'Hexadecimal mix', courtesy of Steve Osborne, of 'Planet Telex'. Again Radiohead's public endorsement of Rock the Vote echoed R.E.M.'s advocacy of the same cause in America. Despite their stance, Ed admitted he hadn't voted at the last general election owing to disenchantment: 'The figures Rock the Vote sent us estimated that in 1992, forty-three per cent of those under the age of twenty-five who were eligible to vote didn't vote. That's 2.5 million people. Those kind of statistics are quite frightening. It means that we could have had a different government in power for the last four years.'

The band were honing new material written on the road in the past year. The first idea usually came from Thom. He and Jonny would sketch out the basic song before bringing it to the rest of the band. Colin: 'The only concept that we had for this album was that we wanted to record it away from the city and that we wanted to record it ourselves... He [Thom] wants to do something that is more like a collection of snapshots of images and impressions that he has had from the external world. That's where little phrases like "jack-knifed juggernaut" [from the first track, 'Airbag'] come from. It's very much a record that encourages you to try to find a space, your own space mentally in the contemporary world. Just trying to get away from some of the obsessive internalizations that were on *The Bends*. That record was very inward-looking. This is more about engaging with things in the outside world.'

The musical arrangements for most of *OK Computer* were completed by mid-March. A new US tour began on the 16th in an effort to promote the release of 'High & Dry', which was previewed on *The Tonight Show*. Paul Cunningham was brought in for his direc-torial debut for the promotional video. An earlier effort, set in a desert, had been vetoed by the band. Cunningham's treatment featured assorted members of the band in an American diner, with a storyline woven around a couple who have just pulled off an armed robbery. However, the explosion of the couple's car in the final frames caused the video to run into trouble with MTV. Clark Staub: 'It was a little controversial and MTV wouldn't play it until we took the car blowing up out. But again, it was a very eye-catching video that got a lot of critical acclaim because of the way it was filmed.' Though the video was impressive visually, the narrative (the heisters are double-crossed by the man who hired them) was probably lost on most viewers. The single peaked at seventy-eight in the US charts.

The tour continued through Canada. The dates included a radio session on 22 March at Vancouver's Real Time Studio, where the band were joined by Ken Stringfellow and Jon Auer of the Posies. The songs attempted included a jokey stab at Oasis's 'Wonderwall', which lasted about a minute before Thom decided he really couldn't remember the lyrics. The tour then swung through Seattle, Portland, San Francisco and San Diego, before further dates in the Midwest. The band returned to Canada for a sold-out show in front of nearly 5,000 at the Varsity Arena in Toronto on 4 April, where Thom introduced 'Black Star' as 'a song about sex in the morning... It's the cheeriest number we have.' He was evidently in good spirits – a review in the *Toronto Sun* noted that his backward somersault took some by surprise that evening. The ensuing tour saw the honing of further songs written since *The Bends* – particularly 'Electioneering' and 'Lift' (which so far remains unrecorded).

The support for the tour was singer-songwriter David Gray, whose band destroyed their Canadian hotel room in time-honoured and tiresome rock 'n' roll fashion. Radiohead dutifully cleaned up the room, protesting that it was only some poor cleaner making $4 an hour who would have to look after the mess otherwise. This anecdote was revealed in an interview with Jon Wiederhorn of *Rolling Stone*, alongside revelations about Radiohead playing bridge while on tour and concealing pots of Marmite, rather than cocaine, in their flight cases. Tales of such sobriety leaked out and condemned the band to a press reputation as unflinchingly polite, which Ed shrugged off: 'We were all brought up in middle-class Oxford, and there's an air of politeness that's hard to escape.' Later he admitted that there was also a degree of pretence. 'The thing is, it's much better to come from that angle, where people think you're readers of books and bridge players, because it means they don't have rock 'n' roll expectations. We camped that up to an enormous extent in '93 or whenever, purposely. And we don't get hassle from customs.'

However, members of the band were also drinking heavily to cope with the boredom of touring. Thom: 'It's like being one of those Russian astronauts who stayed out circling the Earth for a year in a metal fuselage – it's a physical and emotional challenge. The only constructive element is the limbo aspect – it's quite useful for writing and reading and general brain stuff.' He also recalled Ed's ill-advised solution to the post-tour comedown. 'He tried to adjust to coming off the road by getting blind drunk every night. After four days, the guy who lived in his house said, "I've had enough. I'm off." [*Laughs*] So he lost his flatmate.' Phil: 'When you're back at home, there are an awful lot of domestic matters to deal with, and when you're on tour you're removed from those. But if there's someone at home actually dealing with them for you, it sends you on a guilt trip. We're all aware of what a mess we leave behind us.'

After the American and Canadian dates, they headlined the Pink Pop Festival in Holland before returning to Canned Applause for rehearsal and four weeks of 'breathing space'. That breathing space constituted either working till eleven o'clock at night on most days or hitting the pubs with friends in or around Oxford. One of the first songs they began work on was the retitled 'No Surprises'. They would eventually record sixteen takes but, typically, it was the first version that ended up on the album.

Other songs they committed to tape were 'Electioneering', 'Subterranean Homesick Alien' and 'The Tourist' – the first song Jonny had written by himself. 'I was surprised that the other four let me do it,' he recalls. '"The Tourist" doesn't sound like Radiohead at all. It's a song where there doesn't have to be something happening every few seconds. It has become a song with space.' Thom's vocal on this song, which he can't remember doing, was an example of the group's studio technique – recording a rough cut, elaborating on it and losing the original's dynamism, then reverting to the original version. Thom: 'It was left on the shelf for months. When I listened to it again it had obviously been, "Go out and sing a rough vocal." There's no emotional involvement. I'm just, "Yeah, yeah," sing the song and walk off.'

Jim Irvin at *Mojo* later pressed Thom on the subject of 'The Tourist', not realizing that it was Jonny's song. 'I said "The Tourist" was the really key track, and that it seemed a microcosm of the whole record. The subject matter, the notion of a kind of spacewalk – a guy in his own bubble moving through a landscape. Thom went, "I suppose you're right." It was only afterwards I was told Jonny wrote the song. Either they discussed the subject matter so closely that Jonny picked up on that, or they're so like-minded that they both independently wrote material in that vein. It was interesting that he didn't mention the fact that it was Jonny's song. If he's the guy who sequences the record, why put it last? The last track has more kudos and status. I thought that was very interesting.'

'Electioneering' had also changed somewhat, losing the closing line 'Doin' it all' that had been employed on tour. The song on the album most redolent of R.E.M. (in their years on the IRS label), it has opening chords that offer a delightful Beatles pastiche. It is the album's most polemical lyric, and Thom later described it as 'an incitement to riot'. His memories of the 1990 poll-tax riots – 'the moment when the horses broke through the barriers and everyone started smashing windows' – explain the song's undertone of violence. As he told *The Times* in June 1997: 'I switch on the TV, and there's all these irons and fridges coming at you. Watching a Tory MP electioneering, cheering wildly when someone threw eggs at him, but feeling I'd seen this once too often.' He also talked of deliberately invoking a feeling of nausea, of sensory overload and information fatigue, whereas *The Bends* 'was a record of consolation'.

In another interview, he admitted that the song was partially influenced by Canadian academic Noam Chomsky, the linguist, social theorist and author of texts including the brilliantly persuasive *Manufacturing Consent*. Thom: 'Like a lot of songs I write, it came from two places at once. I had this phase I went through on an American tour where we just seemed to be shaking hands all the time, and I was getting a bit sick of it and upset by it. So I came up with this running joke with myself, where I used to shake people's hands and say, "I trust I can rely on your vote." They'd go, "Ha ha ha" and look at me like I was a nutcase. But the phrase sort of carried on. It was like a mantra. As well as that, I had been reading a lot of Chomsky, and I had that feeling when you read Chomsky that you want to get out and do something and realize, in fact, that you're impotent.' Thom came up with pages of words about the Third World and political structures, but writing something so explicit evidently unnerved him. In the end he boiled the sentiment down to a single line – 'Cattle prods and the IMF'.

Later he talked further about the impact Chomsky had on his thinking, recommending *Profit Over People* and *Year 501: The Conquest Continues* to fans via e-mail. 'Well worth a read (unless, of course, you're thinking of ever getting any sleep again with a clear conscience).' The song also owes a debt to Thom's reading of historian Eric Hobsbawm's *Age Of Extremes* and Will Hutton's *The State We're In*.

As a testament to the more relaxed recording regime, at the beginning of July the band found time to play two warm-up shows at the venue they now partially owned, Oxford's Zodiac. One of the nights was restricted to those aged under eighteen – a shamefully ignored and patronized minority on the British gig circuit. A succession of festival appearances followed during the summer, including dates in Belgium (where 'Paranoid Android' was played live for the first time) and T-in-the-Park in Glasgow. Radiohead's appearance at the Dublin Olympia saw them receive *Hot Press*'s award for best International Live Act before they joined the line-up for *The Big Day Out* at the end of July. The critical response to the band was universally strong, though some wondered aloud at the wisdom of their next pairing. The band's subsequent US engagements were to be as support to Alanis Morissette – having met America's first lady of neurosis at T-in-the-Park.

The tour began on 12 August at the Darien Lake Performing Arts Center in New York State and ended two weeks later at the Pine Knob Theater in Clarkston, Michigan. Clark Staub noted to Nick Johnstone: 'It gave the opportunity to test out the new material from *OK Computer* and to play in front of an audience who really had no idea who Radiohead were. I was in Detroit and Radiohead played all new songs with the exception of "High & Dry", and this was an Alanis Morissette crowd at an amphitheater that held 17,000 people, and if they'd been allowed an encore, Radiohead would have got an encore. It was amazing watching them work their way through "Paranoid Android" and "Lift" and "Lucky". I saw Alanis Morissette three times on that tour and every time she came out and wore a Radiohead shirt for the whole set, which was just fucking incredible.'

Colin admitted that, as well as giving the band the chance to play their new songs in, the Morissette tour was worth 'silly money'. Thom: 'I think the fact that, here we were standing in front of 10,000 people in a shed who really weren't that interested in what we were doing, forced us to do a lot of tidying up of the songs really, really fast. I know it sounds stupid, but there was something about playing in really, really huge, sterile concrete structures that was really important to the songs. Because a lot of the songs needed to sound quite big and messy and like they were bouncing off walls. When we went back into the studio, we were actually trying to create the sound of a shed soundcheck, or a big baseball stadium thing, without sounding like bloody Def Leppard or anything. Just the fact that you have this trashy, volatile thing going on around you, which we discovered was really important to the way we did the songs.' Morissette was so besotted with Radiohead that before she was joined on tour by the band, she regularly performed a version of 'Fake Plastic Trees' in her set. As Ed conceded to *Melody Maker*: 'Her music's pretty terrible, but she's a lovely person.'

Irrespective of the non-stop touring, in America Radiohead were still widely considered to be one-hit wonders. *The Bends*, despite going gold, had only sold half as many copies as the band's inferior debut. However, their success had been noticed by a number of creatives working in Hollywood, who approached them to contribute a song to *William Shakespeare's Romeo & Juliet*, a big-budget adaptation directed by Baz Luhrmann and starring Leonardo DiCaprio and Claire Danes. The result was 'Exit Music (For a Film)'. 'Talk Show Host', with its amusingly incongruous theme and a line about waiting 'with a gun and a pack of sandwiches', was also included in the movie, and the band were also asked to write a new song to accompany the closing credits.

Among the new songs the band had broken in on the Morissette tour were 'Let Down', 'Karma Police', 'Climbing Up The Walls' and

'Paranoid Android'. There was an opportunity to try out the new material in front of a domestic audience at a secret gig at London's Tramshed venue on 10 October, a few weeks after returning from America. As the special guests at a party celebrating the twenty-fifth issue of fashion magazine *Dazed And Confused*, Thom and Jonny played semi-acoustic versions of 'Lift', 'Let Down', 'No Surprises' and 'Exit Music (For a Film)' – as well as older songs such as 'Fake Plastic Trees'. Journalist Robin Bresnark witnessed the gig and recalled: 'From the second he [Thom] came on, he was agitated and tense and he didn't really seem to want to be there.' The huge stage backdrop of Radiohead's singer staring down on the gathered worthies hadn't lightened his mood. Thom particularly enjoyed playing 'Exit Music (For a Film)' to the assembled freeloaders. 'It was quite good, actually, because I got to sing, "We hope that you choke" at all those people.'

The group had decided they wanted somewhere isolated but more luxurious than their current recording arrangements at Canned Applause afforded. After toying with the idea of relocating to France, they found a vacant Elizabethan mansion near Bath, owned by actress Jane Seymour (who played Solitaire in the Bond movie *Live And Let Die*, but is perhaps best known for her TV role in *Dr Quinn, Medicine Woman*). Colin: 'In a reaction to that stark, dreary place [Canned Applause] we recorded the other two-thirds of the record in this opulent country house.' St Catherine's Court is a late-Tudor or early Jacobean house built in the Renaissance style and costs approximately £10,000 a week to rent. Jonny: 'She [Jane Seymour] said to us, "Come and stay", handed us the keys and told us to feed the cat.'

The band's sole collaborator was Nigel Godrich. Thom: 'We got on with him really well during those sessions, because he's sort of our age and he's up and about and keeps us going. And he works very fast, which is important for the way we want to record. And he's very passionate about the album: he was really obsessed with it while we were making it.' The band were effectively able to work as their own producers, leaving Godrich to oversee mixing under their direct supervision. By the end of the project, Godrich is variously described as 'losing hair', 'having a nervous breakdown' and 'refusing to speak unless spoken to'. The reason may have been the group's tenacity in chasing perfection. Although the songs were mainly written before they worked on them in the studio, Thom notes: 'We'll get ninety per cent of the way there and really, really love it, but that last ten per cent just drives us absolutely fucking crazy... We basically had all the recordings five months before we finished the record, and then we fucked around trying to finish it.' According to Jonny, the band would indulge in endless tinkering only to go back to the original versions they started with.

With the success of *The Bends*, Radiohead had re-established control of their careers. That meant an end to 'helpful' phone calls from America. Thom: 'As five people, whenever external opinions are voiced before something is finished, we are sort of neurotic enough to actually listen to them and everything goes wrong! See, that was the problem with *The Bends*, when we first started work on it. So we have to be left alone to make the decisions ourselves, and sort of stay true to them and actually know what we're doing. People were allowed to come to sessions, but only once we started getting happy with what we were doing. It's kind of that fragile, really.'

The plush environment offered a refreshing change. Jonny: 'It's just that most times, you go into a recording studio, and you can still smell the body odour from Whitesnake, or whichever band was in before you.' St Catherine's Court was certainly a much grander affair than the house they'd shared together in Oxford – their last attempt at communal living. Thom enjoyed the contrasts between the house's ancient grandeur and the highly contemporary lyrical subjects he was addressing. 'The songs themselves were about the present, very much photographs of where we've been, and then to take these quite transparent ideas about technology and so on – the general images I'd written down in the lyrics – to a place that had all this incredible presence and spirit, it just brought them all to life, as well as the performances themselves. There was this thing about, "Well, why am I singing about these things? What do they mean?" They mean nothing really. They're so important to you, and then you take them to a place like that and it's just so irrelevant, in a way... For the first two weeks, me and Colin literally didn't leave the house, and then we went into Bath, which is the local town, and it was like landing on another planet.

We were sort of touching the walls and seeing all these people and just running away from them because they were coming so close. It was like landing from Mars.'

The house had previously been used by the Cure for *Wild Mood Swings*. Singer Robert Smith rated it his favourite place to record, although sadly it helped to incubate his worst record. Country legend Johnny Cash is another former temporary resident. Phil: 'I think it was sufficiently cut off for us to immerse ourselves in the album, but not so cut off that it turned into a scene from *The Shining*.' Thom noted that the location produced a forced bond within the band, plus an improved work ethic. 'It's about as far removed as you could get without going to a deserted island. The house had the most incredible sound signature to it. We'd recorded in our rehearsal room previous to that, but it was too near [to where we live] and we all just popped off home every night before we could get it together, so it was a kind of enforced exile really.' Ed admits to the stimulation the band gained from their new surroundings: 'Nigel Godrich said during the first two weeks, "We're in somewhere that's completely new and alien to us, we [need to] really respond to it." There's something that lets us completely concentrate on the music because we're unfamiliar with the surroundings and get off on that.' Godrich himself noted: 'We made it our own and developed this real sense of freedom. We could play croquet in the middle of the night if we wanted.'

Thom had fulfilled his commitments to *William Shakespeare's Romeo & Juliet* by composing 'Exit Music (For a Film)', whose intro was inspired by listening to Johnny Cash's *Live From Folsom Prison*. He'd originally intended to shape the lyrics from Shakespearean couplets, before abandoning the idea. Although Thom's central inspiration was the scene from the film where Claire Danes holds a gun to her head, he was also thinking of the doomed romanticism of Franco Zeffirelli's 1968 film version. He saw this aged thirteen, and it made him cry his eyes out. The rest of the band were stunned when he played 'Exit Music (For a Film)' for them for the first time, and didn't think there was any way they could embellish on it. That was until they took delivery of a Mellotron they had ordered. They used this to doctor the voices on the track, layering its haunting refrain. The voices themselves were the disembodied cries of children recorded at a playground near the space needle in Seattle, another example of Radiohead employing 'found sound'. The song portrayed lovers escaping, breathless and terrified. Finally, amid a chaotic maelstrom of drums and guitar, Thom observes of those who would deny his protagonists: 'We hope that you choke'. 'Exit Music (For a Film)' was as cinematic as its titular billing suggested.

Another new song, 'Let Down', was pieced together in the mansion's ballroom at three in the morning. The song's keynote line was a mental reminder to Thom not to get sentimental, because 'it always ends up drivel'. Thom later admitted to *Q* that his contrition was born of embarrassment by his contribution, however indirect, to the bombardment of fake emotion that constitutes end-of-the-century culture. Jonny had a different view: 'Andy Warhol once said that he could enjoy his own boredom. "Let Down" is about that. It's the transit-zone feeling. You're in a space, you are collecting all these impressions, but it all seems so vacant. You don't have control over the earth any more. You feel very distant from all these thousands of people that are also walking there.' As if to emphasize that diagnosis, there is an under-belly of static tension through the song that sounds like a modem connecting. Nearly left off the album, the song presented its challenges – the band had played it live using an acoustic intro from Thom; the recorded version featured Jonny introducing the song in 5/4 time.

Those complexities were nothing compared with those of the grandiloquent 'Paranoid Android'. The title was inspired by Douglas Adams's creation Marvin the Paranoid Android, from his *Hitchhiker's Guide To The Galaxy* TV and radio series. The depressive robot came equipped with a 'genuine people personality', in this case, morbid, melancholic and misanthropic. No wonder it appealed to Thom. The song's allusion to 'kicking squealing Gucci little piggy' was based on an incident witnessed by Thom in a bar, when a woman, part of a bevy of coked-up revellers, became enraged when she had a drink spilt on her. The look in her eyes, according to Thom, was demonic, and the incident kept him awake all night. It also partially inspired the artwork on the album – the protective 'Against Demons' hex of the inside rear cover. Thom: '"Paranoid Android" is full of images of people that I saw in a pub the night before we went to the studio. Most lyrics on *OK Computer* are actually Polaroids inside my head.' However, the critics homed in on one couplet suggesting that when Thom became king, 'they' would be first against the wall. Further, his victims' opinions were 'of no consequence at all'. To them, this was Thom Yorke exacting his revenge on the music press, an absurdly self-mythologizing conclusion. Thom: 'Again, that's just a joke. It's actually the other way around – it's actually MY opinion that is of no consequence at all.'

The music was drawn from three separate musical sketches the band had developed but didn't know what to do with. But the eleven-minute tour version (widely recorded on bootleg tapes) required editing. The long Hammond organ ending was dispensed with, which trimmed five and a half minutes off its length. Ed: 'With "Paranoid Android" we got bogged down. It was a six-and-a-half-minute song with three parts. How do you record that? We tried to play the whole song live, incorporating the tempo and mood changes, but it didn't work. So we recorded three parts differently at different times and then spliced them together. There were no philosophical disagreements. The arguments came when we had to decide what the best take was. Ultimately, Phil, our drummer, had the final say. He has to be happy with the drum take.' Jonny closed the song with a riff he'd been unable to place elsewhere: 'It was something I had floating around for a while and the song needed a certain burn. It happened to be the right key and the right speed and it fitted right in. Rarely do we have riffs *per se*. When we do they only have the lifespan of a few weeks, so if they don't find their place quickly we discard them. We don't have a catalogue of riffs.' They were all pleased with the finished product, and somewhat amused by their own indulgence in writing something so extraordinarily unwieldy.

Having already used the ballroom to record 'Let Down', Phil found an appropriately sized child's bedroom in which to lay down his drum tracks. Thom recorded his vocals for 'Exit Music (For a Film)' in the front hall. After a while, Godrich had to reign the band in, as Thom asked if he could record vocals, variously, in the garden and from inside one of the chimneys. Thom was trying to drag something extra from his voice – he claimed to other members of the band that he wanted

148

twelve different sounds on each of the album's tracks. In the end he limited himself to creating twelve different personas behind each voice.

Encouraged by 'Paranoid Android', the band indulged their experimental appetites. Phil constructed a drum track based on the work of Mo' Wax artist DJ Shadow. The resulting rhythm was spliced up on an Apple Macintosh and an Akai sampler. The 'three best seconds' were then mutated into an angular track that became 'Airbag', replete with a sleigh bell. All the band were pleased with the results, though Phil regretted it didn't turn out to be the homage to DJ Shadow that he had intended. Thom: 'I remember mixing "Airbag". Nigel played it back really loud and I thought: "This is something we never dreamed we could get done." I was so happy, I rang my girlfriend just to say, "Wow, we've done something really great." That's the height of the experience.'

'Climbing Up The Walls' was written about playing early-evening support slots in America, singing impassioned narratives about domestic homicide while the audience munched popcorn. However, it's a case of Thom coming to a lyric from two directions at once, a method he has admitted informed many of the songs on *OK Computer*. 'I used to work in a mental hospital around the time the government was getting passionate about Care in the Community, and everyone just knew what was going to happen. It was one of the scariest things that ever happened in this country, because a lot of them weren't harmless. It's like those huge eighteenth-century paintings: if you get really close to them, you can see these little figures in the corners, these amorphous little monsters. And that's what some big towns are like now: the shadows contain amorphous little monsters.' Elsewhere, Thom refined this fear of society's ill-begotten homunculi: 'Some people don't dare to sleep with the window open, because they're afraid that the monsters that they see in their imagination will come inside. This song is about the monster in the closet… I found the sentence 'the crack of the waning smile/15 blows to the skull' after I had read in the *New York Times* that eight out of ten mass murderers in American history committed their crimes after 1980, and that they were all males between thirty and forty, who had just lost their job or had just been through a divorce.'

For the song, which recalled mid-eighties Cure or Tricky at his darkest, Colin was tutored in keyboards by his younger brother, as the opening was composed using a Novation Bass Station synthesizer. For subsequent live performances, Jonny had to place coloured spots on the keyboard to ensure Colin would connect with the right notes. On stage, the song was further distinguished by Jonny's use of local radio reports played into a microphone before the opening chords. 'I find two or three classical stations and two or three talking stations at the soundcheck and use them during the gig,' he explained. 'I know what kind of music it is in advance – I don't want [the Wonderstuff's] "Size of a Cow" to come out during the show.'

The atonal sound at the close of 'Climbing Up The Walls' was achieved by sixteen violins playing at quarter-note intervals from each other. Jonny: 'It may sound blasé, but we were a bit fed up with rock arrangements. They haven't evolved since "Eleanor Rigby" by the Beatles. We discovered the Polish composer Penderecki. Since then, all we do is steal from him!' Penderecki's compositions hover between the worlds of classical music, traditional ecclesiastical harmonics and electronica. He prefers not to restrict his music to conventional intervals, but concentrates instead on quarter and semi-tones. Little wonder that his vision appealed to Radiohead.

Both 'Airbag' and 'Climbing Up The Walls' encapsulated the band's suck-it-and-see attitude to the sessions. Jonny: 'It was like being at home with your friends one day after school and doing a record. We set out not knowing how we were going to do what we wanted to do. *OK Computer* is what results when you're struggling and thrashing about.' He elaborated on this in an interview with Dave DiMartino on what Thom has called a 'workshop' environment: 'The main difference in the atmosphere of this record was in the recording – the studio experience. We were all of the same age, mid- to late-twenties, and doing a record in the middle of nowhere. And there were no established professionals there. It wasn't a real recording studio, and we had our friend doing the artwork in the studio at the same time. We were all at the same stage of our life and all working together for something, it was quite a buzz.'

That buzz reached Oxford, where Nick Burton of the Candyskins was between flats. He was generously provided rent-free accommodation in Colin's spare room for a few months before making a permanent move to London. There he started writing songs for a new Candyskins album. 'I was really pleased with how the writing was going. Then Colin got back and played me the *OK Computer* tapes. I thought: "Great! He's playing me bits of 'Paranoid Android'." I kept thinking: "You bastard." Then he'd come back again and it would sound even better. And he kept worrying about them. I was thinking: "You keep worrying about these songs, you so don't have to." But that's Radiohead for you.'

In October, with recording virtually complete, the group took a break from sessions. This allowed them time to look back over what they'd produced and to choose the best versions of songs from the several they had assembled. Thom used the hiatus to contribute vocals to Drugstore's 'El President' – a tribute to Chile's Salvador Allende. Sessions were booked at Eastcote Studios, but singer Isabel Monteiro conceded to the press that she had to tell Thom that his first attempts were 'shit'. More accurately, the song was in the wrong key for his voice. Further sessions were convened. Monteiro: 'We tweaked it up a few octaves and it came out wonderfully. He's a great person to work with, because he really appreciates honesty, and will really stick his neck out if it's something he believes in. There's plenty of shit-heads in bands who aren't getting anywhere who are so far up their own arse and convinced the world revolves around them. He's in this huge band and he's still really committed to helping out others and doing his best.' However, owing to the demise of Go! Discs, the song was not released until early 1998.

After declining invitations to headline at the Phoenix and Reading festivals, the rest of the band worked on setting up an official Web site – in addition to the hundred or more unofficial sites currently extant. Given that these contained all the information (and much more) that anyone could ever want about the band's history, they opted for something different. They employed artist Stanley Donwood, who had provided them with artwork since the 'My Iron Lung' EP, to design the site, and collaborated with him on its content.

On their return to recording, they found themselves ill at ease in the mansion. Thom had long complained about the noise of vixens who inhabited the estate, and now he could get no sleep at all. 'We made jokes about it, but there was fear everywhere, coming out of the walls and floors. It took me by the ankles and shook me until there was nothing left. There was really horrible wallpaper in my room. Maybe it was just that and my imagination.' Subsequent complaints of inexplicable equipment failure and bad luck are almost certainly the result of over-exercised imaginations. '...it was in a valley on the outskirts of Bath, in the middle of nowhere,' Thom told *Spin*. 'So when we actually stopped playing music there was just this pure silence. Open the window: nothing. A completely unnatural silence – not even birds singing. It was fucking horrible. I could never sleep.' Then again, perhaps there was a reason why old Gothmeister Robert Smith loved the place.

Whatever forces informed its history, what emerged now from the house was an album that rejoiced in its own unorthodoxy. The most unconventional of all the tracks was 'Fitter, Happier'. This computer-voiced monologue-cum-litany had a title reminiscent of the Fall's 'Fit and Working Again' – and shared the same cynical outlook. Thom's words were mouthed by an Apple Mac computer programme (akin to Stephen Hawking's electronic voice) which emphasizes the sense of emotional detachment and impotence. This stark rejoinder to contemporary living ('Fitter, healthier and more productive/A pig in a cage on antibiotics') returned to Thom's old themes of disease and decay. But its monotonous wish list-style delivery pilloried a superficially healthy lifestyle as another irrelevant attainment, a pointless, self-defeating exercise. The pig-on-antibiotics image was adapted from a novel by Jonathan Coe (*What A Carve Up*) which deals with the recent revolution in farming practices.

The song was recorded one night when Thom got drunk and sat in front of the DAT machine, armed with a series of one-line observations he'd been saving up. It has been suggested the words resulted from an e-mail exchange between Thom and a female fan, or from self-help books he'd collected. Thom: 'I bought a whole load of those how-to-improve-your-life books, and we'd been trying to use them in different ways. One said something like, "You will never make friends unless you like everyone, genuinely." Oh, well, I'm fucked then, aren't I? And the legacy of those books goes on. You still meet people who really believe that the way to succeed is to adopt that smile and that smile will sell: "Unless you believe in the product, you will not sell the product."' It was initially envisioned that these random epigrams would form the basis of a more conventionally structured song, but when the list-poem was presented to his bandmates, no one could do anything with it.

Other songs also reflected the world-weariness of 'Fitter, Happier', with the result that there was a sense of detachment not evident on *The Bends*. Thom produced this analogy for *Q* in October 1997: 'It was like there's a secret camera in a room and it's watching the character who walks in – a different character for each song. The camera's not quite me. It's neutral, emotionless. But not emotionless at all. In fact, the very opposite.'

The musical reference points, too, were far removed from the band's own orbit. Thom: 'We weren't really listening to any bands at all – it was all like Miles Davis and Ennio Morricone and composers like Penderecki, which is sort of atmospheric, atonal weird stuff. We weren't listening to any pop music at all, but not because we hated pop music – because what we were doing *was* pop music – we just didn't want to be reminded of the fact. *Bitches Brew* by Miles Davis was the starting point of how things should sound; it's got this incredibly dense and terrifying sound to it. That's what I was trying to get – that *sound* – that was the sound in my head. The only other place I'd heard it was on a Morricone record. I'd never heard it in pop music.'

In 'Subterranean Homesick Alien', a song Thom wrote after purchasing an electric piano, the narrator travels country lanes at nights and, inconsolable, ponders aloud why aliens won't come and take him away from all this. Thom described the song to *Launch*: 'That was supposed to be a joke song anyway – as much as my jokes are ever funny. I was interested in the fact that there was a lot of misdirected spirituality placed toward the "*X-Files* Syndrome". Like at the end of the last century, everyone started seeing bleeding statues of

Jesus on the cross and so on. Suddenly, everyone sees sightings, though some people claim we always see them. It's the angels-versus-aliens thing, which is fascinating, but not really the issue. Actually, a lot of the song stems from the idea of when I was at school, the first essay I wrote was: "You are an alien from another planet. You've landed and you're standing in the middle of Oxford. What do you see? If you're an alien from another planet, how would you see these people?" And that's a lot of where it came from, from someone who is not involved. Laughing and recording, taking home movies back to their home planet to show to their friends.'

It's a complex song, and another that proved difficult to translate to a live setting. Thom: 'I have to play piano and I get pissed off because I look like I'm into 10cc or something.' Several Bob Dylan Web sites expressed outrage when they subsequently learned of the song's titular similarity to the old master's 'Subterranean Homesick Blues'. ('How dare they touch our Bobby!' screamed one Dylan fan.) However, the real similarity is to Roger McGuinn's 'Mr Spaceman', which also refers to alien visitors and the protagonist's desire to join them on their spacecraft. McGuinn's song, like Yorke's, uses the adjective 'uptight' in reference to human behaviour. 'Subterranean Homesick Alien' also offers the one readily identifiable moment at which *OK Computer*'s much-discussed Miles Davis influence can be located – in Jonny's Hammond organ riff.

By Christmas the band were satisfied with the recording and proceeded to the mixing stage. It was at this stage that they began to reconsider 'Lucky' for inclusion. The original intention was to present it in altered form, but after several attempts they decided the original was superior. That meant fourteen completed songs. The two which didn't make the cut, 'A Reminder' and the overwrought 'Polyethylene', were both employed as B-sides on the 'Paranoid Android' CD singles. Other songs premiered on earlier tours – 'True Love Waits', 'Lift', 'Man-o-War' and 'Motion Picture Soundtrack', one of Thom's favourites – were nowhere to be seen. Neither was 'Last Flowers Till The Hospital', a David Bowie homage that Colin was particularly fond of. Thom: 'Some of the songs we discarded were ones that worked with just guitar, bass and drums. But because we didn't have that head on, we just left them for now. And that's what *OK Computer* was all about – just wandering off down paths and getting lost.'

Sooner or later they had to finish the album. Thom: 'In the end we just called time. It could have gone on for another year. Jonny came in, in January, into the studio one morning and said, "Right, that's it. We have to stop now. We have to finish what we've done and stop." So we wrote down what we'd done, and went, "Yeah. OK."' Jonny: 'It wasn't quite that precious. I didn't say, "That's it, darling, my artistic juices are fully spent, I'm creatively drained," and throw the back of my hand to my forehead. It was more that I'd had enough, rather than I couldn't do any more... It's only forty-five to fifty minutes of music, it was sounding great to my ears, we were just being nervous, being Radiohead.'

Over several tense days the band discussed the running order. Thom confesses that he had the casting vote, which caused him some discomfort. The most controversial choice was the album's opening track. Before they settled on 'Airbag', 'Paranoid Android' and 'Fitter, Happier' were both considered. Thom: 'In retrospect, *The Bends* had a very obvious and comforting resolution, which was by accident, not by design. But this one didn't. For two weeks before mastering the record and deciding which songs would go on it, I got up every morning at five a.m.; I've got one of those MiniDisc machines where you can swap the order of the tracks, take tracks off, put them back on. I couldn't find the resolution that I was expecting to hear once you put the songs together, and I just went into a wild panic for two weeks. I couldn't sleep at all, because I just expected the resolution to be there – and it wasn't ... When we chose to put "Tourist" at the end, and I chilled out about it and stopped getting up at five in the morning and driving myself nuts, we did find that it was the only resolution for us – because a lot of the album was about background noise and everything moving too fast and not being able to keep up. It was really obvious to have "Tourist" as the last song. That song was written to me from me, saying, "Idiot, slow down." Because at that point, I *needed* to. So that was the only resolution there could be: to slow down. If you slow down to an almost-stop you can see everything moving too fast around you and that's the point.'

The only thing they needed was a title for their magnum opus. The one they came up with, according to Thom, was not the result of love or disdain of the cyber revolution – more a fascination with its effects and repercussions. *OK Computer* was also an old song title. Jonny: 'It was a very bad song but a good title that hung around and started attaching itself and creating all these weird resonances with what we were trying to do.' Thom: 'It's like the Coca-Cola advert from the seventies – "I'd like to teach the world to sing." Imagine the same thing with a lot of little tiny home portable computers, kids of all creeds and colours, on top of a hill, all waving back and forth, going, "OK Computer…" That's sort of it. On the surface, it's a positive and nice, neat advertising slogan, but on the other side of that … it's fucking terrifying.'

Finally the artwork was selected, with Stanley Donwood adapting images originally created by Thom. Though Phil liked the way the image evolved, Thom was less pleased with the final effect, which featured blurred human figures and a road intersection: 'It's awful, I hate it. It's fucking rubbish.' Thom is right: it's messy and juvenile and hardly prepares the purchaser for the album's contents. The Fall are a band worth emulating, but their artwork isn't. Far superior was the more expansive work Donwood originally planned to be encompassed as part of a sixty-page sleeve booklet. When this was vetoed by Parlophone, Donwood used the excised material to create Radiohead's visually arresting official Web site.

Alongside Godrich, Donwood was the other collaborator who spent time with the group at St Catherine's Court, developing his distinctive blend of photography, sketches, video stills, paintings and digital manipulation as the group worked on its songs. Donwood: 'We [Donwood and Thom] were both obsessed by the idea of noise. But not just music noise – background noise. Everything is background noise. Our whole lives, the way our minds work. And the album is about that, levels of mental chatter. The artwork is bound up with the idea of white noise – every page of artwork is stuff being painted out. Layers and layers of books and whatever we had hanging around, pasted on, then rubbed away. But in rubbing it away you don't quite get rid of it.' It was the new-old world of Bath itself that inspired their methodology. 'Since we spent a lot of time around Bath, we were noticing how this really old city has been added to and altered over the years, but still some of the original buildings peak through in gaps in walls and above signs, even after the old shop fronts have been destroyed and rebuilt, bits of the old buildings will still be there. We tried to convert that into the artwork.'

This theme that developed was one of scratching at an old wound, of trying to erase an uncomfortable memory. Donwood: 'While they were working in Jane Seymour's house they found a lot of 1950s-era sci-fi books that all had images of the world in the year 2,000, everybody living a life of pleasure with household robots doing all their daily chores, being driven to work in a driver-less electric hover car that would whisk them to and from work in the greatest of comfort. Not one book showed people driving through a smog-filled housing estate out to a main-road traffic jam where they could sit for an hour every morning and evening pumping more pollutants out into the already choking air.'

Thom: 'All the artwork and so on – we chose to pursue it after we did the track. More relevant is the reason I wrote the words in the first place. These were things I was being told to do. I showed it to the others and they liked it, and then Stanley – who does the artwork – was playing around on the computer and made it say it. After that, it went from being a list of things that had a lot of emotional meaning for me and that was it, to coming to life. In fact, it was all the things that I hadn't said in the songs. Stanley was really just pushing into it, and I was as well in the end. It was like, "I'm not going to hide this thing that I wrote, 'cos I'm really proud of it."'

When tapes of the album were passed to Parlophone's managing director, Tony Wadsworth, he was convinced he had the most influential album of the nineties in his hands. In an interview with *Billboard* magazine in May 1997 he made some pretty extravagant predictions: 'The unanimous reaction to this record is that it's something very special. The single is a brilliant piece of music. It might fly in the face of all the rules and conventions, but everything we've ever done with Radiohead that's worked has broken the rules.' A typical piece of industry hype in *Billboard*'s cosmetically fluffed pages, but there was no doubt that Wadsworth genuinely believed in his charges. According to Phil, however, other executives were not so sure. 'When we first delivered the album to Capitol, their first reaction was, more or less, "Commercial suicide". They weren't really into it. At that point, we got "the fear". How is this going to be received?' John Harris recalls being invited over to PR firm Hall Or Nothing's office to listen to an initial tape of *OK Computer*. 'All the talk was – it's a move forward, but it's very difficult. They were gunning for a front cover, obviously. So I went over to hear it, and Caffy St Luce put it on and let me listen to it. I thought initially it was very obtuse. I remember thinking: "No one's going to get this."'

-ten-

global echoes and
mud-soaked heroes

Before the album's release, and before the ensuing promotional circus consumed Radiohead's lives, there was a small window of opportunity for extracurricular fun. Thom and Jonny joined forces to work on the soundtrack to *Velvet Goldmine*, a homage to the glam-rock era, executive-produced by Michael Stipe. Alongside the usual suspects (Brian Eno, Pulp, Teenage Fanclub) who contributed, two bands were specially created for the project. One, Wylde Ratttz, featured Mike Watt of fIREHOSE, Ron Asheton of the Stooges and Thurston Moore of Sonic Youth. The other band, Venus In Furs, took their name from the classic Velvet Underground song, and comprised Jonny and Thom, plus ex-Suede guitarist Bernard Butler, Andy Mackay (saxophone player with Roxy Music), Paul Kimble (formerly of Grant Lee Buffalo) and vocalist Jonathan Rhys Meyers.

Venus In Furs offered covers of Roxy Music's '2HB', 'Ladytron' and 'Bitter-Sweet', with Thom on vocals and Jonny on guitar. The sessions allowed Jonny and Bernard Butler to form something of a mutual admiration society. Butler: 'Jonny was amazing. I'd never played with another guitar player before, but it worked really well. I'm a big fan of his and it turned out he really liked my stuff too.' They are heard to best effect at the end of '2HB', providing a devastating finale to the keynote track from Roxy's eponymous debut album. Venus In Furs were also responsible for two other songs on the soundtrack – versions of 'Baby's On Fire', an old Brian Eno song, and

Steve Harley's 'Tumbling Down'. Both featured Jonathan Rhys Meyers as vocalist. Paul Kimble: 'Michael Stipe put it all together, and Michael is, like, social insanity – he knows everybody in the entire universe, and if he doesn't know them he wants to meet them. So one morning we had breakfast with Jarvis Cocker, Brian Eno, Bryan Ferry, Thom and Jonny from Radiohead, Bernard Butler, me, my engineer, and God knows who else, all sitting at this one table in this weird-ass hotel in London called the Hempel, which was, like, designed by Stanley Kubrick. And I'm sitting next to Eno, who, to me, of anybody ever in music, Eno was *the guy* ... it was all the people I like in music sitting at one table for an hour and a half in this weird hotel with a hangover having English pancakes ...'

OK Computer was officially released in Japan on 21 May 1997. A carefully choreographed European media premiere in Barcelona was scheduled for the following day. This saw the band subjected to the press call to end all press calls, answering question after inane question from journalists flown in especially from around the globe. Typically, they faced down a thousand flashguns while maintaining their traditional getting-the-job-done tenacity and unshakeable diplomacy. The apotheosis, possibly, was Ed doing an interview with Germany's Radio Fritz.

Eventually, however, Thom decided enough was enough. 'When it [*OK Computer*] was launched in Barcelona, I was doing about five interviews a day. For six days. Which was cool. And then I started to get really nervous, because the reviews started to get over the top. A few people write in specific magazines that are really influential, and everyone just reiterates it again and again and again. And whatever sentiment was in the original review turns into this garbled echo. Which really winds me up. And the received opinions started jarring, because I guess they started feeding into the interviews I was doing, so I stopped. Expectations got really high.'

The fallout was recorded by Grant Gee, a confidant of the band who had been commissioned to record a video diary of a year in the life of Radiohead. They had seen his video for the band Spooky – animating stationary objects to dance – and thought his documentary idea has some merit. Ed: 'You make a record ... then after that, you go out and tour this record and that's when it gets bizarre. Then it's the rock 'n' roll circus thing. It's not normality and it's not real. It's his slant on that and I think it's going to be quite interesting.'

However, despite some objections, Radiohead make much better interviewees than some believe. The group are incredibly candid in interviews, Thom often offering detailed observations on his songs, which is far from the case with many more precious and less talented writers. In an age where Chris Heath of the *Observer* recently noted: 'Too many people give too many interviews to too many people who don't really care what they say', the band's copy is generally as lively and humorous as it is self-effacing. When not tired or sick from touring or frustrated by the inanity of the line of questioning, they're all (with the possible exception of Jonny) highly conversational. They are, after all, paid-up members of the chattering classes. Otherwise, the only thing 'received' about Radiohead is their impeccable pronunciation.

In America, of course, things are different. 'Americans have this thing about confessing,' notes Thom. 'You can meet someone in a bar and within a few minutes you find out they've had three abortions and split up with two husbands. You've been talking to a complete stranger and you know all this stuff. There's this bizarre confessional aspect which I'm kind of into sometimes when I write and I think that's what they pick up on.'

Obtusely, the band chose 'Paranoid Android' as their opening single, released on 22 May. Close to seven minutes long and split into three sections – offbeat jazz part, angular rock section and a closing movement dominated by high-harmony vocals and Thom's soul-scraping falsetto – it was as if Radiohead had wholly given up on radioplay and just decided to go their own way. This time, however, they were not ignored. After initially requesting shorter mixes of the track and being told no, commercial radio began to play the single during its rise to number three in the British charts. Ed: 'We wanted to make a cross of Queen's "Bohemian Rhapsody" with the Pixies. No, it didn't become a "Bohemian Rhapsody" of the nineties; it's not complex enough for that and it contains too much tension. It's the song that we played to our friends when they, a long time ago, wanted to know what the new album was going to sound like. You could see them thinking: "Fuck, if that's the new single, what will all the rest be like?"'

The video was once again fascinating. While Thom and Jonny were working on *Velvet Goldmine*, Phil and Ed had travelled to Sweden to meet director Magnus Carlsson. They'd previously seen his show *Robin*, and were beguiled by the lopsided storylines as the protagonist stumbled from one misadventure to another. They needed something special to accompany 'Paranoid Android', and Carlsson agreed to adapt the storyline to his character. The resulting sequence became Thom's favourite video, though broadcasters were less impressed. They expressed particular discomfort with a pair of cartoon nipples and an animated scene in which a man in a spiked G-string chops off all his limbs and jumps into a river. Thom: 'When it came time to make the video for that song, we had lots of people saying, "Yeah, great, we can have another video like 'Street Spirit', all moody and black and dark." Well, no. We had really good fun doing this song, so the video should make you laugh. I mean, it should be sick, too. The whole thing about the lyrics is that they're very twisted, but because of the way we played it, it permitted me to write something I wouldn't normally write: humour.'

Thom liked the fit between Carlsson's put-upon cartoon character and the song's equally hapless but determined subject. 'Robin is quite the vulnerable character, but he's also violently cynical and quite tough and would always get up again. And the rest of the video is really about the violence around him, which is exactly like the song. Not the same specific violence as in the lyrics, but everything going on around him is deeply troubling and violent, but he's just drinking himself into oblivion. He's there, but he's not there. That's why it works. And that's why it does my head in every time I see it.'

OK Computer was officially released in the UK on 16 June 1997. Reviews were ecstatic, James Oldham in the *NME* talking of an 'age-defining' record, 'one of the most startling albums ever made'. John Harris in *Select* and old-stager Nick Kent in *Mojo* were similarly flattering. Kent's opinion appealed to Thom for its view that 'it wasn't the best thing we would do by any means and we'd overstretched ourselves but it was admirable for that. I thought: "Thank goodness someone's said that."' Caitlin Moran's piece for *The Times* was even more effusive, typical of several critics who had been won over by Radiohead: 'It claws at the skies and gets clouds caught behind its nails; it grinds its hips into the ground; it burns, it soothes, it heats the blood to 1,000 degrees and watches with delight as your veins explode. There's rarely been this much passion, this much strip-knuckled emotion in a 50-minute LP. And I used to think they were poo. I have never felt so foolish in my life.' Wading through press cuttings, it's hard to find a single dissenting view, though some members of the band believe that the UK press was overcompensating for giving *The Bends* lacklustre notices.

If, as Jonny says, all Thom's lyrics are ultimately influenced by how he's feeling when he writes them, then *OK Computer* was the work of a more sanguine author – hardly complacent – but clearly on better terms with the world than on *The Bends*. And it reflected his relationship with the outside world, instead of merely himself, which provided much of the album's expanded range and reference points. *OK Computer* is a concept album only in so far as Radiohead had perfected their own unique brand of dramatic tension, which characterized the songs throughout. As Pat Blashill noted in an article for *Spin*, it was a record that explained nothing, leaving everything suggested or implied. Perhaps because of that, it is also the one record of the late nineties that takes time to reveal itself, inviting audiences to come back to savour more of its nuances and to unravel its secrets. Its honesty, integrity and emotional reach left the whole Britpop conceit smelling like cheap perfume.

Yet for all its kicking against the pricks, musical adventurism and antagonistic lyrics, Radiohead had recorded another album of global appeal. Thom: 'I don't think it's uncommercial, in the sense that if we'd set out to make an uncommercial record, we could have done a much better job. I think it has an atmosphere. We had a sound in our heads that we had to get on to tape, and that's an atmosphere that's perhaps a bit shocking when you first hear it, but only as shocking as the atmosphere on [the Beach Boys'] *Pet Sounds*. *Pet Sounds* is an incredibly amazing pop record, but it's also an *album*. It doesn't quite fit the "format", or whatever, but then the sort of things we were listening to were so removed from all that anyway.' Jonny conceded that the band were not overly obsessed with commercial concerns: 'We've made the wrong third album if we were. But I remember when we finished it, I was very keen to have my friends hear it and make sure they liked it. It was that kind of atmosphere. And that's the kind of atmosphere we take on tour with us. We want people out there to think the same as our friends back in Oxford.' His one regret about the record, he maintained, is that several songs were left off that the band either couldn't complete or perfect in time.

For all the esoteric avenues of sound the album finds itself wandering along, there is something persuasively linear and unifying about its evolution from track to track, as *Mojo*'s Jim Irvin notes: '*OK Computer* has an odd structure, the second song is seven minutes long and then the album floats away. After "Electioneering" it just drifts off, and there's something affecting about that structure – it's very gripping. Therefore people listen to it as an album, rather than flick on to individual tracks. Therefore, people do treat it as being up there with the great albums. It's a record that doesn't just spoonfeed you a formula. It makes you work at it.' Thom: 'It's funny when people say to us that it sounds like a complete work, when the way we actually did it was very fragmented. It was never all one album with one sound. It was really, really random. Most of the songs on this record are one performance, with virtually nothing changed but with months of analysis. Because of the instruments we used and because it was the same five people doing it, it has a cohesive sound.'

Q's review of the album was the first of many to cite Pink Floyd's *Dark Side Of The Moon* as a near-neighbour. The magazine noted how the opening five-song cycle also dealt, in some manner, with alien life, stars or the universe. Whereas *The Bends* was characterized by economy, *OK Computer* is the most recklessly expansive album released in British rock music in the last decade. Thom told Davie DiMartino: 'It's an absorbing record, for good or bad. It's whatever was around and picking up on it. It's not really a personal record.' Jonny, too, fought against the idea of a unifying concept to the record. 'It's just describing what the previous year was like for us.

I think this album is too much of a mess to sum up. It's too garbled and disjointed, and the title is only supposed to introduce you to the record; it's not meant to sum anything up, really.'

That didn't stop people trying. There was plenty of purple prose flying about from smitten critics, not least in that bastion of the establishment, *The Times*. 'Anyone in love with humanity is currently in mourning for the present, watching it becoming infected by takeaway burgers, superpubs, shivering, oiled Page Three misses and strip-neon megamalls. Anyone who even semi-understands the political and economic workings of the Western world longs to turn away, furious and hungry for change; and determined to ramraid the untouched future in search of hope... It is this disgust, tempered with a belief that every emotional extreme can lead to release and redemption, and that a kicking tune can save the world, that Radiohead have laid out in their new album, *OK Computer*.' That Radiohead were likely saviours of rock, a singular antidote to British music's inertia and obsolescence, seemed to become a common theme. 'We're not interested in saving rock,' shrugged Thom. 'It should have been dead years ago.'

As writer Jack Rabid astutely pointed out in his interview with the band for *The Big Takeover*, *OK Computer* was not the only great record released in 1997. However, with bands like Oasis sagging into celebrity-whoring mediocrity, it was the only one by a band operating within mainstream waters. Whereas Oasis were once able to produce memorable, insistent pop records, they never possessed the capacity to produce an album of the intelligence, momentum and invitation of *OK Computer*.

Other critics became fixated on the album's title. Despite the band's reluctance to identify too strongly with technological themes – or with impotence in the face of technological progress – the intrusion, possibility and disappointment that new mediums create were all present when the album was recorded. Thom: 'We have the Net running in the studio, and Jonny surfs the Net quite a bit. I hadn't even written all of the lyrics when we began performing some of these songs, and we'd be in the studio with one computer on the Web most of the time. We'd go to the unofficial Radiohead sites, and find that people had gone home with these bootlegs of our shows and typed up the lyrics they thought I was singing to our songs. So there I'd be in the studio trying to write my lyrics, and then I'd look on the Web site to see what other people had written down, what they'd transcribed. That was amazing. It was very odd. I liked that bit of it. That was hilarious.'

There are well over one hundred Radiohead Internet sites currently operating, some of them extremely complex and ornately designed. If, as has been (completely wrongly) noted in the media, ninety per cent of all Internet searches are for pornography, a fair proportion of the remaining tenth must involve Radiohead nuts. True, Thom's lyrics dealt in fragility and helplessness in the age of technological advance, as well as claustrophobia, alienation and those old standbys – transport-fear and physical and mental decay. However, there is also a good deal of humour, of snatched victory in the face of overwhelming odds.

On 7 June, just over a week before *OK Computer*'s UK release, the band had appeared at the Tibetan Freedom Festival in New York City, raising money for the Mariposa fund, alongside organizers the Beastie Boys, Michael Stipe, Noel Gallagher of Oasis and Eddie Vedder of Pearl Jam. Thom talked to the press about his commitment to the cause, revealing he had been reading *The Tibetan Book of Living and Dying* by Sogyal Rinpoche, and also begun meditating. 'Buddhism was really everything that was missing from my life. That book fucking blew my mind. I grew up with a very normal church-going view of spirituality, and this book unlocked a whole new world for me. I've begun to meditate – to just empty my mind of all the shit and let it fill up again like a well, a well full of new thoughts and views of the world. That's why I wanted to play the festival, because I feel like the Tibetans' view of life can change the world.'

Pop stars getting religion, in whatever form, is always an unpleasant, ugly business. So far, thankfully, it hasn't spilled over into Radiohead's music. Not that there is anything wrong with protesting against China's human rights record, especially in relation to Tibet. Jonny: 'We feel like we have to be quite careful, because we're not American citizens, and some of the emphasis has been on pressuring

Bill Clinton, so he doesn't represent us. We're more here to point out that it is an international problem, with solutions that all countries can contribute to.'

The concert was a turning point for Thom. 'I actually believed for a moment that it would be possible to change things. I'd never thought that before. My generation grew up with the legacy of Live Aid and Margaret Thatcher taxing the proceeds. But actually being at the Tibet show – it wasn't like that. It was incredibly moving. In a completely different way, the death of Princess Di really affected me. It was so fucked up, as if we were really grieving over something else, which I can't quite put my finger on. I felt very sympathetic about what her brother said. That made me cry.'

As well as books by Sogyal Rinpoche, Thom was consuming Situationist texts – a choice of reading matter prompted by the Manic Street Preachers' constant references to the Paris student riots of 1968. The contrast between Radiohead and the Manic Street Preachers is an arresting one. Enjoying their breakthroughs at roughly the same time, they share the same PR company, Hall Or Nothing. Neither had any truck with the late-eighties' ethos of the indie ghetto, instinctively opting for major-label deals when they were offered. Both groups were also college-educated but suspicious of student chic, though Radiohead have always fought shy of advertising the breadth of their reading. The Manic Street Preachers' cherry-picking of cultural symbols, their scavenging of soundbites, was, however, anathema to Radiohead. Between them, the two bands have some of the most ferociously dedicated followers in British music. Richey Edwards's disappearance in February 1995, shortly after Kurt Cobain's suicide, saw Thom became the subject of ghoulish media speculation about his own mental health. After all, Edwards, Cobain and Yorke were judged to be complaint rock's leading lyricists. It seemed to some only a matter of time before Radiohead's singer did the decent thing and joined them. Thom: 'That was all sort of happening as *The Bends* came out. I had people warning me a few months before Richey disappeared, before he went away the first time, warning me that he was in a bad way and his behaviour was... I thought that basically it was the British press that did it to Richey. Full stop. Although I've got lots of

friends who are journalists, the few who I think were basically responsible for him having a breakdown I will always hold responsible and I
will always see what we do in that light.'

On the Monday evening following the Tibetan concert,
Radiohead were fêted by New York's glitterati at their Irving Plaza
show. Michael Stipe, Bono and Adam Clayton, Marilyn Manson,
Lenny Kravitz, Sheryl Crow, Courtney Love and the Gallagher brothers were all in attendance, alongside three supermodels – Helena
Christensen, Amber Valetta and Bridget Hall. Madonna was also
there, though her alleged request to have part of the auditorium
roped off for her and her entourage was turned down. Thom introduced 'Creep' thus: 'We're going to do this next song because we still
like it. We've never had a problem with it. Sing along if you like.'
Michael Stipe did more than that, performing some primeval air
guitar to the tune. Jon Wiederhorn watched the show and was later
told by Thom: 'Far be it for me to throw stones, but I started to find
that whole self-loathing thing pretty offensive pretty quickly. I think
there was a genuine point where it really was important for me to say
things on a personal level to get these things sorted out for myself.
But once it was out, it was done. With this album, I am moving on.'

Later that night Blur, in town for their own promotional
purposes, raved about the show on radio. Only Liam Gallagher was
not won over, calling Radiohead 'fucking students'. There was no
rivalry between the bands as such, but Thom took a dim view not just
of Oasis's antics, but more especially those in the media who encouraged them to behave in the way they did. 'They're a joke, aren't they?
It's just lots of middle-class people applauding a bunch of guys who
act stupid and write really primitive music and people say, "Oh, it's so
honest." It's just like the art world where they'll pick up on people
outside the art world, on the periphery, and bring them in. The things
they love about them are that they're out of their environment –
they're working-class, thick or mentally ill. It's a freak show – they're
laughing at them but at the same time they can say, "Look how
wonderfully varied and cultural we are."'

The band were utterly unimpressed with the cult of celebrity, as
Jonny told the *Toronto Sun*: 'We're in Hollywood and we've just had

the phone call – "Can these people come to the show tonight?" A list of actors, basically. It's a bit odd, and I don't think actors know anything more about music that anyone else. It only happens here.' Just as unedifying was their experience on K-ROQ's Weenie Roast bill on 14 June, the day after they'd played the Troubadour in Hollywood. Sharing a bill with Blur and the Mighty Mighty Bosstones, they were confronted with a disinterested, disaffected audience. Despising the multi-band, wheel-'em-on, wheel-'em-off format, Thom berated the gathered masses following their lacklustre reception to 'Exit Music (For a Film)': 'You really fucking hated that one, didn't you? You're all fucking mindless anyway, so you'll probably like this one.' A chant of 'Radiohead sucks' filled the air. The closing song, 'Fake Plastic Trees', was introduced as 'another song to fill your barren lives'.

Exactly a week later the tour to support *OK Computer* reached the Royal Dublin Show. Thom: 'It was by far the biggest show we'd ever done, and we were headlining in front of about 33,000 people. It was sheer, blind terror. My most distinctive memory of the whole year was the dream I had that night. I was running down the [River] Liffey, stark bollock naked, being pursued by a huge tidal wave.' Also on that bill were Massive Attack, a mutual admiration society quickly forming between the two bands. In fact, rumours began to circulate of the them co-operating on an album of *OK Computer* remixes, but time constraints eventually made that impossible.

By mid-summer Radiohead's place as headliners at the Glastonbury Festival on 28 June had been confirmed. It would be their first British concert since the album's release. They warmed up with performances in Utrecht and at Denmark's Roskilde Festival. But it was the 'secret' appearance at Glastonbury that kept Thom and the boys awake at night. In the light of their album, much was expected.

Flying in from Europe, Radiohead arrived at what remained of the rain-drenched site in dismay. The deluge had created a mudbath of epic proportions, likened in the press to the Somme. When the band finally took the stage, they began with traditional set-openers 'Lucky' and 'My Iron Lung'. However, when they attempted to launch into 'Airbag', their third song and the first 'new' cut from *OK Computer*, things started to go awry. Thom was distracted by the intensity of the set lights, and his monitor was turned off. As he recounted to *Q*: 'The lighting system programs were wiped clean so these two white lights were pointing straight at me from the floor and I couldn't see a thing, not a face, until I screamed at the lighting guy to kick the lanterns round the wrong way so that they weren't in my eyes. Until then I hadn't seen the audience, it was a completely isolated experience. I'd played six songs to a pitch-black wall of nothingness.'

Keith Wozencroft was alongside his girlfriend in the crowd, and recounted his feelings to *Mojo*. 'I was laughing for the first two songs, it was unbelievable. I couldn't quite deal with it. It was surreal for me, a bit of an old hippy from Gloucester, who went pretty much every year to Glastonbury to see Hawkwind, Gong or Taj Mahal. So to be there and see the band I'd worked with headlining was fantastic, hilarious. Hearing people behind me singing along and listening to what they were saying. Then I couldn't enjoy it. When they went into "Talk Show Host" I knew they were in trouble.'

Disgusted by the sound problems, Thom thought about leaving the stage but was dissuaded by Ed. He continued to shout at the sound technicians throughout their performance. 'It was hell, in the sense that you were playing into a black hole and yet you know that that black hole is 40,000 people, and you can't see one of them. Your worst nightmare. The lighting computer has blown up, and it's giving you burning white light strain into your retinas. Like you're being interrogated. It was the best day of my life and the worst day of my life. Without doubt. I was going to kill. I was going to kill. If I'd found the guy who was running the PA system that day, I would've gone backstage and throttled him. Everything was going wrong. Everything blew up. And I was the one at the front standing in front of 40,000 people while that was happening.'

However, the band were not cowed, and the result was one of the most life-affirming sets ever seen at Glastonbury. Thom: 'It suddenly dawned on me that actually everything was all right. That it didn't fucking matter whether the speakers blew up. In fact, we turned off the monitors and I just sang to what was coming out of the PA at the front, because they couldn't make them work.' Halfway through

'High & Dry', a series of unscripted fireworks lit the night sky. The moment was perfect. Jonny stepped forward, at Thom's request, to point the floor lights at the crowd during the encore, before setting up for an inspired version of 'You'. Paul Trynka reviewed the show for *Mojo*: 'Jonny's guitar playing was literally terrifying. As he hit the wrenching chords in "Paranoid Android" that signal the full-blown riff, several people in the audience around me literally flipped, just spun into the mud with pleasure.'

By the time the last strains of 'Street Spirit' closed the set, reviewers, like the fans, were delirious, praising Radiohead as the band who saved the event from despair. Trynka: 'Just after Radiohead went off-stage I bumped into a friend I'd been trying to find for hours. We were both in some kind of altered state; all we could say was, "Did you see that?" When I've talked to people since who witnessed that performance, it's been galling to hear the odd person describe it as merely "a good gig". It wasn't. It was something far more profound.' On 3 July 1999, Michael Eavis, having just lost his wife, reflected on the most successful Glastonbury ever. He had one simple regret. 'The two greatest bands in the world are not playing here this year – Oasis and Radiohead.'

OK Computer was released in America on 1 July 1997, entering the charts at twenty-one before beginning a rapid descent. Capitol, bemused when first handed the album, launched a promotional campaign which was odd to say the least – review copies of the tape were glued into Walkmans. The company also announced plans to make videos for each of the album's twelve songs. 'Let Down', for example, was filmed half live and half in slow motion, before the band vetoed it, at great personal expense. Ed: 'The video came out appallingly bad and we scrapped it. There's $100,000 down the tubes, half of which comes out of our pockets. We were devastated. Videos are about trusting. We trusted the producers and they let us down.' The idea to film all twelve songs was eventually abandoned, not only for financial reasons, but also because of the 'emotional time and space' each video required.

The band kept busy with further dates in Europe, including festivals in Germany, France and Belgium. Their show at Cologne was watched by Wim Wenders and his son – the filmmaker later talked of his amazement at the band's ability to re-create the complexity of *OK Computer* on stage. Yet another tour of America followed, with band favourites Teenage Fanclub enrolled as their support act.

At the end of July Thom undertook further extracurricular work, recording 'Rabbit In Your Headlights' alongside DJ Shadow for James Lavelle's U.N.K.L.E. album, *Psyence Fiction*, in San Francisco. The sessions were completed in George Lucas's Skywalker Studios. Significantly, Lavelle is another local Oxford boy, who ran his Mo' Wax nights at various venues in the city before moving to London. Long a fan of the band, he had earlier remixed 'Planet Telex' ('The Karma Sunra Mix') in 1995. The U.N.K.L.E. album featured contributions from Richard Ashcroft of the Verve and Mike D of the Beastie Boys. Thom had originally expressed interest in the project in 1995, but was unable to commit any time to it until after he'd finished work on *OK Computer*. 'Rabbit In Your Headlights' was a joint composition, Shadow providing the music and Thom writing lyrics on his way to the studio. However, the general reaction to the album was one of disappointment, given the talents involved. 'Stunningly underwhelming,' wrote one critic.

The video for 'Rabbit In Your Headlights' was nominated for a best breakthrough video gong at the 1999 MTV Video Awards, though MTV themselves had been loathe to play it. The clip, directed by Jonathan Glazer, featured an insane man walking through a tunnel, where he is repeatedly mown down by the oncoming traffic. The sequence concludes with the destruction of the final car to strike him. Glazer was astonished by MTV's decision not to air it. 'The idea is obviously controversial, which was why we agreed to make certain compromises for MTV. Firstly, they said they'd show it if we pixelated the collisions and, because so many people had worked on it and we really wanted it to be seen, we agreed. Then we had to remove the sound of the impacts. And they *still* refused to show it because the actor playing the madman was too unnerving and subversive. They won't show the video because the actor is too good! What they're saying is anyone on the edge of society shouldn't be seen on television.'

-eleven-

karma police and
ethical ambassadors

Its title a catchphrase the band employed to alert them to anybody, themselves included, 'behaving badly', 'Karma Police' became the album's second, and only marginally more commercial single, on 12 August. Eventually awarded an Ivor Novello Award for Best Contemporary Song of 1997, it was released while the band were nearing the end of their American tour. It's often cited as an illustration that Radiohead do, indeed, have a sense of humour, not least in the throwaway, playful title. 'This is what you get when you mess with us,' implores Thom, though his tone is self-mocking and apologetic rather than threatening. The song collapses in on itself at the end, as the tape drags to a halt. Godrich: 'At the end, there's Ed playing his guitar and I'm feeding it back into a delay and then I pitch it down so it goes, "eeeoooowwww". The very last noise on "Karma Police" is my turning this thing off.' This was not caused, as Phil Jupitus suggested on *Never Mind The Buzzcocks*, by the band forgetting to put a coin in the meter. Among the many fans of the song is cult author Iain Banks, who included it on his *Personal Effects* compilation for EMI. The B-side tracks were the xylophone-led 'Lull', a convoluted confessional piece by Thom, seemingly about losing control, and 'Meeting In The Aisle', which many considered the group's tribute to Brian Eno's *Music For Airports*.

The video for 'Karma Police' was once again memorable. Jonathan Glazer returned as director, and shot the sequence in June on a deserted stretch of English country road. Filmed largely from the front seat of a car, its single point of view recalling Stanley Kubrick's work, it featured the relentless pursuit of a running figure, until the fugitive turns the tables by igniting a trail of gas leading back to the car. It's not the first time a Radiohead video concludes with a burning car and explosion – British television had earlier used 'Creep' to soundtrack the closing scenes to a documentary on arson. MTV, who had faced problems themselves over the use of fire in videos (with *Beavis and Butt-head*), nevertheless put the clip on rotation. Lewis Largent, MTV's vice-president of music, told Pat Blashill: 'All their videos are intriguing. Everyone has a different interpretation of them. The videos aren't cut and dry – like their video for "Just", when the guy dies – that sort of mystery makes them watchable time and again.' It was not the first time Thom found himself in a potentially perilous situation while filming a video. While he sat lip-synching to the song in the back seat, carbon monoxide fumes started to pour into the car. He later revealed that, as consciousness began to slip away from him, he thought he was about to die.

It was only when 'Karma Police' began its rotation plays on MTV that *OK Computer* began to pick up sales. James Lavelle analysed its slow-build success for *Spin* magazine in 1999: 'The whole sound of it and the emotional experience crossed a lot of boundaries. It tapped into a lot of buried emotions that people hadn't wanted to explore or talk about.' The group's subsequent US tour left fans and reviewers breathless. Micah Robinson of *Addicted to Noise* had a foot in both camps when reviewing the band's performance at Atlanta's Masquerade club on 10 August, claiming Thom had never looked happier nor the band sounded more invigorating. After three encores, the audience began to head home. Robinson: 'Finally, while roadies tore equipment down and the audience filed to the exits, Yorke picked up an acoustic guitar and stepped to the last microphone on stage, where he began strumming plaintively and moaning softly as if singing a lullaby to a child. The ballad left fans so hypnotized that many stood stunned for a few minutes, seemingly lost in the moment – one they will likely not soon forget.'

Just as memorable was the show at the Hammerstein Ballroom in

New York on 26 August, which saw Thom in unusually talkative, albeit pugnacious, mood. Introducing 'Karma Police', he referred to the group's upcoming appearance on *The Late Show With David Letterman*: 'In two days' time we have to do this song on a TV show called *Mr Letterman* [*sic*]. Bullshit.' 'No Surprises' was dedicated to Lou Reed and Laurie Anderson, whom Thom had spotted 'walking their bikes yesterday. You probably see them every day, but I was floored, y'know? Luckily, I didn't say anything. He probably would have hit me or bit my head off.'

As with most performances on the tour, 'The Bends' was humbly dedicated to support band Teenage Fanclub – 'the band we used to listen to when we started being a band. And now they're supporting us, which we kind of think is pretty fucking weird.' However, Thom's exhaustion with touring poured out in his closing remarks: 'This is the end of our American tour. This is the final show. But this is a business and in four days' time we start another tour. So as you can tell, we're fucked.' Attendees at the show included Marilyn Manson, Calvin Klein, Lenny Kravitz and Claire Danes – star of *William Shakespeare's Romeo & Juliet*.

A sold-out tour of Britain followed the band's return, including a fan club-only show at London's Astoria and ending with dates in Reading, the Brixton Academy and the Brighton Centre. The show at Plymouth Pavilions proved the most interesting, with signs erected reading: 'Radiohead regret to inform you that crowdsurfers will be ejected from the building.' However, drunks once again dominated the gig, leading to Thom denouncing sections of the audience as 'fucking wankers!' Reports leaked out of disagreements between Thom and Jonny after the show about whether the audience deserved an encore. Coaxed back to the stage, Thom reluctantly introduced first-album favourite 'Lurgee'. 'It's about when you... Oh, you don't care. I'll just play it.'

After Radiohead's appearance at the Brighton Centre, Michael Stipe reflected on their show at the Reading Rivermead two days earlier, when Thom changed the words of 'Creep' from 'I'm a weirdo' to 'I'm a winner': 'They played Reading on Friday night and a band can't really lose on a Friday, because for everyone there, it's fuck-or-fight. But they were really great on top of that. When we toured with them two years ago, they played "Creep" every night. But now, they've taken that song back from the fans, and they've made it really beautiful.'

Further dates followed in Holland, Belgium, France, Italy, Germany and Scandinavia. Possibly the highlight was the set at the Forest National in Brussels on 14 October. Colin: 'We adored playing that concert, and Rotterdam [the previous evening] too. It was the first of our bigger shows, and we were very nervous.' The tour continued in Italy, where John Harris met up with the band again for a cover piece in *Select* magazine. 'Now, in order for Thom to be comfortable, he has quite a distant existence compared to the rest of them. The rest were quite happy to talk to me, sitting having their tea, or by chance in the dressing room. Thom was the whole thrust of the piece – they were a sidebar. They said Thom's interview would happen after the gig. An hour and a half after this gig, I'm in this freezing cold sports centre on the outskirts of Florence, thinking: "Will this happen?" Caffy [St Luce] came over and said, "Mr Yorke will see you now, Thom's ready for you now." You go to the tour bus, knock on the door, go in. Thom's sitting in this darkened lounge at the back with a plate of pasta, cross-legged on the floor. No one else on the bus – it was a bit Colonel Kurtz in *Apocalypse Now*, the inner sanctum. And he was great, fantastic. That interview, we talked about most things. You could ask him about Princess Diana, what that meant, about new Labour getting in. We talked about Douglas Coupland the author and all kinds of stuff. But there's a big contrast between that and talking to Ed, for example, which is a more knockabout conversation.'

Caitlin Moran is another journalist who had endured the 'Thom is ready to see you now' summons. 'Thom is sick of interviews,' she recorded. 'You feel it seeping from every pore as you approach his chair. You can tell from the resigned slump in his back as you sit down.' While several writers have noted that Thom can be moody and withdrawn, the truth is almost certainly that he is bored of explaining himself and answering the same questions time and again. Doubly so when journalists attempt to convey the 'bleakness at the heart of Radiohead's music' in something as frivolous and ephemeral as a

1,000-word article on pop music. Yet several fine authors have written about the band in an engaging and enlightening manner. With limited exceptions, the press have supported Radiohead throughout their career. There are thousands of bands who have been treated more shabbily, and that is where Thom's bunker mentality seems most perverse.

On 19 December the band played a memorable return set at the Hammerstein Ballroom in New York that was recorded for MTV's *Live at the 10 Spot*. In the audience were Marilyn Manson (again) and old hero Morrissey. To many who considered the Smiths the guiding light of the eighties, Radiohead were unquestionably the band of the nineties. At the Ivor Novello Awards in May 1998, Morrissey was asked about assertions that Radiohead were 'greatly inspired' by the Smiths. He replied: 'They never say that in the press, do they! So smack on the head to Radiohead.' However, not every Smiths fan had converted their angst stock. As a message posted on a Morrissey fan site recently railed: 'Radiohead are a bunch of upper middle class A-holes who have never experienced angst in their lives.'

Comparisons with the Smiths always carried more substance than earlier ones with U2. The Smiths, too, had the best guitarist of their generation, and the most distinctive frontman – both Morrissey and Yorke have been declared the 'last great pop star' by numerous commentators. Both have also been attacked for their Little Englandisms, become the subject of uncritical idolatry by fans and been hailed as saviours by critics. Morrissey was quickly undone when he left the performers who anchored his lyrical spite, leaving him as the reluctant godfather of Britpop. What *British pop* – and there is a seismic difference – needed was a nineties' group, like the Smiths in the eighties, who stood apart and sounded like nothing that had preceded them. The joy of both was that, while each possessed a deep affection for contemporary pop history, you couldn't guess what was in their record collections by merely listening to them.

The year closed with a further wave of adulation from the British and worldwide press. It reached its zenith when *Q* commissioned a poll to determine the one hundred greatest albums in the universe. Radiohead had two albums in the top ten, with *The Bends* at number six, eclipsing established artists such as the Rolling Stones. Number one in the poll was *OK Computer*. Some journalists could understand why. Jim Irvin: 'It's got a majesty that many records haven't aspired to lately. I can imagine people that haven't heard Pink Floyd and prog rock and some other things, they might think the Radiohead record was extraordinary. Three or four of the songs on it are incredibly moving – "No Surprises", "Lucky", "The Tourist" and "Exit Music", they can move people to tears. "No Surprises" live, I was holding the tears back myself. Any record that does that for people, they'll treasure it.'

The band were sceptical about the poll's importance, and the frankly ludicrous result. Jonny: 'They had the same poll a year earlier and *Pet Sounds* won. It was number five this year, so it's all a bit irrelevant, really. For instance, *Revolver*, which amazingly came in at number two, is – in all sorts of ways – far more the better album. It's like it doesn't really mean as much to me as some Pixies records I got when I was at college. People have just gone berserk, haven't they?' Jonny, in particular, seemed uncomfortable in the glare of acclaim. 'I don't think it's that good an album, really. There are good songs on it but there are songs that just sound like dead ends, that sound like it's the last time we can do it like that. I don't think we've finished yet.'

Nineteen ninety-eight began with a tour of Japan, preceding the release of 'No Surprises', an exquisite song of admission and resignation, which reached number four in the British charts. Of the stark but universal images – a heart 'full up like a landfill' and a job 'that slowly kills you', Thom noted: 'I find landfills really curious. All this stuff is getting buried, the debris of our lives. It doesn't rot, it just stays there. That's how we deal, that's how I deal with stuff, bury it.' It's one of the songs critics point at as embodying the bleakness of Radiohead's work, but its tone is lightened to that of a lullaby by the lilting glockenspiel played by Jonny. The original version from 1995 had featured radically different lyrics – 'He was sick of her excuses/To not take off her dress when bleedin' in the bathroom'. The closing image of 'Such a pretty house/Such a pretty garden' has more than a passing resemblance to the Talking Heads' domestic primal scream 'Once In A Lifetime'.

In conversation with *Rolling Stone*, Thom argued against the perceived wretchedness and misery of lyrics such as 'No Surprises': 'I don't think it's pessimistic. I put the stuff in the songs because I can't say it elsewhere. If you write it down on a sheet of paper, it may sound like that, but it's actually the lyrics to a song, so it's redemptive in its own way. Anyway, it's compassionate, not condemning.' Jim Irvin at *Mojo* agreed: 'It's a beautiful song, the lyric is genius. Totally under-rated. It says a lot about a modern, mortgaged malaise.' Thom has also admitted: 'We wanted it to have the atmosphere of Marvin Gaye. Or Louis Armstrong's "Wonderful World"… I wanted a song that sounded like new double-glass: Hope-giving, clean and safe.' One assumes he was being sarcastic, as there's something incredibly eerie and ominous about the song. Colin: 'It's our "stadium-friendly" song. The idea was – first, frighten everyone with "Climbing Up The Walls" and then comfort them again with a pop song with a chorus that sounds like a lullaby.' The B-side track, 'How I Made My Millions', was a demo recording Thom made at home on his four-track studio. The background noises are of his girlfriend Rachel engaged in domestic chores.

The 'No Surprises' video, alongside 'Street Spirit (Fade Out)', again illustrated how maturely Radiohead dealt with the video medium. Like a great deal else with this late-developing band, it had taken them time to come to terms with and gain confidence in their own choices. On one occasion they worked with an American direc-tor who kept asking 'if the little guy could jump up and down a bit'. Now they handpicked their directors. For the duration of the song, Thom is pictured in full frame, inside a diving helmet filling with water. His head is submerged for what seems (and indeed is) a very long time. The distortion of his face as the water envelops him is chill-ingly cinematic. Grant Gee was reluctant to talk too much about the video. 'Going into the nuts and bolts of the shoot just undermines it. It was the situation that was interesting, and it's exactly how you see it… It was a very intense thing to do. The process, how we achieved what we did, was entirely mechanical. But the situation was … odd.' He had originally sent the band a basic proposal, and only later thought about scrolling the song's lyrics over Thom's face to prevent the video looking too static.

Dilly Gent, who commissions videos for Parlophone, told *Promo*: 'I don't think Thom considered the possible dangers, he knew he could hold his breath for a minute or so ... there was no deep significance about it. I just thought it was an excellent script.' Extensive footage was shot of the filming of 'No Surprises'. Again and again Thom's head is immersed in water. Again and again he is seen spluttering for oxygen, scowling, swearing and crying at his inability to hold his breath sufficiently long enough to get the vital take. It is undoubtedly one of the most harrowing, intense scenes ever committed to celluloid in the name of a pop video. Gee conceded that, if nothing else, the 'No Surprises' promo offered him 'fantastic documentary material' for his ongoing video diary, *Meeting People Is Easy*, which was nearing completion.

The spring is traditionally viewed as the record industry awards season. The band duly collected a Grammy for Best Alternative Music Performance for *OK Computer* – having also been nominated for Best Album. Ed: 'The fact that we won a Grammy was really, really unexpected. I think [it] is a testament to the fact that the record has moved quite a few people and has touched people, and people have "got" it.' In the domestic Brit Awards, *OK Computer* lost out to the Verve's *Urban Hymns*. Radiohead were also nominated in the categories Best Group and Best Single, for 'Paranoid Android'.

By February they were once again on tour, visiting Australia, where they hadn't played since 1994. The reception was much warmer this time. Indeed, their opening date at the Melbourne Festival Hall, which lacked air-conditioning, was notable for the extreme heat. Thom: 'Is it hot in here, or is it just me? We'll have to pretend we're in a sub with some Germans.' 'Why Germans?' volunteered an audience member. 'Because they're always stuck in a fucking sub,' came the reply. In Perth, 'Paranoid Android' was introduced as being 'about Hollywood, a place that believes you can justify anything if you become famous'. After growing problems on American and British tours, an announcement was made before Radiohead took the stage stating their disapproval of moshing or crowdsurfing: 'Anyone who comes over the barrier will be marked on the hand. If they come over a second time they will be ejected.'

On their return to Oxford, the band were asked to record a track for the forthcoming *Avengers* movie. They attempted to resuscitate a song, 'Man-o-War', which dated from the 1994 John Leckie sessions and was originally described as Radiohead's answer to the Bond themes. In fact, at one stage Radiohead were offered the chance to record their own 007 theme, but had to decline for lack of time. 'That was about the most exciting thing that's ever happened to me,' recalled Thom. 'Man-o-War' was retitled 'Big Boots', but they struggled to get it into a shape they were happy with. In the end they conceded that the track 'just wasn't happening' and, later, that they were never likely to release a version because of the 'intense frustration' it caused them.

Another series of dates in America began at the end of March, with Spiritualized as support. This time the band found themselves playing much bigger stadia, and filling them with ease. Several critics noticed that they looked tired and less motivated than on previous tours, and by the end of the trek they were candid in interviews about the exhaustion they were feeling. They did break in a number of new songs, however. 'Nude' had developed from its original acoustic airing in Japan, with both Thom and Jonny playing keyboards. 'This Isn't Happening' had changed title to become 'How To Disappear Completely And Never Be Found' (the title of a self-help book by Doug Richmond for those attempting to fake their own disappearance).

On 1 April a plot was hatched by the band's old sparring partners K-ROQ. The station broadcast an interview in which an impostor Thom (Ralph Garman) was interviewed and pretended to play acoustic versions of 'Fake Plastic Trees' and 'Creep' (actually taped versions of older acoustic recordings). One of the DJs, Bean, then made fun of Thom's eye in a series of ill-judged wisecracks – 'The cool thing about interviewing Thom is that he can look at us both while answering the questions'. After remaining stoical for a while, the impostor Thom lost his temper during 'Creep' and lunged at the DJ. The station cut to music, playing several songs in a row before reporting that Thom had been rushed to St Joseph's Medical Center in Burbank for an X-ray. The phone lines lit up as over a thousand fans deluged the show with complaints, unaware of the nature of the hoax, which was only revealed a few days later as the station's April Fool's joke.

The real Thom Yorke could also be incredibly indulgent with fans. Barbara Violani, who moved to Oxford from Italy and worked in Cult Clothing to satisfy her Radiohead obsession, followed the band through America and Canada on that tour. When she turned up in San Francisco, with little money or forward planning, Thom came to the rescue. 'He "ordered" me to sell all my tickets for the following shows, 'cos he was going to put me on the guest list for the rest of the tour. That's what he did. I travelled around the USA and Canada, taking part in every single show, and meeting the band backstage without spending a dollar!'

Thom was still uncomfortable with the actions of some American audiences. He had begun to take a very hard line on anyone in the moshpit endangering other fans, and at the band's show at the Salem Armory on 4 April he insisted one prime offender was removed, stopping midway through 'Lucky'. 'I fractured two of my breastbones during that gig...' Barbara recalls. 'I was in a panic, I didn't know what was going on.' Thom took up the microphone to insist: 'Kick that guy out. Yeah, you. This guy has been hurting people the whole show. Hey, tell you what, if you want to hurt people, come up here and hurt us and we'll show you how it feels.' The antagonism festered through the rest of the gig. 'This is a song called "Creep",' he announced mid-concert, surfing the wave of excitement and cheering that followed, before announcing: 'Oh, no, not going to play it.' The payoff for the injured Violani came during the encore, 'Pearly*'. 'He whispered, "This is for Barbara." I broke into tears. It meant more than anything else...' At other concerts, faced with the crowd chanting for 'Creep', Thom simply replied: 'We're not playing it, it's a boring song. We're bored with it.' Two days later, in Seattle, 'The Tourist' was testily dedicated to 'all the people out there who take the pictures, buy the merchandise, and read the books, but don't know what the fuck is going on.'

While frequently irritated at their audience's behaviour, Radiohead more usually remained responsible, safety-conscious entertainers. At their next show, at an oversubscribed Coliseum venue in Vancouver, the gig was nearly abandoned because of Thom's concerns over crushing at the front of the auditorium. A minute into set-opener 'Airbag', he began gesturing wildly to Ed, who eventually communicated the singer's wishes to the crowd: 'There's a lot of people getting squashed, so if you want us to fucking go off we will. Please don't. We really, really want to play to you.' The gig resumed, but throughout Thom kept a close eye on the crowd to make sure no one was hurt. Denise Sheppard attended the gig and noted: 'He may not be an easy man to get along with, but Thom Yorke is a gentle man, a thoughtful man.'

At their show at the Max Bell Centre in Calgary two nights later Thom attempted to ridicule crowdsurfers by cracking jokes, pointing specifically at them during 'My Iron Lung' and emphasizing the 'suck your teenage thumb' lyrics. One particularly drunk audience member surfed to the front of the stage, where security grabbed him. Thom pretended to bash his guitar against the guy's head. 'I didn't think anything of it until one of the management pointed out, as white as a sheet afterwards, that I could have cracked his head wide open and spent the rest of my life being sued down to my underwear. So remind me to think twice next time.' Other dates saw Thom dedicate 'Paranoid Android' to Microsoft's Bill Gates – 'the most paranoid man in the world'. Meanwhile Drugstore's much-delayed single featuring Thom, 'El President', was released on 20 April. Thom started some playful rumours about he and Isabel Monteiro appearing naked in the video – after a suggestion made by a video director – but this was never truly envisaged.

The US tour concluded with two performances at New York's Radio City Music Hall, the band's final 'official' dates of 1998. Both nights had an end-of-term feel, Thom repeatedly stating how happy they were to finally be heading home. He generously thanked support act Spiritualized and, on the last night, got Nigel Godrich up on stage and praised 'the best crew in the world'. American fans were left with a memento before Radiohead returned to Britain – the 'Airbag'/'How Am I Driving' EP, released in the US on 21 April. Despite having no supporting video and being largely composed of previously released B-sides, it debuted at fifty-six in the *Billboard* charts. The number written on the sleeve, 1426148550, when prefixed with the UK's international dialling code, +44, was answered by a pre-recorded 'Hello' from Thom. It was actually his old pager number. The wheeze was originally intended to be a repository for fan messages that the band would use in some way, though this idea was eventually abandoned.

One of the songs on the B-side, 'Palo Alto', was the group's homage to California's 'Silicon Valley', where the HQs of a number of computer companies and Xerox are located. The Xerox PARC (Palo Alto Research Center) developed the first GUI or graphic user interface computer-operating system, which inspired the development of the Macintosh operating system and Windows. The band had undertaken a series of tours of the corporate 'city of the future' when they played there in March 1996. 'Melatonin' was titled after the hormone supplement used in treatment of the elderly, which allows the body to adopt regular sleeping cycles. Thom: 'Melatonin is a drug that sends you to sleep. Only it doesn't send me to sleep, it gave me the scariest dreams I ever had. And those were the words. Not what I'd really define as sleep.'

Other tracks appended to the 'Airbag' EP included rejected album efforts 'A Reminder' and 'Polyethylene', which graced the B-side to the 'Paranoid Android' single, 'Pearly*' and 'Meeting In the Aisle'. 'A Reminder' is one of the most endearing non-album tracks the band have ever recorded, with its restless vocal and becalmed keyboard motif. 'Polyethylene (Parts 1 and 2)' was less successful, inexplicably lunging from acoustic ballad to guitar rock overload – a feat the band was normally capable of achieving with much greater dexterity. 'Pearly*', like 'Polyethylene', returned to Thom's suspicion of antiseptic conformity as a crumbling artifice under which real terror lurks – in this case revealed by the closing line, 'Daddy hurts me'.

On 27 April *7 Television Commercials* was released, a compilation of the videos for the group's last seven singles – 'Paranoid Android', 'Street Spirit (Fade Out)', 'No Surprises', 'Just', 'High & Dry' (US version), 'Karma Police' and 'Fake Plastic Trees'. Despite its brevity, it is quite possibly the best video collection ever released by a contemporary rock band, a supreme example of art and craft in a devalued, oversubscribed medium.

In June Radiohead once again participated in the third annual Tibetan Freedom Festival, ignoring threats that any performer taking part would be banned from playing China for ever. The event climaxed in a rally on Capitol Hill where President Bill Clinton was asked to raise the Tibetan issue on his upcoming state visit to China. Thom serenaded Slick Willy with an acoustic version of 'Street Spirit' (Fade Out)'. However, the festival itself was dogged by bad luck. On 13 June, before Radiohead were due to take the stage, the weather turned stormy. A member of the audience was struck by lightning and left in a critical condition, with ten others also seriously injured. Radiohead, alongside R.E.M. and Sonic Youth, had their sets rescheduled for the following day. The band used the opportunity to arrange a gig at the 9:30 Club in Washington, with Pulp opening for them. Admission was free for the first 800 Tibetan Festival goers to show up with a ticket stub. Michael Stipe joined the band on stage for its encore of 'Lucky' (reading lyrics taped to a mic stand), after having opened the show with his cover version of Fleetwood Mac's 'Landslide'. Beastie Boy Adam Yauch was in attendance and declared the conflagration 'cool'. Stipe reprised his guest spot the following evening, and Thom returned the favour by singing lead on 'Be Mine' and backing vocals on 'E-Bow the Letter' – taking the place of Patti Smith, who had appeared on the original studio recording and couldn't make the festival because of the bad weather. The group also played 'Creep' for the first and only time during their current American tour.

On their return from America, Radiohead were allowed the rare luxury of a holiday with their wives and girlfriends. On 24 November 1998 *Meeting People Is Easy*, Grant Gee's documentary of his year on the road with Radiohead, had its premiere in London. This multimedia scrapbook is an enlightening, often depressing look at the way a successful modern rock band operates and endures. Radiohead, keen to oblige, find their patience stretched and their strength sapped by mercenary industry types, hysterical fans and opinionated media bullies. Among the more pertinent images are the band having to parrot radio IDs and slogans *ad nauseam*, saying thank you until they're blue in the face and consoling distraught fans at a Japanese airport. What's fascinating about the footage (which is full of Gee's intelligent edits and expansive use of colour) is that, rather than simplifying the process, technology's saturation has exacerbated the demands on a modern rock band, clogging up an already torturous process. The band, resolutely obliging and compliant up to the point where either tiredness or disbelief kicks in, come out of it well. Revealingly, under pressure to characterize the impact of *OK Computer*, Thom delegates that responsibility to the critics and insists: 'We've done our job.'

Gee's original treatment for the documentary is revealing: 'The basic premise is that here are a bunch of articulate, essentially shy people who, somehow, are able to create this huge, astonishing music and as a result find themselves in the strange/insane/seductive world of end-of-the-century celebrity with thousands of people wanting to meet them, thousands of cameras and microphones constantly siphoning off little bits of them... The film would work on similar levels to the music. So while it would be accessible and combine great looking performance footage with cool, moody, intimate documentary-style material, it would also use this basic form to explore aspects of the weird and scary, paranoia and vertigo-inducing, end-of-the-century blues and to push the notions of music documentary to some kind of limit.'

By the time Gee approached broadcaster Channel 4, he had spent a great deal of time with the band already. 'The scene in Barcelona last month was a perfect example: Funny and frightening. So much media. Sucking out the quotes and pictures to be chopped, spliced, distorted and fed back into the world. Everyone trying to get their own "real" snapshot of the band. So many different agendas.'

However, in a development piece, Gee later revised his own brief: 'The proposal is rather too heavy-handed on the "what the media do to the band" angle. They're not on the celebrity circuit and compared to those who are, Radiohead suffer very little press hounding. They also have, in comparison to most successful bands, a great deal of control of their own PR, promotion and press, so again I can't honestly portray them as victims of this tyrannical system. Also, as my own involvement with them has increased, I can't pretend to be any different in using them as media fodder.'

Gee's close collaboration with the band helped define the finished product. Thom provided key phrases (including the title) and also some of the graphical ideas. The band were shown a series of rough cuts of the final document, for comment rather than approval. The only major deviation from the original treatment is that Gee abandoned his original idea for the finale (the band watching themselves on screen). Instead the footage closes with the band playing a new song, '(Don't Get Any) Big Ideas (Cause They Aren't Going To Happen), alternatively titled 'Nude/Neut'. Otherwise, not one of the live songs was filmed in its entirety. This was actually due to the limitations of the portable camera equipment Gee used (which had a three-minute barrier), but it added to the feeling of transience and impermanence that was such a part of Radiohead's world in 1997. Other footage was drawn from MTV, *Later With Jools Holland*, and the band's performance at Glastonbury. Asked about the new songs featured in the documentary, Ed told reporters that 'I Promise', 'True Love Waits' and 'Motion Picture Soundtrack' might end up on any new album, and that the band had already worked on material in the portable studio situated in the back of their bus while touring *OK Computer*.

The documentary was eventually issued on video, with the artwork reminding Radiohead's audience: 'You are a target market.' Thom e-mailed this answer to those fans who felt patronized: 'I felt very much like we were being sold down the tubes at that particular moment, and the people who liked our music were being patronized and manipulated as well as us. Despite spending so much time and effort trying to avoid being just another desirable bar of soap on the shelf talked about in a lifestyle magazine, it just happened anyway. It also gave us an insight into how the crumbling machinery of record companies and the press and TV work. And if you try to explain how you feel about it to ANYONE you are accused of being precious and moaning. So I decided to just keep my mouth shut. And then Stanley had a copy of a marketing survey that our record company commissioned on what type of person bought our music, like humble little witless Pavlov's dogs, which section of the population involuntarily salivates at the mouth, and it just became funny. That is what the bar chart and "you are a target market" comes from. Because you are, and so am I.'

If you can judge the popularity of a band by the number of bonkers hangers-on, weirdos and ingrates they attract, Radiohead were clearly now superstars. Dean Testerman's homage to the lyrics of Thom Yorke – *The Untitled Radiohead Project* – took to the stage on 12 November at the seventy-seater Hollywood Court Theater in Los Angeles. It featured several characters in hospital rooms, bars and domestic settings mouthing the words to the group's three albums and EPs in lieu of dialogue.

Radiohead, though not censorious, were hardly amused. A statement was issued to clarify that 'they have no connection whatsoever with a play called *The Untitled Radiohead Project* ... and they are upset that no attempt had been made to ask for, or obtain, permission from themselves or their publisher. Something that would have been at least courteous.' Testerman told *Sonicnet*: 'I got a call from a lawyer representing Warner Chappell, the company that owns the publishing rights to Radiohead's lyrics, saying if they didn't hear from me instantly, they would be filing an injunction. I don't know if, when I go to the theatre tonight, they'll have me locked out.'

Testerman went on to claim something approaching altruism in his motives: 'We're not making any money. If they want the money that we as a non-profit [group] are making, they can have it. This has never, never, never been about profit. We thought it would give us a great chance to set up scholarships for kids who can't afford to go to music schools or theatre schools. We had no idea this would be a problem.' Testerman, also a freelance journalist, explained how the idea had taken hold while attending an acting audition two years previously. Asked to present a monologue, he spontaneously recited the lyrics to 'Creep' – which helped him realize the 'subliminal power' of the words. Testerman later related this anecdote to Thom during an interview he conducted.

Testerman stated that the thrust of the play was about society's emphasis on technology: 'I think that's what the audience will get from this – the way that we're getting technologically raped – we're losing touch with life. It talks about the memories that we have from being abused as children, from alcohol, from technology, from drugs, from repressed selves.' The central character (naturally enough, known as Thom) drives along remote roads, hoping to be abducted by aliens (as in the lyrics to 'Subterranean Homesick Alien'). A car crash then leaves him in a coma – and he has to choose whether to return to his body and the life he once knew. The first lines he utters on waking are 'A green plastic watering can', and from there the dialogue took in forty other Radiohead songs. The lyrics were delivered unchanged, including some of Thom's vocal mannerisms and non-syllabic moans. Michael Poulin, who played Thom, told *Sonicnet*: 'I think the whole thing is just a brilliant concept. This is something that's never been done before. It's Dean's story, based on Thom's lyrics, and he's done a great job with it.'

The band apparently discussed the play with EMI, saying it should be allowed to continue on the proviso that any profit would be donated to charity, and stating that they would 'supersede' their record company and publisher in order to allow the project to complete its run. Testerman passed on his gratitude at the band's indulgence. However, as Miriam Jacobson of the *LA Weekly* opined: 'You'll watch this show waiting in vain for some humour or sexiness, let alone a dramatic pay-off. Nor are there even snippets of Radiohead's gorgeous music to relieve the pointlesss human suffering of the central character, not to mention the audience.' Band sources were said to be less than pleased with this latest effort to jump on the Radiohead bandwagon. However, their restraint in embarking on legal action demonstrated a healthy commitment to artistic freedom.

On 10 December Radiohead took part in the Amnesty International Concert at Bercy Stadium in Paris, alongside such worthies as Alanis Morissette, Tracy Chapman and Peter Gabriel. The performance, their sole European date of the year, was later released on video. It was a rare outing for the band, who were continuing to enjoy some time off after a hectic schedule over the preceding decade.

Thom concluded that his performing for Amnesty International was a way of 'addressing my guilt, I guess'. In an interview for

Channel 4 News he went further: 'Radiohead came out of the grunge culture of complaint. I think we've grown up and it's dawned on us that our problems are utterly, utterly irrelevant and it's offensive to have them rammed down your throat on MTV... What I find really offensive is the way our culture – once anyone has any degree of success – gets into the realms of *Hello* magazine – "Have a look at our glamorous lifestyle that you should all be aspiring to – come look at the homes of the rich 'n' famous and look at them doing charlie in the toilets. This is your future – this is success."' In conclusion, he said he felt comfortable using his celebrity to help the cause of Amnesty International because 'I don't really use it for anything else'.

In an on-line debate on the subject, when questioned about the dubious relationship between rock and good causes, he went further: 'I spent the first few years of being in Radiohead not aware of outside issues like these. I had tunnel vision, but as we travelled a lot it became very obvious that the wonderful West was not the wonderful West we thought it was. The trip to Mexico and Thailand made that bloody obvious. My personal experience was in some way feeling that every-one was trying to be Western but it was obvious that the countries were only doing this because, culturally, they had been destroyed and they were at the West's mercy. I think any artist or any writer or any creative person is more acutely aware of their surroundings which is unfortunate sometimes, but it does mean sometimes it's difficult to ignore wider issues. It's hard to sing about "humping your baby" when you're seeing all this other stuff. It's difficult to live with a bad conscience.'

Phil, meanwhile, was spearheading a new campaign by the Samaritans, urging young people to contact them when they were in distress. Having been a volunteer Samaritan for eleven years, he was the first high-profile musician to support the organization. The Samaritans said Phil was asked to be a figurehead in order to help them connect with the under-twenty-fives, '...because the emotional subject matter of Radiohead's songs strikes a chord with disaffected young people'.

Figures show that in the UK suicide accounts for nineteen per cent of deaths among people aged between fifteen and twenty-four.

'That translates into two young suicides in Britain every day. Most of whom are young men,' Phil told the *NME*. 'Talking through emotional problems and feelings, whatever they are, is a major step in taking some control over them. But finding the right person to open up to can be very hard, especially for young people.' As part of the campaign, Phil visited schools to talk about his work. He also posted his personal reasons for membership of the Samaritans on the organization's UK Web site. 'Most people want to do something positive in their community. For me, becoming a Samaritan was a case of using my skills in an appropriate way. I have been extremely touched and impressed by the care and patience that I have seen in the organization. I would miss being a part of that.'

In December Radiohead made an unexpected appearance on a single by the Oxford group SPU.N.K.L.E ALL STARS. 'Where Will You Be This Christmas?', on Shifty Disco, employed snippets of Thom's between-song banter, including 'And now, to further our argument that pop is dead...' before Radiohead launched into a 'Hooked On Classics'-style instrumental medley of classical pieces set to a cheesy disco beat. The sample came from an early performance at Oxford's Jericho Tavern in December 1992, where they also performed covers of Glen Campbell's 'Rhinestone Cowboy' and the Beatles' 'Money' (it was part of a series of 'Your Song' evenings run at the venue). A Radiohead spokeswoman told the *NME*: 'We get calls every day about people doing Radiohead stuff in one way or another. Honestly, they're really not bothered.' Another Oxford band, Holy Roman Empire, also released their 'Carter meets Adam and the Ants' version of 'Street Spirit (Fade Out)'. Before its release, Colin had attended one of their gigs and was apparently bowled over, declaring, with a huge grin: 'You kill that song better than we do!' Other have-a-go-heroes to pillage the Thom Yorke songwriting canon have concentrated on covers of 'Creep' – notably the Pretenders, Mark Owen (ex-Take That), pseudo-lounge singer Frank Bennett, rapper Chino XL and punk band J Church.

Early in 1999, Jonny guested on Pavement's final album, *Terror Twilight*, as auxiliary harmonica player. The sessions were recorded in New York and London and produced by Nigel Godrich, who brought

Jonny aboard. Pavement's Steve West later talked of the 'nice British shine' Godrich lent to the album. Godrich had also been busy recording Beck's *Mutations* album in California and Travis's UK number one, *The Man Who*. By 1999 he was being acclaimed by *Q* as an 'end-of-the-millennium sonic guru'.

He was also the automatic choice to helm sessions for Radiohead's fourth album. Jim Irvin: 'I'm intrigued by what Nigel Godrich brings to Radiohead's new album, based on his recent records. He seems to be a fan of restraint, he likes things to be reigned in and have a calm about them. Yes, they sometimes have the storm, but the promise of the storm is what's thrilling.' Despite rumours that the album would emerge at the end of 1999, the group had no real intention of delivering new material before the millennium. Work officially began on 12 April. The sessions were spread between Paris, Copenhagen and another English country house, this time in Batsford, Gloucestershire. However, the band would end up doing most of the real work at Canned Applause.

On 13 June Thom and Jonny (on Hammond organ and guitar) once again played at the Tibetan Freedom Concert, this time at the Rai Parkhalle in Amsterdam. They presented acoustic versions of 'Street Spirit (Fade Out)', 'Exit Music (For a Film)', 'Lucky' and 'Karma Police' in a twenty-five-minute set which included a new song, 'Nothing To Fear', and a cover of Elvis Costello's 'I'll Wear It Proudly'. They also played alongside R.E.M. at the equivalent Washington concerts. Of considerable interest were Thom's comments in Amsterdam about recent events in the former Yugoslavia: 'Even though at the moment everybody's waving the flag, in Britain I'm profoundly ashamed of their actions, simply because I don't see what right NATO had to do what it did. The re-write of history going on is incredible, and I find it extremely unnerving. In 1949 Britain turned a blind eye when China invaded Tibet. How can a government claim to work for the people yet never ever listen to them. I'm totally ashamed to be part of the West, the way they've dealt with the rest of the world.' Thom obviously felt strongly about the subject, but comparing NATO's action in Kosovo with the supine capitulation of previous administrations over Tibet is woefully inappropriate. Regardless of the appalling arms links the West in general and Britain in particular enjoys with atrocious regimes worldwide, the thinking is clouded here – a genocide was occurring and for the first time the West didn't shove it under the carpet and offer succour to demagogues.

On 30 June 1999 Thom and Ed travelled to Glastonbury. Thom was there to bolster support for the Jubilee 2000 Drop the Debt campaign on site, as Jamie Drummond, who helped to organize the campaign, recalls: 'Thom did some great interviews for us, but he was selective about whom he spoke to. He wouldn't talk to anyone from Sky, for example. But he gave very good value in those interviews he did do.' While Thom and Ed were glad-handing it with the celebs (or not, as seems to be the case) Phil and wife Cait had become the proud parents of a bouncing baby boy, Leo, in May.

Ed was there to have fun. John Harris: 'Both times at Glastonbury I've had to get Ed O'Brien in. As an indication of how humble Ed is – crazy – he turned up in 1998, and he appears back-stage, near the Portakabin where we do the newspapers. "Can you help me? I can't get in." I said, have you said: "I'm Ed from Radiohead, we played the epochal show that defined last year's festi-val'? "I can't do that, I can't do that." So I had to take him in the press Portakabin and say, "This is Ed from Radiohead, get him a car pass." And they all start fussing. This year, exactly the same thing happened. "Ed, tell them you're from Radiohead!" "I can't do that..." In return for that favour, I said, "Do you mind going up the Green Field with one of my journalists and filling a two-page spread, because Super Furry Animals won't do it." He said, "No problem, man, I owe you a favour, no problem. Let's do it tomorrow at one o'clock." He was staying in a caravan with Nigel Godrich, Thom had been down. I went round at one and knocked on the door, and Nigel says, "Ed's asleep, come along in an hour." Forty minutes later Ed appears, his hair all in a mess. "Sorry, man, sorry. I was in bed, I'm really sorry, can we still do this?" It's a heart-warming story about what a great guy he is. With the possible exception of Thom, that's exactly what they're like. They've got no heirs and graces, and I think they are fantastically good, and I think that's still to do with living in

Oxford. And also the fact that they're intelligent. I think, to start doing rock star behaviour implies a lack of self-awareness.'

Thom was becoming increasingly active in the Debt Collective – an alliance to put pressure on governments to end the vicious cycle of Third World debt. His involvement was inspired by reading a book on world economics by Eric Osbourne. Thom, Bono, Perry Farrell and Bob Geldof headed 35,000 demonstrators calling on world leaders to cancel the debt. The four rock stars handed in a petition signed by nineteen million people to Prime Minister Tony Blair and other premiers at the G8 summit in Cologne, as part of the Jubilee 2000 campaign. Afterwards, a new initiative for dealing with debt was announced, though Thom criticized the measures in a press release: 'I recently became involved in the Jubilee 2000 campaign and travelled to Cologne on 18 June to show my support. I was one of a chosen delegation, along with Bono and Youssou N'Dour, who submitted the petition to the G8 summit of world leaders. There were seventeen million signatures on that petition and 50,000 people in a human chain around Cologne, yet we were patronized, trivialized and bullied by the G8 and the media.'

Jamie Drummond: 'We went as part of the ongoing grass-roots campaign to democratize international governors. Decisions are being made for people that they don't know about. Democratic govern-ments form cabals and cartels, regardless of whether they're in our interest or not. That's our agenda, and it's one that Thom is a very passionate advocate of. When I first met him, I expected to give the normal pop star briefing, but he's by far the best-informed musician I've met, and he's willing to talk about the technical issues. He was right on the ball. Bono and Geldof are articulate, but it falls out of Thom's mouth more passionately, because he's so well read. He knows about the Washington consensus, the world bank and the IMF's orthodox monetarist policies and the damage they cause both in the long and the short term.'

Thom watched as the celebrities were treated to the outstretched hands of German premier Gerhard Schroeder ('stood there with the smile of a used-car salesman'). Nevertheless, being the polite Englishman, he took the proffered hand. As Ed noted: 'If Tony Blair

can behave as a pop star, why shouldn't we feel a bit like politicians?'
Jamie Drummond: 'If you really want to help, you have to be a diplomat. Bono's a master diplomat. Thom is not yet, his views are still
passionate, from the heart, in a very raw form. But that also means his
voice is stronger with a younger crowd as a result, who are extremely
important to a campaign like ours. I put that form of eloquence
alongside Liam from the Prodigy's eloquence, having his back
tattooed with our message. He's never said anything for us, but when
he does that, he doesn't need to.'

Meanwhile Ed was involved in writing the instrumental sound-
track to a new BBC drama series, a TV adaptation of *Eureka Street:
A Novel Of Ireland Like No Other* by Irish author Robert McLiam
Wilson. This was a well-received and extremely funny four-part series
aired in September, and the soundtrack featured dialogue from the
characters in the series alongside twenty instrumentals – composed by
Ed's friend Martin Phipps. Ed was responsible for co-writing
'Sometimes My People Shine', 'Jake', 'Oh, God, a Riot', 'Easy To
Live Without' and 'My Cat's a Wanker' – its title taken from a line in
the book.

-twelve-

the millennium
album and beyond

'I think we have reached a peak here. I sometimes
find it hard to imagine we'll do anything better. Most
bands start going rubbish around their fourth album,
don't they?'
Jonny Greenwood, interviewed in The Times *during 1997*

Although it didn't feel like it, not everyone in the world was a
Radiohead convert. Some people will instinctively hate glossy maga-
zine-led consensus anyway, while others tired of what they saw as
the group's ceaseless moping. An editor of a major music ency-
clopaedia, who didn't wish to be named lest his inbox be cluttered
with avenging e-mails from Radiohead fans, can't see at all the
attraction of the band 'and their constant carping'. That seems to be
the most frequent line of attack from critics, such as Kid Rock: 'Quit
crying, you babies. "Waaaahhh! I don't like making lots of money
because I've got to actually talk to my fans." How wack is that?'
Tony Wilson of Factory Records, a figurehead of the post-punk
scene which originally inspired the members of Radiohead to form
a band, wasn't won over either: 'Radiohead and the Manics, that
type of music, I call it the dead generation ... this lot, this
Radiohead generation, this lot are ripe to be blown away when the
next thing happens, the next cycle. It's like the music scene before

punk.' Mogwai called Radiohead a fake stadium band, but then Mogwai hate everybody anyway.

Others, like John Robb, admired the craft behind Radiohead and acknowledged their importance, but cannot find it within their hearts to love them. 'They're well designed records, well constructed. They're capable of doing some really bizarre things on record and yet still making it sound like a pop song. But for me, listening to Radiohead is like looking at brilliant architecture, say a Norman Foster building. It's emotionless. The fascination comes from structure. The music doesn't do anything to change my mood at all.'

For most, however, Radiohead are due back to save the universe from humdrum trad-rock sometime around the summer of the year 2000. Jim Irvin at *Mojo* explains why the appetite for Radiohead's new record is so voracious: 'People expect more of a Radiohead record at this point, because they've decided with Oasis they'll get more of the same. They trust Radiohead to come up with something intriguing. Some bands get obsessed with ringing the changes. As long as they're doing something different, it must be better. With Radiohead, that actually seems to work. I gather that recording all the albums has been painful, because it's not just about recording some songs, it's all been about questioning the whole process. They like to jump in and make it as difficult for themselves as possible, and what comes out displays the tumult that went on in the recording. I gather with *OK Computer* they thought they had a bunch of copper-bottomed stadium fillers, but they never released them. It's almost as if they don't trust the material when they go into the studio.'

Radiohead's last two albums set a benchmark for intelligent rock music and broke the shackles of Britpop's Beatles fixation. Not that their influence on British rock has been entirely benevolent. As Fiona Sturges noted in the *Independent*: 'Part of the Oxford band's legacy is a mood rather than a musical style.' Citing acts as disparate as Go! Beat's Ben & Jason and the John Leckie-produced Muse, she continued: 'In interviews, many of these bands complain that you can't have a good wail on record without being compared with Thom Yorke. That may be true, but our response to music is as much to do with immediate associations as tapping our emotions. It is also to do with the fact that no one has done it so well as Yorke, or [Jeff] Buckley before him.' These days *Nightshift* editor Ronan Munro has to deal with a weekly mailbag of Oxfordshire bands desperately attempting to emulate Radiohead. 'I just wish they'd take the influence of Radiohead. Aspire to what they've done, not how they sound.' Jim Irvin shares that concern: 'I was worried that Radiohead would just lose interest when they heard all this stuff coming back at them that sounded just like them, only worse.'

Asked if Radiohead's album is the most keenly anticipated of the new millennium, *Select* editor John Harris is unequivocal. 'Yeah, it has to be. Totally. Especially given the fact that things are in such an awful mess. Things are so quiet, bands are dropping like flies. Also, loads of bands have come back with really disappointing records. Suede put out a disappointing album, Oasis did it with *Be Here Now*, Pulp did it with *This Is Hardcore*.' Blur's *13* was the other flop album from 1999. 'I remember saying to Ed at Glastonbury, "Don't do a *13*." I think that's one of the reasons it's taking so long. They are so – it's not even media literate – it's culturally literate. They know where they fit in. It must prey on your mind.'

Jack Rabid, who has documented the passage of contemporary rock music for over two decades in *The Big Takeover*, reiterates his assertion that Radiohead offer the last great hope for guitar rock: 'Yes, I will stand by that.' So too does Thom's former Exeter collaborator, sHack: 'Although I was brought up on guitar music, my interests were always in sound itself, and whilst I personally feel that guitar music has exhausted most of its sonic possibilities, Radiohead are one of the few existing bands who defy the norm. I love the boldness of their production, the off-kilter way in which they write their music, and the way in which they can make the least obvious thing sound like it's the *only* thing that they could have done at the time. They've also managed to maintain a consistency of excellence which most bands can only dream of.'

Those testimonials help to put the expectations about the group's fourth album in context. However, rather than hide themselves away and work in secrecy, the band shared with the world the sessions for their fourth album via a studio diary written by Ed for their official

Web site. It seemed few of the songs they had premiered but not recorded on previous tours were judged up to standard, with the exception of 'How To Disappear'. Others, like 'Lift', were mothballed. 'We haven't lost the song,' revealed Thom. 'We played it too much in a certain way that didn't work in my opinion. It didn't feel right, so we need to approach it in a different way but at the time of *OK Computer* it was impossible to get into rearranging it because everyone had fixed ideas on what to play and we'd all just got into a habit we couldn't break, like staring too long at strangers, know what I mean?'

Ed candidly noted how the sessions could prove as frustrating as they were rewarding. From the diary entry dated 4 August: 'The problem we have found is that we are essentially in limbo – for the first time… We have nothing to get ready for except "an album". It's like, how do we start this? When we made our last three albums there were time restrictions – we no longer have those. Are we going down Stone Roses territory? The result of this somewhat frank discussion is that we need a plan and something to aim for.' On 2 September the diary recounted another interesting chapter: 'What has been interesting about this is that for me, this is the first time I am aware of the cyclical nature of our behaviour; patterns emerge. Today was much like a day four weeks ago. Things came to a head. And although you wish that there weren't days like this, it actually probably aids the creative process. So maybe the next few rehearsals will be great. Time to swig back a bottle of wine and contemplate the frail nature of it all.'

By December, Ed was able to advise that at least six songs were ostensibly complete. Intriguingly, 'Everyone – The National Anthem' utilized a full jazz band and Jonny was talking up the possibility of using a classical orchestra in an 'unconventional' way.

With the band having already namechecked hip hop star Missy Elliott, it was revealed that former A Tribe Called Quest rapper Q-Tip had approached Radiohead about appearing on his debut solo album, *Amplified*. Ed also talked about the impact of David Upshal's documentary for Channel 4, *The Hip Hop Years*: 'There was a wonderful moment this week when we were all crowded round the TV watching this programme documenting the story of hip hop, and it was the classic years from '86 through to '92, with Run-DMC, Public Enemy and NWA, etc. Some of the greatest records ever made. And they interviewed Hank Shocklee... And he was explaining their [Public Enemy's] methodology – the way they recorded. Basically they all set up with samplers and drum machines in the same room and recorded. Now most of it, he said, sounded like a mess, but apparently, there were some great moments, that were then cut up and from that the basic track was constructed. Why the fuck can't we do this? It could be so exciting. We have the means to make a communal racket, so why not harness some of this technology and use it within our own sphere? I mean, we're not going to make a hip hop record, much as we'd like to, but what was exciting was the idea of that kind of approach. Something similar offered us a necessary alternative to the way that we have largely worked up until now. Once we have done this, then we might really get somewhere.'

However, as The Bigger The God's Andy Smith points out, the group's enthusiasm for hip hop should be taken with caution. 'They went on and on about how much they loved DJ Shadow when they were making *OK Computer*. They came up with a fantastic album, but I can't hear much trace of DJ Shadow in it.' Contrast this new-found love of hip hop with this amusing, curtailed interview taken from the souvenir programme to the Tibetan Freedom Festival in New York City. 'Q: What impact do you think the deaths of Tupac and Notorious B.I.G. have had on the music industry? A: No impact. Who are they? Sorry, don't know what you're talking about.'

As an adjunct to Ed's diaries, members of the band also contributed to Stanley Donwood's official site, contributing thoughts (marked in red or blue to prevent misrepresentation) in reply to fans' questions and observations. As Jonny noted, self-deprecatingly: 'Radiohead reserve the right to abuse all positions of authority and/or influence.' There is plenty of entertainment to be had. Fan: 'I have never been in love but I have found music. Should I be happy or sad?' Thom: 'Love takes a while. It starts off like feeling sick. Music is easier and more friendly, but tends to repeat itself.'

Thom has alluded to these sessions as 'wallpaper in my skull', but it also gave him chance to air his views on the sessions, and, in partic-ular, writing new songs: 'We talk about it [the way new songs are composed] a lot at the moment. It's not really to do with piano or guitar but more about trying to write in a different way completely. This is really hard because no one knows what is really happening and I have such a short attention span. We have kind of complete songs, but in some ways that is just as hard because we know how we should do things, so by definition that will sound tired. We really want to just get up and bash through everything and then bugger off, but it ain't gonna work like that, so just got to be patient. All of the stuff we've done so far that's worked has been by dragging ourselves through the hedge backwards.'

The message board did not offer a completely idyllic forum, however, as Thom discovered. 'There was something on the message board the other day that upset me a lot. I can't remember, but it was just really spiteful. I showed it to Nigel [Godrich] and he just said they're just looking for attention. But I can't get over sometimes (when my resistance is low) that people believe it is their right now to slag you off to your face, to insult you personally in public, accuse you of being a caricature of yourself (only a journalist can reduce life to such mind-fucking double think), come up to you and tell you that you wrote the most bloody depressing piece of music they ever heard and expect to walk away and you not to react. As if you are just two-dimensional and everybody else is 3D. So no, I am no more immune now than I have ever been.'

Later versions of the studio diary were 'scrambled' via Ed's own handwriting, in an effort to stop 'dodgy muso mags cutting and pasting straight into their pages'. If this wasn't explicit enough, Stanley Donwood replied to one fan's plea for a typewritten manuscript: 'I can read it, try harder, or do you work for *Select* or something?' Melanie, head of Radiohead's fanclub/merchandise operation, replied on-line to queries from fans about whether the band was mad at *Select*'s 'lifting' of pieces from the site: 'No, not mad ... maybe a tad confused and bewildered that the site could become press features by lifting chunks from it. I think everyone was surprised by the coverage the site has had. It wasn't set up for press and was done for the people who enjoy the band. We are all astounded by the interest and have realized the power of the Internet.' They shouldn't have been surprised, really. A band who can record a record themed *OK Computer* ought to be aware of the function not only of the technology but of its media context and application.

Elsewhere on the site, Thom contributed some bizarre, seemingly random thoughts to a section called *Primetime*. He offered this to a fan who suggested that this was 'diarrhoea': 'You can take it or leave it, it is of no consequence to me. A lot of the work that appears in primetime is transitory, is noise, you flick through at will like channels on your TV. If you think it is dribbling droning shite then probably so do I. But what you have to perhaps bear in mind before pulling it to shreds is that much of this work was done during a time when I firmly believed I was finished, that I had no right to work any more, that I no longer had anything to say. If you agree with that then I am happy for you. For myself, putting it into the public domain was a way of moving on, good or bad. I feel no need to prove anybody wrong or right about me or what I write in words. For a while I did and it almost destroyed me. But now I am excited again about what we are doing and what I have written, and a lot of that is based on what you see on these pages.'

To John Harris, Radiohead's interaction with their own Web site points to their future as a group: 'I think that the Web site is quite indicative of what, given technological developments, Radiohead will do. That Internet diary is vastly significant. I know the record company were really bemused by it. The point is, the music business hitherto, you put out your album, you tour it, and no one sees you for two years. That's ludicrous. What the Internet allows you to do is keep that contact up with your fan base. Not on the level of cynically exploiting it, I think Radiohead just enjoy doing it. They go on the chat site, and so on. I think, if they like doing that, given the chance, they'll put material out on there. You'd have to ask them, but I think that's the way it'll go. And I think Radiohead, because they understand the technology so well, will be one of the trailblazers. They obviously like that idea of constant contact. I think they'll blaze a trail for – it won't be MP3 – but downloadable music. In the end, because they're so self-sufficient, they'll book their own studio and probably dispense with the record company altogether.'

Given Thom Yorke's frigidity in dealing with the music industry, Harris believes this will offer Radiohead the optimum solution. 'A lot of Thom's rhetoric, he doesn't like the demands of the music industry at all. A lot of people say they don't like it, but he *really* doesn't like it. He says, "Every time you make your record, you're blackmailed into going on tour for two years..." I don't think he likes that, I think he likes constant creativity. But creativity isn't anything without them releasing it to the public.'

Mac, the promoter who gave the band their first major gig, is less convinced: 'That's a good theory. But I would have thought that any man would be tempted by the sort of money they can earn through the outlets that would be afforded them. Basically, you're looking at the sort of deal R.E.M. signed three or four years ago. They're going to be up for that and then some next time. I would have thought John's angle plus the traditional way of doing things would be financially impossible to turn down. It might be your last chance before the whole world's a big computer terminal – "We want £50 million for two or three albums, but radiohead.com will be releasing them as well." And they'll probably get away with that and maybe even get a one-album deal.'

Jim Irvin, too, believes the new record will not be Radiohead's last conventional release: 'It's like people saying in the sixties everyone would buy their clothes mail order. It's a misnomer that people will want to do everything through a screen. Everyone still has an emotional connection to the artefact. Most people like to mingle. You go to a record shop and hear something you haven't heard before. It's much more about immersing yourself in an experience.'

The band gave a strong indication of their willingness to harness the technology on 9 December 1999, when they Webcast an unannounced show on the Pirate TV Network, an underground Web site which regularly features 'virtual club nights' hosted by Timmy B of Dreadzone and dance music veterans Mixmaster Morris and Coldcut. Jonny and Thom, returning to his student role, were the house DJs. As well as selections from the Fall, Captain Beefheart, Syd Barrett, Iggy Pop, Sonic Youth, Can, Talking Heads and PJ Harvey, there was a smattering of jazz (Charlie Mingus and Miles Davis), ska (Prince

Buster) and country (Johnny Cash). Also included was an acoustic version of a new Radiohead song, 'Knives Out', performed around a Christmas tree. Timmy B: 'It was them who wanted to do it, and they knew that I know about music on the Internet. They ended up playing a new tune. Nobody recorded it; it was just for the people who tuned in. It was really good.'

Ed related his excitement in the studio diaries. 'It's a bit like having our own TV station for three or so hours. There was little/virtually no planning for it, so everything was done on the hoof. So refreshing to do, as it seems to take an eternity to get anything done quickly in this business. And yes, it was completely shambolic at times but surely there's nothing wrong with that. I'd love to see more people doing this. Can you imagine Tony Blair and his boys and girls doing a similar thing? – Prescott on the wheels of steel: "This one goes out to Ken, this is 'Going Underground'."'

Other highlights of the three-hour set, which was estimated to have attracted an audience of 250 – a sharp contrast to the much-hyped Paul McCartney return to the Cavern the following week, which registered 500 million Internet hits – included a sock-puppet show, directed by Phil, and ironic dancing as the band members larked about in seemingly effervescent spirits. It may be that others feel the pressure on Radiohead delivering their fourth album more keenly than the band themselves.

postscript: where do we go from here?

Whether Radiohead ever leave their physical vessels behind and become our first non-corporeal, virtual rock band, remains to be seen. But even if they drop the biggest turkey of their career in the summer of 2000, which hardly seems likely on present expectations or past experience, they will remain unarguably the finest rock band we have produced in the past ten years. A year from now, critics may be dismissing *OK Computer* as an appetizer, a creative primer, for the majesty of the first great album of the new millennium.

The waypoints on Radiohead's career are self-evident. They formed at school, but it is difficult to imagine any other band surviving the four-year hiatus imposed by college, then reuniting and prospering in essentially the same format. Whatever forged that alliance at Abingdon School – belief, ambition, fraternity or plain pigheadedness – has produced a stubborn bond that has weathered whatever's been thrown at it since.

The overwhelming response to 'Creep' and the subsequent pigeonholing of the group was certainly unhelpful. So too the exhaustive touring and the relationship fractures that almost holed the group beneath the water before they recorded *The Bends*. But we should not exaggerate these crisis points. The truth is that Radiohead have had it pretty good. They've worked at it, as they'd be the first to tell you, but there is no great melodrama to relate in their story. It's essentially a simple tale of well-intentioned, talented young men who have used whatever gifts they possess astutely, even studiously. As well as behaving with tremendous decency, they've applied themselves, as school reports used to say. As otherworldly and extraordinary as *OK*

Computer is, it is a child of capable, active minds and honest endeavour. And if you're disappointed that there isn't more to it than that, you're reading about the wrong band entirely.

A final word from chairman Thom: 'Thinking I have any influence is bullshit. I'll do my thing and that's it. I am not answerable to the consequences as if at a trial. Any artist holds a mirror up. The image that is reflected may not be very nice. Tough, if that is what she or he sees. You can't scrub it out and go and look for a nicer, more palatable one. That's when it all goes down the tubes. I'll make mistakes and I'll enjoy it and I'll learn from it.'

uk discography

ON A FRIDAY DEMOS

DEMO 1 (cassette only, 4/91)
What Is That You Say?/Stop Whispering/Give It Up

DEMO 2 (cassette only, 10/91)
I Can't/Nothing Touches Me/Thinking About You [EP version]/
Phillipa Chicken/You [EP version]
Demo 2 also known as the 'Manic Hedgehog demos'.

RADIOHEAD SINGLES and EPs
(all released on Parlophone)

'DRILL' EP (5/92) CD/12in/cassette:
Prove Yourself [EP version]/Stupid Car/You [EP version]/
Thinking About You [EP version]
Limited edition of 3,000 for each format.

'CREEP' EP (9/92) CD/12in/cassette
Creep/Lurgee/Inside My Head/Million $ Question
Limited edition of 6,000 for each format.

'ANYONE CAN PLAY GUITAR' EP (2/93) CD/12in/cassette
Anyone Can Play Guitar/Faithless, the Wonder Boy/Coke Babies

'POP IS DEAD' EP (5/93) CD/12in/cassette
Pop Is Dead/Banana Co./Creep (live)/Ripcord (live)
Live tracks recorded at Town and Country Club, London, 14/3/93.
'Banana Co.' recorded live for Signal Radio, Cheshire.

'CREEP' EP (SECOND VERSION) (9/93) CD/7in clear vinyl/
    cassette
Creep/Yes I Am/Blow Out [Phil Vinnall] remix/Inside My
    Head (live)
Live track recorded at the Metro, Chicago, 30/6/93.

'MY IRON LUNG' EP (9/94)
CD1: My Iron Lung/The Trickster/Punchdrunk Lovesick
    Singalong/Lozenge Of Love
CD2: My Iron Lung/Lewis (mistreated)/Permanent Daylight/
    You Never Wash Up After Yourself
12in: My Iron Lung/Punchdrunk Lovesick Singalong/
    The Trickster/Lewis (mistreated)
Cassette: My Iron Lung/The Trickster/Lewis (mistreated)/
    Punchdrunk Lovesick Singalong

HIGH & DRY/PLANET TELEX (3/95)
CD1: High & Dry/Planet Telex/Maquiladora/Planet Telex
    (hexadecimal mix)
CD2: Planet Telex/High & Dry/Killer Cars/Planet Telex (l.f.o. jd mix)
12in: Planet Telex (Hexadecimal mix)/Planet Telex (l.f.o. jd mix)/
    Planet Telex (Hexadecimal dub)/High & Dry
Cassette: High & Dry/Planet Telex
Hexadecimal mix and Hexadecimal dub by Steve Osborne.

FAKE PLASTIC TREES (5/95)
CD1/cassette: Fake Plastic Trees/India Rubber/How Can You
    Be Sure?
CD2: Fake Plastic Trees/Fake Plastic Trees (acoustic)/Bullet Proof
    ... I Wish I Was (acoustic)/Street Spirit (Fade Out) (acoustic)
Acoustic tracks recorded at Eve's Club, London, 16/2/95.

JUST (8/95)

CD1: Just/Planet Telex (Karma Sunra mix)/Killer Cars (Mogadon version)

CD2: Just/Bones (live)/Planet Telex (live)/Anyone Can Play Guitar (live)

Karma Sunra mix by U.N.K.L.E. Live tracks recorded at the Forum, London, 24/3/95.

STREET SPIRIT (FADE OUT) (1/96)

CD1: Street Spirit (Fade Out)/Talk Show Host/Bishop's Robes

CD2: Street Spirit (Fade Out)/Banana Co./Molasses

7in white vinyl: Street Spirit (Fade Out)/Bishop's Robes

PARANOID ANDROID (5/97)

CD1: Paranoid Android/Polyethylene (Parts 1 and 2)/Pearly*

CD2: Paranoid Android/A Reminder/Melatonin

7in blue vinyl: Paranoid Android/Polyethylene (Parts 1 and 2)

KARMA POLICE (8/97)

CD1: Karma Police/Meeting In The Aisle/Lull

CD2: Karma Police/Climbing Up The Walls (zero 7 mix)/ Climbing Up The Walls (Fila Brazillia mix)

12in: Karma Police/Meeting In The Aisle/Climbing Up The Walls (zero 7 mix)

Zero 7 mix by Henry Binns and Sam Hardaker at Shebang Studios, Fila Brazillia mix by Fila Brazillia.

NO SURPRISES (1/98)

CD1/cassette: No Surprises/Palo Alto/How I Made My Millions

CD2: No Surprises/Airbag (live)/Lucky (live)

'Airbag' recorded live in Berlin, 3/11/97; 'Lucky' recorded live in Florence, 30/10/97.

ALBUMS

PABLO HONEY (2/93) CD/cassette/LP
You/Creep/How Do You?/Stop Whispering/Thinking About
You/Anyone Can Play Guitar/Ripcord/Vegetable/Prove Yourself/I
Can't/Lurgee/Blow Out

THE BENDS (3/95) CD/cassette/LP
Planet Telex/The Bends/High & Dry/Fake Plastic
Trees/Bones/(Nice Dream)/Just /My Iron Lung/Bullet Proof ...
I Wish I Was/Black Star/Sulk/Street Spirit (Fade Out)

OK COMPUTER (6/97) CD/cassette/Double LP
Airbag/Paranoid Android/Subterranean Homesick Alien/Exit
Music (for a film)/Let Down/Karma Police/Fitter,
Happier/Electioneering/Climbing Up The Walls/No
Surprises/Lucky/The Tourist

bibliography/sources

Material used in the preparation of this book was drawn from magazines, newspapers and Web sites including:

Alternative Press; [The] Big Takeover; Billboard; Calgary Sun; Curfew; Dazed and Confused; Details; Entertainment Weekly; Guardian; Guardian; Guitar Player; Guitar World; Hot Press; Irish Times; Jockey Slut; Lime Lizard; Local Support; Making Music; Melody Maker; Mojo; Musician; New Music Report; New Musical Express; New York Times; Nightshift; Options; People; Promo; Q; Raygun; Raw Vision; Request; Rocket; Rolling Stone; Rolling Stone Australia; Sassy; Scene; Select; Sounds; Spin; Times; Toronto Star; Toronto Sun; Total Guitar; Uncut; Vancouver Sun; Volume; Vox.

ONLINE ARTICLES

Addicted to Noise; Launch; Planet Telex; Radiohead.com; Sonicnet.

The following articles were especially useful:

DiMartino, Dave. "Give Radiohead to your Computer." *Launch* May 1998.

Harris, John. "Radiohead." *Volume 7.* World's End July 1993.

Harris, John. "Renaissance Men." *Select* January 1998.

Irvin, Jim, and Barney Hoskyns. "We Have Lift-Off." *Mojo* September 1997.

Irvin, Jim. "Thom Yorke Tells Jim Irvin How OK Computer Was Done." *Mojo* July 1997.

Lester, Paul. "People Have Power." *Uncut* August 1998.

Lowe, Steve. "Revolution in the Head". *Select* November/December 1999.

Malins, Steve. "Scuba Do." *Vox* April 1995.

Masuo, Sandy. "Subterranean Aliens." *Request* September 1997.

Moran, Caitlin. "Head Cases." *Melody Maker* 10 June 1995.

Morris, Gina. "You've Come a Long Way, Baby..." *Select* April 1995.

Myers, Caren. "Creep Show" *Mademoiselle* 1995.

Rabid, Jack. "Radiohead: the Last Hope?" *The Big Takeover* Issue 42 (1998)

Steele, Sam. "Sound Bytes: Thom Yorke's Track by Track Guide to OK Computer." *Vox* July 1997

Wiederhorn, Jon. "Radiohead Transform Emotional Turmoil into Kinetic Pop." *Rolling Stone* September 1997.

Yorke, Thom. "That's Me in the Corner." *Q* October 1995.

BOOKS ABOUT RADIOHEAD

Clarke, Martin. *Hysterical & Useless*. London: Plexus, 1999.

Hale, Jonathan. *From A Great Height*. Canada: ECW Press, 1999.

Johnstone, Nick. *An Illustrated Biography*. London: Omnibus, 1997.

Malins, Steve. *Coming Up for Air*. London: Virgin, 1997.

Stone, William. *Green Plastic Watering Can*. London: UFO, 1996.

WEB SITES

Official –   www.radiohead.com
          www.parlophone.com
Unofficial – Planet Telex: www.underworld.net/radiohead/
          Green Plastic Radiohead: http://radiohead.zoonation.com
          Against Demons: www.underworld.net/againstdemons/
          Oxygen Kiosk: www.underworld.net/kiosk/

The latter site has links to many other unofficial sites, plus reviews of each.

index